HAMARTIA

RAQUEL RICH

Edited by Victoria Bell

HAMARTIA

Paperback ISBN: 978-1-7771-1051-2
E-book ISBN: 978-1-7771-1050-5

Cover art by Maria Fernanda Avelar Sardo
Author photo by Christine Albee
Visit the author: www.raquelrich.com

For Gregory and Liam.
Repeat after me: "Yes I can."

CHAPTER 1
NOW

For the tenth time, Kay nervously looks up at the departures hologram as we pass through security. Our flight details haven't changed since the last time she looked: Toronto to Las Vegas. It's like she's expecting them to spell it out: "Destination: 2000." What part of "secret mission" does she not understand? Everyone else is actually going to Las Vegas, as the hologram says. They're just not going back more than eighty years in time like we are. I wipe my sweaty palms on my sweater, again.

"So... You'd think when you're travelling back in time, the means of transportation would be futuristic," Kay says. "Where's my shiny golden hovercraft time-warp machine, emerging from the clouds?"

"Ya, I was thinking the same thing," I respond to Kay absently as I press my fingerprint to the scanner and smear it with sweat. I sigh.

The screen directs us to Gate 47. We go directly to the gate, anxious to get started on this journey. My stomach churns as I think about what cloning a new replacement soul for my son, Jordan, actually entails. I bite my lip, hard, trying to stop my fear from taking over the rest of my body as it has my empty stomach and nervous system.

"I don't get it," I say. "We're boarding the plane with regular people? Where's that assistant? She's supposed to be here," and just then, she surfaces from the gate, tucking her hair behind her ear.

She's outfitted in an all-white dress suit, directing people to their seats on the plane. As we approach and she sees us, she smiles, winks and re-tucks her hair. I notice she's wearing a nametag and shake my head in amazement when I realize it's blank. "We're all anonymous," she had told Marc and me when she greeted us at Dr. Messie's home office, right before we were given a chance to save our son's life. But the blank nametag seems to intentionally rub in our faces that we don't even know her name. This whole process has felt like a secret gamble rather than a mission. We're not entitled to know anything, yet we're expected to go along with everything. We're just supposed to trust that a bunch of strangers hold the miracle cure to a disease no one has even figured out the cause of. Metagenesis.

"Ladies, please follow me."

She leads us past the line of people waiting to board the aircraft. No one pays any attention, probably assuming she's an employee. She matches all the other flight attendants. They're all wearing white, too. Maybe she actually does work here, for this airline, or even at this airport. Or could those other flight attendants work for Dr. Messie, too?

We don't put our fingers on the scanner to board like the other passengers.

"We don't need you on the passenger manifest," she tells us as we follow her to our seats near the back. "Most of the seats in this section are vacant. Right after take-off, before the seatbelt sign turns off, meet me in the bathroom." And she's gone to escort other passengers to their seats—doesn't even give me a chance to ask any of my hundreds of questions, including the most recent one that just popped into my head: how long after take-off, exactly? Are we supposed to just guess? Five minutes? Ten?

"Grace?" Kay interrupts my thoughts. "So, what'd you *really* think of that orientation?"

I shrug in response, not really wanting to talk about it again with her. I have nothing new to add about how I feel or what I think. Jordan is dying of Metagenesis, a disease that has plagued the human race for decades now. I've watched my boy deteriorate, his eyes become vacant as his soul slowly fades away, his breath laboured, making him weak and lethargic. I fear the day is near when his soul will leave him, never to return, and he will die just like the millions of victims this disease has already claimed. I'm still trying to accept that finding him a replacement soul in Marc's past life, through a secret, illegal clinical trial is our son's only chance of survival. So secret that Dr. Messie didn't even see us off at the airport. Given that Kay and I are the first to travel to past lives, you would think he'd be micromanaging every step. Dr. Messie made no guarantees. We might not even make it back. So, either way, whether we do or don't go back, Jordan could die.

I don't feel up to small talk, but my former best friend is like a nervous dog looking to bury a bone. It's been a few years since I stopped talking to her—I'd forgotten how chatty she can be. And so she babbles on.

"Don't you think it's weird that the test said Marc has no fears or phobias? He must've had peaceful deaths in all his reincarnated lives. Lucky guy."

I almost chuckle at her calling him "lucky." He's lucky, all right. My soon-to-be-ex-husband is lucky that he can't go on this journey with me. Dr. Messie warned that it would be hazardous for Marc to meet his past life, David Williams. Lucky Marc gets to stay by our son's side, safe and sound, while I risk my life—risk getting stuck in the year 2000. Lucky Marc. I also think about Kay, wonder how the assistant or Dr. Messie approached her about being my supporter. If our reunion wasn't days fresh, I'd ask her bluntly.

I know Kay is just trying to keep the small talk going to distract me or beat around her original question about the orientation—the whole soulmate thing, which is eating away at me. Although we know the name and home city of the donor whose soul we must clone, and Marc spent hours at the regression session, profiling his past life, the science can do only so much. The rest is up to me. If Marc is my soulmate, I will recognize him in his past life. Not by his looks, since our bodies change from life to life when we reincarnate, but by his soul, his energy. I will feel it. But I'm divorcing him. People don't divorce their soulmates, do they?

Kay rambles on, "I never really gave it much thought, but I have a phobia of clowns. How does someone die of clowns? Or was I a clown who was murdered? Or, what if I was a clown who died from suffocation while crammed into one of those little itsy-bitsy cars with twenty other clowns? But then I'd be claustrophobic, right? Not just afraid of clowns, but of tight places and stuff, right? I mean, at least for you, your weird obsession with avoiding turtlenecks, that makes sense. You were probably strangled to death in your past life. But *clowns?*" I feel her glance over at me, seeing if I'll bite at her attempt to engage me in conversation, but I don't reply. "I hope they're right," she says after a long pause, but not to me. I think she's talking to herself. "I hope you and Marc are soulmates."

The engines roar up, and Kay quiets down, leaving me to contemplate.

There are a lot of things riding on "if"s. If Marc is my soulmate. If I find his past life. If we make it back home. If Jordan hasn't lost his soul to Metagenesis while we're gone... I feel that churning in my stomach again, forcing a chill up my spine yet making me sweat. If all those things fall into place, maybe Jordan will be the first survivor of this disease, and then the whole world will benefit from the cure. Metagenesis could be abolished. I don't trust Dr. Messie—all the secrecy I'm bound to terrifies me. Yet I have to trust he'll cure my son because I feel mankind is counting on me, they just don't know it. I am desperate to trust someone, though: Kay, the assistant. Anyone.

Kay and I don't speak during the take-off. I stare outside, watching the world speed up through the oval window. Wondering about the whole idea of what we're about to do: time travel—or, actually, life travel. Travelling back to another life already lived, nearly eighty years ago.

I sigh deeply, trying to release my worries and fears as we

ascend into the sky. Instead, I focus on right now, the trivial, left-out, tiny little detail: how the hell are we even getting to Marc's past life from an airplane thirty thousand feet in the air?

Kay interrupts my nervous internal self-chatter. "I think it's time."

I feel weird about disobeying and getting up while the seatbelt sign is still on. When we undo our belts, with that metal-on-metal click as the flaps open, one of the passengers a few rows up looks back at us, gives us a disapproving look. We duck back into our seats and wait a few moments. When no one else pays us any attention, we head to the bathroom together.

"OK, now what?" says Kay after latching the door shut. "She's not here. Maybe it's the other washroom."

I look around the small room—which smells like bowl cleaner—as if somehow Miss-No-Name is hiding in this tiny little stall. I spot a small backpack hanging on the door, with the same logo from Dr. Messie's clinic and his hologram-boards.

"That must be our kit they talked about," I say. I open up the backpack and find all the stuff described in our orientation: a ceramic pig, a phone book, a pager. "Well, this has to be the right washroom, then."

I put the lid down and sit on the toilet, my knees banging into the wall. How does anyone taller than a munchkin pee in here?

We hear a rustling noise above our heads. I look up and see one of the panels moving out of the way. I have to blink to keep the falling dust out of my eyes. Behold: there she is, tucking that hair behind her ear. She is looking down at us, stretching her hand out. Miss-No-Name.

"Well, grab on and come on up!"

Kay and I exchange a look. I shrug as I rise and clasp the assistant's hand to go first, climbing out of the little bathroom. I step on the toilet lid and then the bitty little counter, clumsily trying to fit my feet into the teeny shelves, using them as footholds. When I climb out on the other side, I reach back and take the bag, then pull Kay up to join us.

We're lying on our bellies. I look around, but there isn't much to see or far to go. It's dimly lit by small openings beneath us, probably vents to the cabin, but the vents do nothing for us up here. It's hot and stuffy. Even the hum of the engine seems muffled by the air we're sucking in. I taste overpowering metallic filth when I breathe, making it difficult not to cough. It's like we're in the airplane's attic; there's no room to stand or even crouch, much less manoeuvre.

"Where are we?" I ask, but the assistant hushes us.

"The ceiling isn't so soundproof—your not-so-'Grace'ful exit from the bathroom was loud enough," she whispers. "People might hear your voices below. We're almost above the galley, which should be empty, but I'd prefer to exercise caution." She crawls away. "Let's go."

I want to tell her it's impossible to be quiet, and if discretion is important, then perhaps they should consider installing a ladder in that pee-hole. "Not-so-'Grace'ful exit," I mock to no one. Back in Dr. Messie's office, I decided I liked her, but now I'm finding it hard to remember why.

We snake along on our bellies toward the back of the plane, further and further. I can feel the dirt getting in under my nails, and the dust almost makes me sneeze, but I hold it in. A wall comes into view right ahead. It looks like we're heading toward a dead end.

"Where are we going?" I whisper-ask.

She doesn't respond. Instead, when we reach the dead end, she disappears. What the…?

It's not a dead end. It's a drop-off, but I can't see where it drops off to. It's pitch-black darkness.

"Just go!" Kay urges from behind me. I hear her suppress a sneeze.

I close my eyes and snake up quickly, and then the ground starts to give way. The next thing I know, I'm accelerating downward as if on a giant slide at a playground, only steeper, more slippery. I feel like I'm skating on my belly on a sheet of ice. I open my eyes wide, trying to see what I'm sliding toward, but there's nothing to look at, just thick blackness. I stop at the bottom with a bang. Kay crashes into me from behind. I get up on my knees, afraid to bump my head, and brush myself off. My adrenaline is pumping from the unexpected ride and relief that I survived it.

"Hello?" I call out, trying to keep my voice quiet.

"Right here. You don't have to whisper anymore, and you can stand up." Just then, a bright light comes on, pointing right at my face, blinding me. "Sorry, sorry. Here…" the assistant throws something at us, "…these are your outfits. You can't go in what you're wearing; you'll stand out. You need to fit in. Leave all your personal belongings here—no accessories, nothing."

"This is exactly what Dr. Messie told us to wear," Kay objects.

"Well, *Dr. Messie* doesn't know anything about the fashion from those days—just trust me."

I raise an eyebrow at the defensive tone she uses when she says Dr. Messie's name. It's the first time she's appeared to be anything but a happy yes-sir assistant. It's also the first time she's used his name instead of just referring to him as "Doctor." I sense defiance in her, which I like.

"You'll also need this—take it with you," she adds, tucking some toiletries into the backpack. "He doesn't know the first thing about being a girl. Just trust me." She looks at me, hesitates. For the first time, I notice her eyes are kind, and she seems to be searching mine for the same kindness. "Trust me, OK?" She doesn't look away until I nod yes. "I'll be right back. Keep the light." Miss-No-Name leaves the flashlight on the ground, beam up, and disappears around a corner.

Kay and I strip off the Dr. Messie–approved jeans and tank tops and change into the shiny silver outfits she gave us. I remove my accessories, reluctantly.

"I'm nervous," I admit in a quiet voice, not wanting the assistant to hear our conversation from wherever she went, but Kay doesn't respond, which probably means she is nervous too. I remember the way she usually keeps positive talk going, but when things are not positive, she doesn't talk at all. She doesn't want to add to the negativity, keep the bad vibes alive. Kay is odd that way. She also sings old show tunes to her plants and doesn't kill bugs. We're nothing alike, which is probably one of the many reasons our relationship died.

11

"Hello-o? Aren't you nervous?" I persist, determined to get a reply out of her. "Throughout the whole orientation, no one told us how we would be travelling in time. They refused to answer any questions about the transportation. Not Dr. Messie, nor the assistant—who, by the way, we're supposed to trust, without even knowing her name. And now, here we are at the back of a plane, unregistered guests, no record of us boarding this aircraft. We've climbed out through the roof of a bathroom to follow a woman with a blank nametag who may or may not work here... Aren't you the least bit concerned?"

"Yes, yes, yes! OK? Is that what you want to hear, Grace? Now quit talking about it—I don't want any more malicious energy to go into my nerves. Your bad talk is like a snake in Eden's garden."

I'm satisfied to have finally got a reaction out of Kay, but don't get to say anything more before the assistant reappears.

"Ready? All dressed? Come right this way, ladies."

We try to argue again about the go-go-dancer–looking outfits—they seem really over the top—but to no avail. At the last second, I tuck my lucky watch into my pocket. I haven't been apart from it in years. I'm not going to leave it behind now. It's the only thing left from my dad. At least I will have one comfort from home, from my past, even if it's an uncomfortable comfort. I adjust the tight new shirt, which is made from itchy I-don't-know-what, as the assistant escorts us through the dark back of the plane. We follow the path her light beam provides until we no longer need the way illuminated, thanks to the sunbeams that have appeared ahead.

She comes to a stop in front of a glass room with natural sunlight shining through. It's the middle of the day, and we can see clouds passing below and above, beautiful blue skies that reach until forever. The whole room is glass—the walls, floor, and ceiling—just like Dr. Messie's home office appeared to be. It's about the size of the bathroom stall we climbed out of.

She turns around to face us and hands us each a glass containing murky liquid with fog rising off it. "Stand in there and drink this," she says.

As if triggered by her voice, a door opens in the glass wall and the assistant motions for us to go through. I peer in. It's a glass room, all right. Unlike Dr. Messie's home office, this is not a trick of the eye. My mind's eye runs wild at what might happen, seeing the blankets of clouds through the floor. I clench my fists. I have a vivid imagination and a terrible feeling in the pit of my stomach.

"Tell us what's going on, please?" I stammer. "How are we getting there? What's the drink? Why are we standing on a glass floor in a little glass room in an airplane?"

But the assistant doesn't look concerned or even fazed by my uneasiness. She doesn't answer my questions. Out of her necklace, she takes something that at first looks like a pendant, then tucks her hair back.

"Put this in your pocket." She hands me a small glass tube, the size of my pinky nail. Again, she's searching my face. Her tone is serious, but her eyes kind and gentle. "Make sure you keep it safe. The glass isn't fragile—it will not break—but keep it safe and don't lose it. This is your son's life in your hands, do you understand?" She focuses on the tube for a beat, then turns her attention back to me and closes her hand over mine, with a gentle squeeze. "When the time comes, you do exactly as we talked about in the orientation. Just a small poke in the donor and the device will latch on for us to read the data of the soul."

She releases my hand but doesn't break eye contact. I have to look away first.

I open my hand to examine the small tube. It's warm and gives off a soft, pinkish glow. I don't see a syringe in it, but from the orientation, I know it will open only when I touch it to the donor. This tube is my son's soul, and that's how I will treat it. Even though it is not fragile, I place it in my pocket as if it's the most breakable little item in the world, as precious as a newborn baby's first breath. I zip up my pocket and pat it. I hold my son's life in one pocket, and my father's death in the other. Vowing to keep both safe, I promise myself that this will be a successful mission. I convince myself that I will know "when the time is right"; I will find Marc's past life—I will feel his energy, recognize him somehow.

I stare at the drink the assistant gave us, sniff at it, look up at her with questioning eyes.

"It will transport you when the glass room opens," she says. "Instead of plunging to your death, you'll fall back in time. Now drink up. It's best to plug your nose—and don't sip it, we haven't got all day. You can't miss your opportunity. As soon as the right turbulence hits, you're out of here." She pauses, a smirk creeping onto her lips, making me annoyed with her all over again. "And the look on your faces is exactly why we didn't tell you anything before. Trust me, remember? Good luck to both of you."

She turns and leaves, her footsteps echoing.

I turn to look at Kay. She looks like I feel, but she's already standing in the glass room, holding her drink out to clink with mine.

"Cheers?" she says in a shaky voice.

I join her on the glass floor. My knees almost buckle as I step over the threshold. The door slides closed behind me; I hear it lock into place, sealing the deal.

We clink glasses and chug the liquid. It's warm and fizzy and tastes like salty tree bark, and I don't get all the way through it before I start gagging. I do everything I can not to throw it up; it almost comes out through my nostrils.

"Oh no, that's awful!" I say between gasps, and Kay laughs nervously at me, nodding in agreement. I take the assistant's advice and plug my nose to finish the rest. And then all of a sudden...

All...

...of...

...a....

...sudden...

Nothing. I don't feel any different. The glass floor is still beneath us, and soft clouds still look like soft clouds, big blue skies above us. Nothing happens.

"So I guess we just wait, then," I mumble.

Kay and I don't talk to each other. I'm nervous, and Kay is being Kay, avoiding bad energy. This feeling is horrible.

My fears are making me want to call all this off, run back in, chase down the assistant and tell her she's made a mistake. Tell her we're not the right people to do this. If it weren't for Kay being here with me—even after I've treated her so badly—taking this crazy adventure with me for my son, for no personal gain... If it weren't for that, I might just run. Chicken out.

But as strange as I feel about it, Kay is here. And she didn't leave after the orientation session, either. She didn't leave when they explained the risks involved in surviving in the early twenty-first century. When they talked about the risk of heart attack from the food we're going to eat, or the risk of cancer due to the radiation we're going to encounter, or the risk of traffic accidents before the invention of the links we use today: she didn't leave. Even when they explained that they don't know if we will make it back. That we could be stuck there forever. Even then. When I asked her why she was coming with me, she told me it was for Peter, her little brother. She was doing this to honour his memory. Kay practically raised Peter because her parents worked so much. She was the only one by his side when he succumbed to Metagenesis, and his soul left him for the last time.

The aircraft shakes, interrupting my thoughts and making my heart skip beats. I hold my breath as I look at Kay. She's holding her breath too, her blue eyes wide. The glass floor shudders, but nothing happens. I just want this to be over with. I guess that wasn't the right turbulence.

I've never been skydiving. Marc's the risk-taker guy. He went skydiving on his eighteenth birthday, the same day we met. I wasn't the skydiving kind and watching the clouds below us... we're really high up right now. I gulp at the thought of plunging through those clouds at top speed, the ground rushing up beneath me, no parachutes, nothing to slow us down if something goes wrong. I wonder if we will come close to the ground and then be zapped into another time. Will we actually hit the ground and go through to another dimension? Or will it be instantaneous: the earth will open up and swallow us whole, and just like that, we'll be transported? Will it hurt? Why didn't I ask the assistant if it would hurt? Whatever is going to happen, I hope it happens soon.

The empty glass in my hand is now slippery from my sweaty

grip. I look to Kay, desperate for her positive small talk, but she doesn't look up to it. She's staring at the ground, the colour gone from her face. She looks pale with fear, or maybe even sick to her stomach.

"Kay? Are you OK?"

She meets my eyes, and I hear her glass drop to the ground and smash. But her eyes widen, and I realize she's still holding her glass. I know I'm still clinging to mine; my fingers are almost numb from the death grip on it. So if that wasn't our glass cups...

The floor drops away from our feet, glass shattering. We're momentarily suspended in the air. What is probably a split nanosecond feels like an eternity. Just like being on a roller coaster, when it reaches the top, and the climb seems to slow to an almost stop when you regret boarding the little car when regret is useless, there's no turning back. And you think to yourself, what the hell were you thinking? And then you get to the top and seem to teeter and totter, right before you...

Fall.

The wind is sucked out of my lungs in one big swoosh. I feel weightless. My hair actually lifts and polar-cold air surges through it, freezing my scalp and penetrating down to each root holding each strand. I don't know why I have all this time to think and wonder if my hair will actually snap off at the scalp and leave me bald when we arrive. I chance opening an eye to look at Kay, but she's gone. And then what seemed like the slowest nanosecond in time abruptly speeds up and I'm ejected out of the glass room. I smack my thigh hard on the way out. The vicious wind twists me around; my hair in my mouth, my collar snug around my neck, the shirt pulled taut under my armpits. I try to pull my knees in, to protect myself, but I can't. My arms and legs flail in all directions; the pack on my back pulls away from me, and I fear losing it. I try to twist around, so my back is against the wind, make the pack suction into me. Eyes closed, I hold as still as I can, trying to relax as much as one can when whipping through the air into the unknown without a parachute. I let the wind push my arms and legs. And then, when I think I'm ready, I pull my right arm and leg in and then twist my body around. I think I've done it. I have two seconds of relief, knowing the pack is safe.

The wind is now at my back. I open my eyes, expecting to see the blue skies above me, afraid I'm now falling backward through clouds, the ground below me. But I don't see the sky. I see the clouds. It doesn't make sense, but maybe I'm not thinking straight; after all, I'm plummeting in a freefall toward... where the hell are we plummeting toward? I try to think it out. If the wind is to my back, then I should be falling down, *through* the clouds, right? But the clouds are further and further from me like I'm falling away from them. And that brings on a whole new panic. If I'm falling away from them, then the earth is coming up beneath me sooner than I thought. Somehow I must've missed falling through the clouds. For some reason, I imagined I would feel them, whatever it is they feel like. Perhaps cool cotton balls, or a misty fog on my skin, but I felt nothing at all.

I still don't see Kay. At last, I find my voice, which was stuck in my throat from fear, and yell for her, scream for her, screech for her. I haven't heard her screaming at all, and I'm suddenly afraid she's not with me. I'm worried about her.

"Kay?"

Nothing.

"Kay? Kay! Can you hear me!" I'm yelling as loud as I can, but the wind snatches the words away; even I can barely hear me. I feel a different kind of panic rising in me. She must be under me, I reason, because I don't see her. Please let her be near me, please. She can't possibly still be in that glass room. I try to look for her, squinting my eyes against the brightness of the day, the sun glaring off the plane. I see the plane, getting smaller and smaller. There is no sign of Kay, which fills me with dread.

What the hell? I see the *roof* of the plane getting smaller and smaller, not the underbelly.

Kay whips past me just then, twirling hard. Thank God!

"Kay, put your arms and legs out—you'll slow down and stop the spinning!"

I know she can't hear me, but I don't know what else to do.

"Kay!"

My screaming is useless. I watch in horror as she spirals and zigzags further and further from me. She looks like a rag doll in the wind. I'm afraid she might be unconscious. She doesn't look right, and I'm powerless to help her.

"Kay!" I yell out desperately, while my mind grapples with why the *roof* of the plane is in my vision. It doesn't make sense. I wonder if it's that drink. Maybe it's a hallucinogenic drug of some sort.

"Kay!" I yell again.

Everything seems to be getting brighter and brighter—the sun is blinding, and the blue of the sky is lightening. We're not falling to the earth, we're flying away from it, up, away from the ground, away from the plane, higher and higher.

Suddenly the air thins out, although I'm sure it's always thin this high up. Instantly I can't breathe. I open my mouth to take a breath and yell again for Kay, but nothing. I can't suck in any air; I'm like a fish out of water. My eyes might bulge from the pressure or lack of oxygen. The wind on my back lets up, and I think I might pass out.

I seem to slow down. I'm still desperate to draw air into my lungs when, right at the very second I think I might lose consciousness, a strike of whiteness penetrates the world around me, forcing my eyes shut; I've been desperately trying to keep them open in an attempt to hold onto consciousness.

I'm weightless, floating almost. I feel like I'm drifting, or maybe I'm passing out, or going into a coma. Everything seems to slow down. It doesn't hurt not to breathe, and I know that it should. Sounds disappear, no rushing wind in my ears, no panicked thoughts in my brain. I feel as though I may be slipping into a trance. I fight it; I want to stay awake. Is this what it feels like to lose your soul to Metagenesis? Trying to hold on, but it's easier to let go?

I try to breathe and realize that I have been breathing already—deeply, actually, and slowly. I've never felt more relaxed in all my life. It's like I'm floating on the surface of a salty lake, where my body feels lighter than it really is. I don't even want to fight it anymore. I want to succumb to it, whatever "it" may be.

I open my eyes lazily and find I'm now in complete darkness. I see nothing, hear nothing, smell nothing, and it doesn't even faze me.

I am floating in nothingness, neither up nor down.

"Kay?" I mumble as my eyes roll back in my head, and I let the darkness take me.

CHAPTER 2
THREE DAYS EARLIER

"Do it again."

I get a blank stare in return from Dr. Messie. He licks the sweat off his fat lips.

"Do...it...again," I enunciate slowly as if Dr. Messie is the idiot—not that locking my son away in a glass observation room for days so he can undergo hypnosis and gruelling physical exams, for the fifth time with a fifth doctor, is overkill or anything. Why would it be? If Jordan were his son, would it be overkill to double-, triple-check, demand more opinions?

I called Dr. Messie because he's supposed to be the leader in the specialist field of Metagenesis, saving lost and old, dying souls. That's what all his huge holograms advertise. My son has been given a death sentence. He is going to die. I can't just accept that—*we* can't just accept that.

Dr. Messie is talking now, but to my soon-to-be-ex-husband, not me. He's addressing Marc because Marc appears calm and rational.

"Marc and Grace," Dr. Messie says, still facing Marc. "As you know, there is a pandemic facing today's society, which is indiscriminately attacking all humanity, regardless of age, gender, race, and socioeconomic status. There is no cure for Metagenesis. There are support groups..." He taps a button on a book, instantly uploading pamphlets to Jordan's medical repertoire and making it vibrate in Marc's hand. "And for young Jordan, I recommend we get him into the clinic right away to prevent him from wandering off alone again. And with your permission, I'd like to use his results for my research..."

I'm trying hard to listen because Marc's not going to remember any of this. He's not going to ask questions. He's not even recording this. He'll just accept anything, not challenge or protest. I hate the way he does that—the way he avoids conflict.

I look around the room at Dr. Messie's plaques, awards, certificates; his name, "Claudio Messie," written formally in italics on degrees and diplomas in fields of study in that new-age reincarnation stuff. The clock's ticking is loud, and suddenly I'm acutely aware of the smell of the leather seats we're sitting in. I can almost taste Dr. Messie's overbearing cologne. My hands are sweating and clammy and sticking to the umpteen coats of varnish on the super-shiny, super-expensive mahogany desk, which has even more expensive marble slabs embedded in the wood. The desk probably weighs a thousand pounds and costs more than Marc and I will earn in all of our lives, past and present put together. I suddenly hate this Dr. Messie, for sitting across from me calmly, for having diplomas and degrees, for his leather sofas on triple-dipped chrome legs, for his fancy desk and stupid antique lamps and loud old clock. Why is that clock ticking so loudly? Doesn't anyone else hear it? Or is that the sound of my head pounding, my heart racing, the sound of my sanity escaping through my ears?

The clock noise is infuriating, deafening, maddening, and before I know it—before Dr. Messie can finish and say, "He's dying," and "you're better off taking the humane approach and euthanizing your son," like the last four doctors have, I run out of there. I cover my ears with my hands and squeeze, tightly, and I run the hell out of his office, bust through the waiting room—surprising the uppity young front-desk snot, Janet.

I run past the fancy lobby, the overpaid security guard, the snooty decorative landscaping that the ultra-rich flaunt in the faces of us poor middle-class. I hate this doctor, I hate that Janet, I hate Marc, I hate that I love Marc, I hate them all. They agree to see us, but they are only humouring me. Even Marc humours me with his passiveness. Those doctors just want us to euthanize Jordan like he's a common criminal. Marc doesn't fight with them.

I reach the parking lot and sit on the curb with my hands still over my ears, squeezing stubborn tears out of my eyes and struggling to find my breath, and with it, my sanity. I feel my husband—*ex*-husband—embrace me from behind, and that's all it takes for me to let go of everything. I let go of my breath and my ears, and I let out a raw cry: no words, just cruel pain into Marc's arms. I turn my body, so I am cradled in his arms, and I don't care about the big fight we had right before coming here. I just need to cry into him. He may be an agreeable conflict-avoider, but he does understand my pain because he shares it.

Jordan is our son, our only child. He is the reason we married and tried to be a family in the first place. Just as our relationship fell apart, Jordan told me he thinks he experienced an episode of "soul loss," and then the doctors confirmed to us that he has contracted Metagenesis and is dying.

As I cry into Marc, I remember sitting beside Jordan, comforting him as he described his symptoms to me. He was petting Lucy, scratching hard behind her ears, and I remember thinking what a loyal dog Lucy was, enduring her ears being manhandled and groped so roughly. That was how I knew Jordan was nervous and something was wrong. But I had never thought that image would be etched in my memory as the last few moments when he wasn't dying. The last normal seconds before our lives changed forever.

I was in the kitchen at the counter unpacking groceries. I could see Jordan through the hatch, sitting on the couch. "I think I'm sick," he said. I wish the memory was cloudy, but it's as clear as the sky is blue. It replays in my mind like a recurring nightmare that I wish I could wake up from or alter, but can't.

His eyes shifted down to his folded little hands. I didn't respond right away. Instead, I continued my chore while I watched him fidget, from the corner of my eye. A few days earlier he had said he had a tummy ache and begged to stay home from school. I'd suspected he was faking, to avoid something or someone, but I played along and allowed him to stay home. I had been waiting to see if he sorted things out at school before I offered advice on his potential problem, so I sort of saw the conversation I thought was coming.

"Like, I'm sick sick, you know?"

Lucy came to sit in her usual spot on his feet. He seemed to welcome the distraction, and he bent down to pet her, his nervous hands going straight for her ears. Lucy flinched, and he grabbed harder.

What vocabulary did my nine-year-old use to describe his imminent death? "Mommy, I have it. That Metagermies."

I giggled a little bit at his mispronunciation. At the time, this confirmed to me that one of the kids at school was picking on him. Jordan was a small child with a small circle of equally small friends. He was shy and definitely not in the cool crowd, although he was not in the crowd that got bullied either. He was in the left-alone, forgotten group of mediocre, quiet kids. But some mean kids pick on all groups equally. It wasn't out of the question that rumours were being spread, as kids often do. It would've explained his fake stomach ache and avoiding going to school.

I joined him on the couch and put my arm around his tiny shoulders. I remember that it was stuffy in that room, unusually warm for a late September evening, and I was thinking mundane thoughts about opening the window to let in some fresh air.

"Why do you think that?" I asked, pulling him into me. "Did something happen at school, Jordan?"

He didn't let go of Lucy's ears, so the poor dog compensated by stretching her neck. I put my hand over his to release his grip on her and felt his ice-cold hands. They were trembling. I thought it weird that they were cold in this warm room. Poor thing was probably so upset and even scared. My blood boiled on his behalf, heat rising to my cheeks as I pictured those jerks spreading rumours that he was infected and taunting him.

"You can tell me, baby, I'm all ears—let's let Lucy keep hers," I said, trying to keep the mood light so he would open up.

I was all prepared for the pep talk about sticks and stones.

But then he said, "I couldn't catch my breath, and then I left my body. When I looked down, I was still there, walking home."

I froze, my hand stilled on his shoulder.

"It was walking without me inside of me, my body. And, and… I tried to chase it, but it wasn't waiting for me, and I couldn't catch it. I couldn't catch my breath, either."

Robotically I pulled him closer like I was the one out of my own body. "What? I don't understand…" I had heard him, but I didn't hear him. A knot formed in my stomach. I bit down on my lip to stop my questions so I wouldn't interrupt his flow, but I wasn't absorbing his stream of information. My skin numbed up, goosebumps crawled up my arms, forming a barrier between his words and my emotions.

"Then I just woke up, but I wasn't awake. I couldn't move, I couldn't breathe, Mommy." He started to cry then, his body heaving as he spilled the rest out between sobs. "I could hear people talking to me, telling me to come back, and I was trying to tell them I was back, but I couldn't say anything, and it felt like a heavy person was sitting on my chest."

Words lodged in my throat as it swelled shut as if I was the one who couldn't breathe.

"That's Metagermies, isn't it, Mommy?"

His face turned up to look at me then, but I couldn't meet his eyes. I was having my own out-of-body experience. I wanted to go back to him just being a boy petting his dog.

I had been mad that Marc wasn't there—not that he would've handled it well, anyway. I had always been the stronger one, the responsible one, but he still should've been there, even if it was my fault that he wasn't; I had kicked him out a few months previously. I was mad that I had been so caught up in the demise of our marriage that I hadn't noticed Jordan's missing medical alerts. When was the last one I saw? Two, three months ago? Then it dawned on me that Jordan must've been intercepting his medical alerts.

I had a million questions in my head at once, but couldn't ask any of them. At that moment, Jordan felt so tiny, so fragile, needy and lonely. When I finally managed to come back to myself, all I could do was squeeze him into me as he sobbed, rub his little arms and shoulders, and kiss the top of his little head. His hair smelled of green apple shampoo mixed with boy-been-outside scent. I'll forever hate green apples.

I remember whispering "it'll be OK"'s and "don't worry"'s and "we'll figure it out"'s. Lies, lies and more lies, because that was the worst news I ever received.

There is no turning back from Metagenesis. When your soul gets too old, when it's been reincarnated too many times, Metagenesis takes your life. And so I rubbed his shoulders and let him sob into mine as I breathed lies through his hair—just as Marc is doing to me, right now, comforting me about the fifth set of results, outside Dr. Messie's office.

"Grace, we have to make his time precious, not let him die while trying to save him," Marc says, and I know he's right. I know that these last weeks, all the doctors, soul-exams, all with the same results, are draining and fruitless for all of us—but mostly for Jordan, who is the victim of this incurable disease. Rather than hope, they continue to reinforce the fact of Jordan's unavoidable death. And obviously, Dr. Messie and his holograms are just false hope, a money-grab, and a way to get subjects and funding for his research.

"Let's make him happy."

Marc's voice is soothing; like always, he manages to calm me, even in my fury and madness. Even when our son is dying, Marc's voice and words bring me just enough peace to keep going. I hate that he still holds power to do that to me.

In his embrace, I catch my breath and slow it down consciously, drawing air through my nose and releasing gradually through my mouth. Each time, Marc mimics me; he doesn't let go, squeezes tighter as I exhale and releases me a bit as I inhale. His arms feel strong, his hands big and gentle. I allow myself to be his wife and the focus of his attention for a few minutes while I gather myself. I remember a time when I felt safe with him. Where did that time go? What happened to us?

"OK." I manage. "OK, I'm ready to go home." I get up and shake myself loose of the short hold Marc has on me, shake off the emotions, remind myself that we're not meant to be. That everything between us is dead, and that even the one thing left—our son, Jordan—is dying, too.

I toughen my skin with each step toward my link-car. Marc doesn't follow me, but I hear him laugh a little. I roll my eyes. What the hell is he laughing at? Then I realize I don't see my link-car on or near the solar loading tracks, and my cheeks heat with embarrassment. I don't have a link-car anymore. Neither of us does. I sold mine and made him sell his to pay for the tests, for all the visits to the doctors with the diplomas and leather and chrome and marble. Dr. Claudio Messie.

"Asshole," I say through gritted teeth, and Marc laughs harder. I find myself trying to hold in my own laughter. I want to be mad at Marc for laughing, mad at him, so it's easier to leave him. But as hard as I try, I just can't. Through my embarrassment and anger, I let out an involuntary half-laugh, and with tears of frustration I spin to face the medical building and shout the pain I feel. "*Asshole!*"

Marc makes his way toward me. He tries to take my hand, which I don't allow, but I do let him walk me home. It's a long walk through neighbourhoods much like my own, filled with empty container homes that were once alive with happy families but are now dwindling, just like the dying population. The walk feels even longer with the thought of having to tell Jordan it's another bad result, and explain the next steps to him. We'll have to check him into the Metagenesis clinic for lost and dying souls. He's already started wandering aimlessly in the night, his eyes empty, vacant and hollow. At the clinic, they can resuscitate his soul, bring it back. Until it can no longer come back to him. Until his soul eventually dies. And then so does Jordan.

The dream is one I've had many times. The one about Dad, and me reaching up for his hand. Except this time, the dream warps and changes into a dream about Jordan. It taunts me with happy times.

Marc and I are taking a younger Jordan and Lucy to the park in our link-car on a sunny afternoon. Back then, we didn't have a lot, but what we did have was good. Our small container home in the once densely populated Toronto was modest, but we owned it. We were a young family, but a happy one. Weren't we?

Jordan chases Lucy around the abandoned park. It was once filled with families and children like our own before the Metagenesis crises began to spread like wildfire. But Marc and I still liked coming with Jordan, to keep things normal—that is, until Marc and I fell apart.

"Gracie," I hear.

"Dad?"

We're suddenly back in my childhood home, where the dream usually takes place. The couch is green, and the wooden stool is where it always is in this very scene.

"Daddy," I repeat.

I can hear him calling my name. I try to grasp it, hold on to his voice. But the more I try to hold it, the louder the knocking becomes. Wait, knocking? That's not usually part of the dream...

I wake up to the sound of my headache knocking. What the hell? That's not my headache—it's the door. *Who* the hell? I roll off the couch, where I've slept every night since Marc left, and tell the music to shut off. The music has been putting me to sleep in his absence. The knocker is impatient and persistent.

"I'm coming! I hear ya!" I shout. I just want to silence the pounding. My head is killing me.

When I slide open the door, a smile-less man with a dark complexion, wearing a super-white suit and super-dark shades perched on his wide nose, stands before me. His shades are out of place, given the heavy rain behind him.

"Good morning, Mrs. Dartmouth," he says in a thick Caribbean accent. "Dr. Claudio Messie would like to meet with you. I'm here to escort you and Mr. Dartmouth right away."

"Marc doesn't live here, we're getting divorced, and you can call me Grace." That is my response. Not "who are you? Why are you here? Or why the hell would a doctor send a personal driver to come get me for?" Instead, I feel the first thing I must do is to clear the air that Marc and I are not together and ensure he doesn't address me by my married name, as if convincing everyone else will help to make my decision irreversible.

"We can pick him up on the way. I will wait in the link-car for you to get yourself..." He lifts his glasses to look me up and down. "...Cleaned up."

I must reek of booze. I was feeling really down last night. At his look, I wrap my knitted sweater around me tighter and cross my arms in defence.

"This is very unusual. What does the doctor want to see us again for? Did he make a mistake or something?" I feel my chest tighten and that damn lump grow in my throat.

"I'm just the driver." And with that, he turns back to his white link-sedan and leaves me standing at my door. The "driver" doesn't even turn around to see if I've gone to go get ready. I guess he's confident. Why wouldn't I go with him?

"Why are you taking me back to the doctor?" I shout at him, persistent.

Without any urgency, he turns around to face me and removes his sunglasses, revealing an icy glare. I take a step back, pull my sweater tighter.

"Do you want your son, Jordan, dead or alive?"

My knees go weak, my heart stops a moment.

"Get in the car, Mrs. Dartmouth."

CHAPTER 3

I call my brother, Charlie, to let him know I am leaving so he can come over and mind Jordan when he wakes.

Fifteen minutes later, we pull into Marc's driveway.

"I'll get him," I announce.

The driver doesn't respond. In fact, he hasn't said much of anything. He calls himself Mister and has said nothing more.

When I reach Marc's door, I let myself in and call out for him. He comes around the corner in his boxers, out of breath and surprised to see me. He looks nervous. I guess I don't blame him. The last time I barged in here, I was screaming my face off at him for I don't even remember what—again.

"We're going back to see Dr. Messie. He sent a no-name driver to come get us. I'll be in the link-car."

He furrows his brows in a question.

"I don't know," I answer before he can ask. "But he was pretty convincing."

I turn to leave and notice a pair of women's shoes by the coffee table. I look over my shoulder at him and roll my eyes, but he's already heading back down the hall and didn't even notice—a complete waste of a perfectly good eye roll. I squeeze my hands into fists and shake my head to rid my brain of the burning thoughts of another woman. A few months and he's already with someone? I slam the door on my way out. He may not have seen my eye roll, but I hope he felt the door slam.

I sit as far away from Marc as humanly possible, pushing my body toward the window and staring outside the whole car ride. I don't know why I'm mad at him. It's over between us; has been for a long time. I'm divorcing him, right? Aren't I? Maybe I'm just focusing on that, rather than the weird request to go back to see Dr. Messie, and the secrecy of a driver who wears sunglasses in the rain and tells us nothing, not even his name. Marc pays no mind. I don't think he even realizes I'm trying not to let his mere breath enter my personal space, and that is even more infuriating to me than the red peek-a-boo pumps by the coffee table. With a deliberate sigh, I ignore his presence and focus my attention on the world outside my window—away from Marc and whatever those shoes may or may not represent.

It's cold outside, the October rain dampening the high-rises and sidewalks and the people outside. A huge hologram of Dr. Messie sparkles and shines above. I wonder if it's a coincidence how the hologram seems to replace the sunshine on gloomy days, as if the doctor is the only hope, like a god.

As we wait our turn to make a right, exiting the link, I watch as a woman and small boy tape up a picture of a missing person onto the post next to all the other signs of missing people. The child clings to the woman as if his grip alone will prevent her from dying, too. He looks about the same size and small build as my nine-year-old Jordan, which makes me assume that he is quiet and shy, just like my boy. It breaks my heart.

There are many missing people; it seems to be getting worse every day, and this Metagenesis pandemic is all anyone ever talks about. The news coverage cycles through images of the suffering families coping with loss, lineups at the shelters and the clinics. The media interviews top researchers, Dr. Messie always at the forefront. Dying from Metagenesis is all anyone ever talks about. People fundraise to help find a cure. Marathons, bake sales. I always donated to the cause but never imagined being part of the cause. There are so many people who die from Metagenesis, or they go missing—wander off when their souls escape them, never to be found again. But their loved ones still hold on to hope, post missing persons signs and ask around at the shelters, hoping beyond hope to find their loved ones so they can die at home.

Will that be us? Will Marc and I be posting pictures of Jordan one rainy October morning? Will Jordan join the countless who have lost their old souls to Metagenesis? The thought makes me shiver. I hear Marc draw a deep breath, something I know he does when he's stressed. We share Jordan and the fear of losing him in common. When Marc squeezes my hand, I let him—for a second, anyway. Then I pull away.

When we reach a long driveway, it's the first time I realize we took a very different route than the one we took to get to Dr. Messie's office last time. It appears we've reached our destination when the car dismounts from the link and I hear the doors unlock.

"Where are we?" I ask.

It turns out to be Dr. Claudio Messie's home, and it's massive, pompous, expensive-looking, and heavily guarded, just like his personality. Nothing like the converted trailer-homes or shipping containers the rest of the general public live in. When we arrive, even Mister can't get past the security at the gates. He lets us out at the end of the long driveway, instructing us to stand near the gate.

"I will wait here," he says.

At the gate, we provide a DNA sample using little swabs and feed it through the sensors. The gates open and then we walk through metal detectors and an X-ray machine, then stare into the pupil reader while standing on something that resembles an old-fashioned scale but displays no numbers. I feel exposed. I look back at Marc, who doesn't seem fazed and simply shrugs when he sees my expression, then puts his hazel eyes up to the pupil reader.

Marc takes my hand to reassure me, which I immediately release, to his disappointment.

We are greeted by a young woman dressed all in white who introduces herself as Dr. Messie's assistant, but she doesn't tell us her name. When we start to introduce ourselves, she smiles politely as she tells us that they prefer to keep things anonymous. It's strange, but we don't question it. We let her lead us to a large, sparkling-clean glass room. She shows us to a white leather and chrome couch set facing an oversized, shiny mahogany desk. It looks identical to the desk in the doctor's office at the clinic yesterday.

"The doctor will be with you shortly." I notice she doesn't use his name. "There are cold refreshments; mint tea with olives for you, sir, and raspberry lemonade with frozen berries instead of ice for you, madam." She pauses. "And I see you left your son at home, but do bring him those candied apple caramel brownie bites he likes so much. I'll go get you some take-out containers." She turns to leave quickly as if to make sure we don't reply.

Marc and I exchange a perplexed look. "So…'*Anonymous*' …." Marc hand-gestures "air quotes," emphasizing "Anonymous." "Don't tell us your name, but we know your favourite drinks and snacks, and do leave us your DNA, scans, and X-rays at the gate," Marc says sarcastically.

"Ya, I was thinking the same thing. What the hell was that?"

We don't get a chance to sip the drinks, or even to sit down, for that matter. Not ten seconds after I agree with Marc, Miss Know-It-All appears from a door in the glass wall, which doesn't look like a door. Dr. Messie is behind her.

"The doctor will see you now."

It's as if the drinks and snacks were just a show of power, flexing a muscle. *We know you, but you don't know us.* I feel uneasy, actually. And where did that door come from? This is a glass room, and yet we can't see the other side?

"Take a seat, please." Dr. Messie gestures toward the sofa, and we obey.

He barely looks up at us as he shines a spot on his perfectly clean desk with his sleeve. Dr. Claudio Messie is dressed in white, matching Miss Know-It-All—or maybe she's matching him, whatever. The white is unflattering around his wide frame. He is sweating even though this room is cold. He carries a small rag, presumably to dab his fat forehead. He doesn't smile and looks as serious and matter-of-fact as he did yesterday when he told us Jordan was dying.

"Thank you for coming," he says, but he doesn't sound or look thankful. Without any prompting, he cuts to the chase, no niceness or small talk. "Marc and Grace, I've asked you here today because your case has been selected to participate in a medical research trial. Your son is dying of Metagenesis."

As if I need the reminder. I stiffen, and he holds up his hand, probably to stop me from running away as I did yesterday.

"I've invited you both to discuss a possible solution."

He has my attention. I'm not running anywhere.

Marc shifts in his seat beside me and clear his throat. "Go on, Doctor," he urges.

Dr. Messie lowers his hand and scooches himself to the edge of his seat. He looks straight at Marc and me, meeting our eyes for the first time, then lowers his voice. "No matter if you agree to participate or not, it is in your best interest not to repeat what I tell you."

"Yes, Doctor," Marc replies, and I nod impatiently. He has just told us he has a solution to saving our son's life—what the hell are we going to say? *Nah, to hell with it, we're outta here!?*

"Of course, we understand. What are you proposing, Claudio?"

He doesn't react to my addressing him by his first name. He rests back in his seat, which I'm glad for. He was making me feel uncomfortable, sitting that close to me and looking at us so intently. He returns to his normal I'm-Mr.-Serious-Too-Good-For-You tone with no eye contact.

"As you may know, my family was responsible for *the* discovery of the century: the discovery that reincarnation is a fact," he brags, and glances at us before continuing. "The study, of course, didn't end there. They also discovered the possibility of travelling to those lives, as you know. Past life travel is going to be the tourism of choice for those who have the means to explore it."

He's not telling us anything new—everyone knows about the ongoing research. Only the ultra-rich are going to get to travel back to visit their past lives, anyhow. Regular people like us won't benefit from that discovery.

"My team of researchers has taken it a step further. Our

research has concluded that not only will one have the possibility to travel back to visit a past life, but it may also be possible to clone a soul from a past life to repair dying souls before they succumb to Metagenesis." He pauses—for what I think is dramatic effect—with an almost-smile that doesn't reach his eyes. He seems self-absorbed in his own discovery. "Are you following me?" Maybe he thinks we should be leaping up to applaud him, but neither of us reacts. I'm feeling confused and shake my head no.

"We've found a potential donor for Jordan's soul, and we would like to send you back to a past life to identify him so it can be cloned," he states proudly.

"A donor, that's great!" says Marc.

I, on the other hand, am in shock. "What do you mean that you'd like us to identify *him*, and travel back? What exactly do you need us to do?" Dr. Messie doesn't respond, and so I repeat myself and rephrase. "Do you mean we're travelling back to meet one of our ancestors? Like a great-great-grandfather?" I ask.

"No, a reincarnated life—not a family member, not an ancestor at all. That's not how souls work. All of this will be explained in the orientation."

"That's great," says Marc, ever the optimist.

Isn't he at all curious about the implications? No one has actually travelled back to a past life. They're still researching it, aren't they?

"So you're telling us that we can travel to a past life? People are already doing this? And... what about that past life person, or donor, as you called him—what will happen to him?" I ask.

"Nothing. His life has already happened, already been lived out. You're not travelling back in *time*, you're travelling to a *past life*. The donor has already completed a full life cycle." His tone implies that my questions are stupid. "Grace, we have thought of everything."

As far as I know, from all the media has shared, all of this past life travel is still in the research stage, and no one has actually done it yet. I don't care that I sound stupid—his answers are vague.

"Why is the donor from Marc's past life and not Jordan's past life?" I ask. Dr. Messie's lip twitches with annoyance. "I need a better explanation of how this all works," I add cautiously. I don't want him to reconsider selecting us for a trial that might save our son, but I want to understand what will happen to Jordan. "Side effects?" I add in a small voice when he still doesn't respond.

"The soul may not take. The donor might not be a close enough match, and Jordan's body may reject it. It's just like getting an organ transplant; the closer the match, the better, but there are never any guarantees."

"I see," I say, waiting for him to continue.

"You have to make it back before Jordan's soul leaves his body for good. The cloned soul will only correct any damage Metagenesis has done to his soul, not actually replace it." He pauses, looking at Marc, then back at me. "As for your question on why the donor is Marc's past life and not Jordan's..." He takes a deep breath, hesitates and folds his arms over his chest, above his fat belly. "Only someone's soulmate can positively identify a past life. Jordan is only a child, and we don't know who his soulmate will be." He lets that sink in a moment before uncrossing his arms and tipping his head down to look at me, like he knows I'm keeping something from him. "But we have a good idea of who Marc's soulmate is—am I right, Grace?"

I sit perfectly still, trying not to look as uncomfortable as I can tell Marc feels from his sudden fidgeting in his seat. I don't want Dr. Messie to have any reason to believe we are not the right people to participate in this, so I nod and steer away from the soulmate subject before Dr. Messie can ask if Marc and I are still getting a divorce.

"So why is this a trial? Why aren't you doing this for everyone? A trial insinuates that it's not working as it should yet—that you're still in testing phases. Furthermore, I haven't heard anything about this. I have researched everything on the topic of Metagenesis from the moment Jordan was diagnosed by the first doctor, and as you know, you're doctor number five." I hold up my hand, spreading my fingers wide to emphasize my point. "Why haven't I seen anything on this?"

Marc is looking at me and places his hand on my knee, in an attempt to pacify me. He probably doesn't want to hear anything negative. He is so naive.

"Honey, there is a chance to save him—let's just go ahead and do this."

I remember the shoes at his place and cringe at his touch and the pet name, "honey." He retracts his hand.

"Marc, would you shut up? Just because you pretend things are good by not asking tough questions, it doesn't make it so." I'm not just talking about this doctor's visit. Marc quiets down.

"Grace, your concerns are valid. Yes, this is still a trial. There are risks, which will be explained during the orientation session hosted by my team. But you haven't found any material on this because it's still in the clinical stage. Your secrecy is imperative while we plead our study to the Ethics Review Board. All trials on humans must obtain approval to avoid human rights abuses. We don't want to stunt the research and allow Metagenesis to continue to spread simply because the boards haven't given us the official go-ahead."

I blurt out the obvious, "So it's illegal."

"Which is why we insist on anonymity," he replies without a firm yes or no, but I get the picture.

"Anonymity for *you*," I counter.

"Precisely," is his reply, which sounds like a menacing threat when followed by a solid thirty seconds of silence while he stares me down.

I may have addressed him by his first name earlier in an attempt to show courage, but I feel like I am being reminded that it's because he allowed it. Dr. Messie is in charge.

"It is very difficult to determine an exact match." He straightens his posture, becomes animated and suddenly passionate about his speech. "The odds of finding your past life are approximately one in five hundred thousand. With the staggering number of deaths and the missing people who are likely also dead, one in three people is affected by this pandemic." He looks directly at me as he continues. "You two are very fortunate to have a donor with a close enough match in the year 2000."

I gulp—that's nearly eighty years ago.

"All you have to do is identify a man who lived a long time ago and let the science do the rest."

The doctor's right. People would do anything for a chance to save their child from Metagenesis.

"You could be the first to prove our research right and help us hone in on the formula of finding the perfect match for others suffering from this disease. To put it bluntly, you've just won the ultimate lottery—the lottery of saving your son's life and making history, eradicating Metagenesis for good. You have nothing to lose by trying. And everything to lose if you don't," he finishes, driving the point home.

He's right. We can save Jordan. He's going to die if we do nothing. It's just that it all seems so farfetched and too good to be true. I'm scared to say yes or no.

"Do you have any more questions?" Dr. Messie asks as he leans back in his chair, like a lawyer resting his case.

I feel like I am not allowed to ask any more questions, like I'm questioning a god to explain his miracles. Dr. Messie looks like he's done entertaining my scrutiny and answering questions, but to my surprise, Marc speaks up.

"If this has never been done before, how do you know it will work?"

"I don't—that's why it's a trial, Marc. Any more questions?"

"No, he doesn't have any more questions, but I'll do it. I'll go." I jump in before I lose my nerve.

Marc looks over at me. I don't look at him, but I can feel his angry glare.

"She means 'we'; *we* will go."

"Like hell I'm going anywhere with you!" I scream at Marc.

"He's my kid too, and if there is a chance we could save him, then I want to help!" Marc screams back.

"I think I can settle this disagreement." Dr. Messie holds up a hand to stop the brewing argument, looking directly at Marc. "Marc, you can't go," he states matter-of-factly.

"What?" Marc asks, confusion and anger in his voice.

I close my eyes, feeling relief and defeat simultaneously.

"You are more than welcome to attend the pre-orientation

session with Grace and her supporter. Everything will be explained there."

Dr. Messie's statement puts an end to the discussion. Marc sits in the chair, sulking. I would almost feel bad for him, if it weren't for the fear growing inside me about what I'm about to embark on without him, alone. But I don't think I'm alone.

"Doctor, you mentioned a supporter?" I bring us back to the topic, subdued now that I'm getting what I think I want: no Marc. I feel weird over how contented I am about leaving him behind.

"Yes, Grace, you may bring someone to help you—your brother Charlie? Or perhaps Kay?"

It makes me very uncomfortable to hear him referring to people in my life by their first names, reminding me that he knows everything about me, not just my favourite drink and DNA profile. And the mention of my old best friend, Kay, is particularly bothersome, as I haven't spoken to her in a few years now. What would make him think I want her support? Last I heard, Kay was still working at that underground casino: a life I left behind when my dad died three years back. We were best friends. How far back did these people dig up information on us?

"If there are no other questions, my assistant will record your confidentiality agreements and begin the orientation session."

As if on cue, the no-name assistant appears through the glass wall door that, strangely, looks completely see-through but obviously isn't. She carries a takeout container with Jordan's favourite brownies, as promised, and hands them to Marc.

"Right this way." She motions for us to follow and we rise to obey.

Before leaving the room, I pause and look over my shoulder at Dr. Messie. "How do we get there and back?" I ask, and the fat man smiles at me.

"There is a nightly shuttle service to bring you home," he replies. His smile doesn't falter, making it clear that he heard me but is choosing not to respond to the other part of my question. I hope this orientation explains everything.

The assistant ushers us out of the room. We walk down the

long corridor which I assume is the other side of the glass office we were just in. The walls are also glass, and I can see the office, desk, plaques and all, but I don't see Dr. Messie. He couldn't have left the room that quickly, could he have?

"It's glass—you're not imagining it. You can see everything except people on the other side." Dr. Messie's assistant clears her throat and tucks a loose strand of dark hair behind her ear. She appears to be nervous. I hope it's just excitement over this mission they've worked so hard to get going. "It's part of the research on locating souls—one of the first breakthroughs," she offers up. "You could watch your past life like a movie through a looking glass: see but not be seen. Or, at least, that was the original purpose. You can see moments in time surrounding the present. Like snippets from dimensions closest to our own." She shakes her head "Never mind."

"Who is the donor?" I ask, making small talk. "What's his name?"

She clears her throat again, re-tucks the same strand of hair.

"I'm not privy to that," she responds with a hint of irritation. "We're all anonymous." She repeats the line from earlier like she's rehearsed it a million times.

"The driver, Mister, knows our names," I mumble, thinking about how he addressed us by our surnames.

The assistant doesn't react to my comment, but she definitely seems nervous, and as soon as she opens the door at the other end of the hall, I realize why.

"Kay, what are you doing here?"

Kay turns to face me, her eyes wet and wide with worry.

Marc steps out of the way. Kay looks exactly the same: tall, thin and busty. Her hair is still that same dark shade of blue, matching her big, round eyes. I guess she loved that colour enough to keep it up. I've let my own hair go back to its normal dark brown. Back then, it was the deepest purple ever.

"I know, I know. They already told me I have to change the colour back or else I'll stand out like a mango tree on Mars, and it's important to fit in."

I'm just looking at her, not sure what to say. I've missed her and her quirky idioms and comments and the way she just jumps on board—her carefree attitude. I love that she's obviously coming with me even if I'm perplexed as to why she was chosen, given the state of our relationship. Although there should be tension between us, she ignores that possibility and instead walks toward me with wide-open arms, like nothing is wrong at all. Not like we haven't seen each other in years. Not like distance and time and lifestyles have come between us.

I embrace my old friend. She cries as she tells me she's so sorry to hear about Jordan. At the mention of my son, I start to sob too and squeeze her tighter. I've missed her.

"I'm so so sorry, hon, so sorry. What you must be going through." She knows all too well. Her own little brother, Peter, died of Metagenesis when the disease first starting grabbing attention before it escalated to where it is now. We were just kids.

"Girls, this is a lovely reunion and all, but we must begin the orientation and record your confidentiality agreement straight away."

I find it amusing that Dr. Messie's assistant calls us "girls." I think she's about our age, if not a bit younger.

"You must carry on as if everything is normal," says the assistant, who keeps tucking and re-tucking her hair; now I think it's a nervous twitch. "You must check your son into a clinic first thing tomorrow. We've reserved a bed for him in the doctor's own clinic. You must tell people that you are going away to earn extra money to pay for the clinical trials, so they don't wonder about your absence while your son's in critical condition. They will assume you've gone back underground to work in the casinos."

I cringe at the fact that she knows that. Gambling is illegal, and we worked hard to conceal that life. I left it years ago, even before my dad's death. How does she know this?

Before I get a chance to interrogate her, Marc speaks up. I'd almost forgotten he was there, with the excitement of seeing Kay.

"What about me—what do I do?"

I suddenly feel bad for Marc. He's standing there, with his hands in the pockets of his shabby jeans. When did he start dressing like that? I give him a once-over, his sandy hair is a mess, outgrown, needing a cut. He looks helpless.

"Sir." The assistant smiles and places her hand on Marc's arm, letting it linger longer than I'm comfortable with. We're still married.

But the look she gives him is a sad one. She seems to pity him. Maybe she senses how left out he must feel, now that Kay is here, knowing he won't be embarking on this journey with me. And maybe the assistant senses that he still loves me. It's hard to miss his feelings for me—even I sense that he still loves me: the way he looks at me but then looks away just as I meet his eyes.

"Sir," she repeats, even more softly, "you will stay here, watch over Jordan. You will be key to keeping his soul intact until your wife's return in a few weeks." Her voice is gentle, and she doesn't tuck her hair once while talking to him, making her seem genuine.

I like that she referred to me as Marc's wife. I decide right then that I like her, this no-name assistant. I need to start trusting someone, and I'm going to start with her. There is something about her, her gentleness, her small display of trust telling us about the glass wall, her sympathetic tone with Marc.

We finish the confidentiality agreement and then leave to go prepare. Tomorrow, we bring our son to the clinic, where people go to die. Except he is not going to die. We're going to make history. Jordan will be the first to survive this deadly disease, Metagenesis. Or he will die while I try, without me.

CHAPTER 4

Jordan clings to his belongings tightly, bringing the sack close under his chin as we nervously tread down the clinic's corridor toward Ward 6, where he will share his room with three others suffering from Metagenesis. Everyone here has been sentenced to death when you think about it. That's what this clinic is: these souls are on death row. Those waiting for a cure come here, but rather than being cured, they die. At least they're not wandering the streets alone, like some others who don't get into the clinics; those who go missing, never to be found or seen again.

Marc's hand rests on the small of Jordan's back, guiding him. I walk a few paces behind, feeling angst over lying to Jordan. He doesn't know we're working to save his life. He doesn't know about the medical trial we're participating in, been threatened to stay silent about. Jordan thinks he's coming here to die. I remember visiting Kay's brother, Peter, years ago in one of these clinics. Not much has changed. Even this place, sponsored by Dr. Messie, still looks and smells just like I remember: sterile, medicine cabinet-y, disinfectant-y—somehow, that cleanliness smells just like a disease to me. The lights don't seem bright enough, yet they are too bright.

When we reach Ward 6, Jordan doesn't even pause at the door. In fact, he lets the sack down from under his chin, dropping his hands to his side, straightens his shoulders, raises his head just so, and walks into his new room. He bravely nods hello to his new roommates and makes his way over to the empty bed by the window. Sadly, it was probably vacated by another victim taken by Metagenesis. Marc follows him in.

I hesitate at the door, to take in my son's new home. Even though Jordan is not here to die, hopefully, I still feel defeated. My uneasiness at leaving him here is not just about honouring the confidentiality agreement, keeping silent so I'm not silenced. I'm scared. I'm really, really scared. Everything is moving too fast. Just a few weeks ago, my boy was doing regular kid stuff, and today...

Last night, right after I came home from the orientation, he had another episode. Charlie was panicked. "You've been gone forever—I didn't know what to do," he said, the second I walked in the door.

I rushed into the back room right away to find Jordan, his eyes semi-open, but unfocused. He was unconscious.

"He was mumbling at first, and I tried to keep him alert, keep him from closing his eyes, but he was slurring his words, lethargic, then he stopped responding altogether. I didn't know what to do—I was going to tie him down. I didn't want him to wander off like he did before. I haven't left his side. What did Dr. Messie say?"

Charlie seemed so desperate, I felt terrible lying to him about what the doctor had really said.

"The doctor said he got him a spot at the best clinic, the most prestigious one with the best care. So we're checking him in tomorrow, where he will be made comfortable while he waits to... you know," I lied as I looked down at Jordan. "It looks like this couldn't have come at a better time." That part wasn't a lie.

I glance around the room and notice that all Jordan's roommates are boys. They all look about the same age as Jordan, the oldest maybe around eleven or twelve. The dark-haired one directly beside my son is sitting up in bed, playing a solo game of chess. He looked like he was concentrating, strategizing, until he noticed us. Now he smiles, ignoring his game, as we approach. He is the only one who does. The two others remain quiet and don't even acknowledge our entrance. He's surrounded by personal articles, probably from his own room. He looks right at home, comfortable. It's disturbing how relaxed he seems—he's probably been here a while. The decorative homemade photogram frame hanging on the wall shows a younger him standing beside a woman in her thirties with almond-shaped eyes that match his—probably his mother.

He looks so pale like he hasn't seen the light of day in quite some time, the blue veins under his dark eyes showing through. But he has a huge, toothy smile as he sets his game aside and maturely stretches his hand out to Jordan.

"I'm Walt."

Jordan shakes his hand and seems to let his guard down, but doesn't introduce himself. Walt nods in our direction and waves at Marc and me.

"He's Jordan," Marc says.

Walt invites Jordan to play chess, and without waiting for a response, he demolishes his unfinished game and sets up a new one. They hit it off well—or, at least, Walt is outgoing enough to counter Jordan's shyness, and I'm relieved for that. I was worried about moving my quiet kid to this new place, but Walt seems big-brother-like. He seems friendly, chatty, and he makes eye contact. He talks to Jordan and fills in the blanks when Jordan replies shyly or doesn't reply at all. I like him immediately.

Marc and I set up Jordan's area with personal belongings from his room to make him feel as comfortable as possible in his new surroundings. I remind myself that this is temporary. Jordan will not die here. This is all just to keep him safe from wandering. Each item Marc or I unpack makes me reminisce; the ancient paper passport I brought back for Jordan as a souvenir is a bittersweet memory. It simultaneously reminds me of my dad's death and of bonding with Charlie. When Dad died three years ago, my brother and I sold off his container home and took a trip to the other side of the world with his ashes before laying him to rest where the Statue of Liberty still stands. It was where he proposed to our mother. As we passed through the old borders, we stamped our old-fashioned passports and wondered what it must've been like living in a time where people were separated by countries, laws, and languages—not just by wealth, as it is today. It all seemed so complicated.

I jiggle my watch, remembering my dad to distract myself from how wrong all of this is. I don't want Jordan to get too comfortable. He thinks I'm leaving to earn money to keep him here—that's the story Marc and I agreed upon. It kills me to think he doesn't know all I'm risking to do this. He doesn't know that I may not even be here with him on his last days in this world. This is his last life. His soul is dying, which means he will never be reincarnated ever again. That I might miss his last moments but I don't have a choice angers me.

Today I am angry, and that's exactly what I want to be. Not sad about today, and not anxious about tomorrow, when Kay and I will be transported to Marc's past life in Las Vegas.

Before we leave, I kiss Jordan hard on his forehead, brush his hair to the side.

"I'll be back soon, Jordan. You understand I have to go, right?"

He looks up from his chess game. Walt doesn't take his eyes off the board, which I appreciate, the little privacy that gesture affords me.

"Do you have to go tomorrow? You can't wait a few days?" asks Jordan in a small voice.

"I have to go." I command myself not to cry. I try not to meet his eyes, distract myself by fluffing his hair, scratching his head like he usually does to Lucy. "But I'll be back real soon. I don't want you to worry because Dr. Messie and his team are working really hard on the research—they're going to find a cure for all the lost old souls. Metagenesis will be a thing of the past. You'll see. Everything is going to be just fine."

I hope.

His hair is soft and wavy, just like his dad's. He looks so much like Marc, right down to the exact shade of his hazel eyes. His expression says "I don't believe you"; his expression says "I know there's no cure" and "I know you're just trying to make me feel better," so "please be back before I die." I finally meet those hazel eyes I was trying to avoid, and they make me melt from within.

"I love you, little man. I'll be back before you can even miss me."

I hope.

"I love you too, Mom."

Marc walks me out of the clinic to the front entrance, through the beautifully landscaped gardens generously funded by the Messie family, which reminds me that this is Dr. Messie's clinic. Only those with money are privileged to visit their families here unless you're Dr. Messie's lab rat.

"Are you sure you want to do this, Grace? What if you don't make it back in time?" Marc asks me, but it's redundant. We've been through this, and I don't like this conversation, given my trust issues with the doctor responsible for my safe passage through past lives and time.

"Yes, stop asking me! Just be there for Jordan and support my decision to do this. If I don't do this, he will die, guaranteed. Saving his life is a risk worth taking."

Marc's not the one leaving everything behind, who may never see his family again. "You know what, Marc? I'm the one risking everything to go!" I feel like a bubble about to burst, and Marc is the needle that got a little too close by exposing my fear and anxiety. My fingers reach for my temples, my face heating up.

"I wanted to come," he protests.

"But you're off the hook! You're not coming!" I want to rip my hair out. "So stop questioning me, because I'm done explaining!" I use the vision of the red shoes in his living room to replace my fear with anger, my voice escalating. "In fact, why do you care if I go or if I stay?" I know I'm just pushing Marc away like I always do, but knowing you're on fire doesn't help to extinguish the flames.

I ignore the nurses and clinic technicians, who are probably staring at us, given Marc's uncomfortable eyes darting around, embarrassed at being scolded in public.

"We're finished, remember?" I snap, and Marc flinches. I hit him where it hurts, and I immediately feel like a jerk for pouring salt on a wound I created when I left him. I bite the inside of my cheek to hold back my venomous tongue.

He stares back at me while I try to read his mind but can't, and as usual, he doesn't speak it. Silence fills the gap between us for several minutes.

"Do you have a better idea?" I ask, defusing the tension, feeling guilty. I know he means well. The stakes are high. Jordan is his son too, and I know he misses me, misses us, his family. Part of me misses him too, I think.

He breaks eye contact and stares down at the ground. He looks like he is gearing up to speak, clearing his throat. Maybe he has something to say after all.

"What about all that stuff they said in the orientation?" He shuffles his feet, shifting weight from one foot to the other. Suddenly I don't want him to speak any more. I don't want him to voice his opinion, because I suspect we share the same fear. "You know, about us being soulmates? What if we're not, and you don't identify the right donor? What if you go for nothing?"

I just stare at him, but he doesn't look up at me, just continues to glare down at his shuffling feet. I don't have an answer. The thought more than just crossed my mind. I haven't been able to stop thinking about it, obsessing over it. Marc spent hours in regression answering questions about his fears, habits, phobias, and dreams, trying to determine the personality of the donor we need to find, a past version of himself. The rest of it is up to me.

This is someone I'm divorcing. Why would I divorce my soulmate?

"I don't know what to say," I admit in a quiet voice, holding back the urge to cry from frustration or fly off the handle again, whichever.

He finally looks up at me, meets my eyes and stops his nervous shuffle. At that moment, I think we both realize that we fear finding out the absolute truth that we really are not meant to be together; not in this life, not in any life. This journey will also uncover without a shadow of a doubt that we are, and always were, a mistake. And if we were an error in judgment, not only is our relationship over and the past decade or so a waste, but our son will die as a result of our mistake.

"Just be back, OK?" he says, matching my low tone.

"OK." I hope I can keep my promise.

CHAPTER 5
NOW

We must be getting closer. In the distance, we see a gathering of sorts. But not like it was described in the orientation. They told us Las Vegas was lively, with overbearing lights and extravagant people, parties and unruliness. I had pictured it looking a bit like the days that followed the ending of the borders that divided the world. I was only a child, but I still remember the celebrations. People thought it would be a good thing. And maybe it would've been if Metagenesis hadn't begun plaguing the world. Some extremists blamed the Metagenesis disease on the world coming together. They argued that losing identities was the first step, and losing souls was an inevitable consequence.

"Why are all those people dressed in black huddled around like someone just killed their dog?" Kay asks, reading my mind.

"I don't know, but we should check it out. We've been walking for hours in this heat, I'm thirsty, we're covered in dust, and that's the first sign of life we've seen," I whine. "My feet are killing me, not to mention my leg from that smack it took." I rub at the already swollen spot on my thigh, picturing the bruise that must be forming.

When we first arrived, it was dark. The sun wasn't even up yet. We awoke after hitting the ground in complete blackness. I don't know what time it is now, but from the increasing heat and the sun blaring down on my scalp, it's got to be almost noon. This is ridiculous. Why would they leave us so far away from civilization, in the middle of a dusty, hot desert, in the month of August no less? We were told we'd be landing in summer and it would be warm. This is more than just warm.

"It's an oven out here," I moan. Toronto is never this hot or dry, and the contrast of leaving there in rainy October to come to this August heat is almost more than I can bear.

"I'm hungry," Kay complains.

It's amusing to me that she can even think about food right now. I'm worried about finding a place to stay or whether we landed in the right city and century, as this is nothing like what was described in our orientation.

As we get closer to the gathering, we realize some of the people are softly crying. They don't seem to notice us approaching, but Kay and I realize we're being intrusive and we stop at a nearby tree for coverage.

"I think it's a funeral," I say, and just as I do, one of the mourners looks right at us.

He looks annoyed. He's not crying like the rest of them, and I immediately look away.

"Great!" Kay exclaims. "Spotted by the cute guy! Nice going. Look, Grace, I'm starving. With any luck, the tradition of feeding people at funerals started a long, long time ago. Let's go in that building over there and see if we can find something to eat before I pass out." She rubs her stomach with a pained look on her face.

"Are you suggesting we crash a funeral?" My pulse quickens. I'm nervous about encountering people from this era. I'm worried about standing out so much: we're wearing shiny silver outfits! Whose dumb idea was that? "Stupid no-name assistant," I curse her out loud. I thought I liked her, but right now, I'm not so sure. "'Dr. Messie knows nothing about fashion from those days,'" I mock with a screwed-up face.

"What? What's Dr. Messie's bimbo got to do with this?

Anyway, I'm not suggesting we crash a funeral—I'm suggesting we sneak in before. Like a pre-crash. And sample the party favours."

And with that, she's already leading the way confidently. Two girls, dressed like hookers from Venus, walking across a cemetery carrying a pig full of money. No, that's not weird.

I follow Kay, not as confidently, and chance a look back to see if anyone is noticing this scene. If they are, they're ignoring us. That cute guy wasn't looking anymore, either. I tighten the straps to the pouch that holds the phone book and other stuff. The pig was uncomfortable on my back, but I wish I could shove him back in the pouch so it would muffle the sound of the money he holds in his belly.

Inside it's better than I expected, more extravagant than any funeral I've been to—not that I make it a habit of attending many. I think back to my dad's funeral, with the few friends who showed. His death was awkward and the circumstances uncomfortable; maybe that's why it was so bare. Whoever's funeral we're at now must've had lots of friends, and died of something honourable because there is plenty of food. There are snacks and sandwiches on disposable platters, with disposable toothpicks and paper napkins and disposable little plates. What a disposable society this era was. Even though we learned about this in our orientation, it's still shocking to see. I can't imagine using something once and then tossing it aside.

We first head over to the bathroom, where we splash cold water on our faces and brush our teeth. I silently thank the assistant for the toiletries, even if I'm mad about the itchy outfit. I'm tempted to stick my feet in the sink, they're so hot and swollen from all the walking, but I refrain. If Kay did it first, I'd go for it. I watch as she pushes a brush through her freshly dyed auburn hair. It's weird to see her stripped of her blue waves. I pull my dark, tangled curls into a tighter ponytail. I wish we could change out of these flashy outfits.

I guess the assistant didn't think we'd be dropping in for a bite at a funeral with fifty mourners dressed in black. We look so out of place we might as well be wearing a sign that says "we're from the future, give us your soul." I look at Kay, and we nod in agreement to hurry this up and get out of here.

"Let's grab a snack and run," I whisper, even though we're alone in the bathroom.

Kay leads the way. Ah, shit, I almost forget the ceramic pig. I go back for him. I tuck him under my arm, and when I turn around, Kay is already gone, the door swinging closed. I put my foot in the door to stop it and peek through the gap to see Kay heading over to the buffet table. The reception must've started. It was empty when we came in, but now people are mingling, exchanging hugs with soft expressions, stroking arms, squeezing shoulders with sympathy. I decide not to follow Kay. Two girls in go-go dancer suits stand out more than one girl in a go-go dancer suit, I reason. My stomach aches with hunger—or, more likely, knots of nervousness—as I watch Kay stashing sandwiches and other snacks into another wasteful napkin. I just stand at the door, embarrassed for her, afraid of someone shouting "hey you!", and yet no one does. No one pays her any attention at all.

I spot the "cute guy," or rather, he spots me, and I can feel him staring at me. Damnit. I hope I don't look like I feel.

I step out of the bathroom and try to appear as normal as possible as if I belong here. He is leaning against the wall, conversing with someone but keeping an eye on me. I'm curious about what they're talking about—if they're talking about us, the intruders. But I'm relieved that I am not close enough to hear what they're saying at all. That means I'm not close enough for him to hear my heart pounding against my chest, as I can, loud and clear. It seems to me like he's just pretending to chat with the older gentleman he's standing with. The other guy does most of the talking, while cute guy smokes a cigarette and steals glances my way.

I make eye contact with Kay, who has now started up a conversation with an old woman at the buffet table. Smiling, they look like they've known each other a hundred years. How does she do that? Fits in everywhere—even when she stands out, she still fits in. Maybe that's why she was chosen to come with me. I'm trying to understand why she's here, with me, chasing Marc's soul.

I give her a firm stare and tilt my head toward the exit. She catches the hint and heads toward the main doors, where we meet. I take a last look over my shoulder as we leave the building. The cute guy is gone. I'm relieved that no one stopped us.

"I told that lady we were from out of town and were looking for a recommendation on where to stay near the action for cheap. She made a few suggestions for us."

"That's bold," I reply.

"Ya, well, we're on a time crunch—no time to waste, right? Anyway, when I asked her how to get there on foot, she laughed and gave me this." Kay holds out a green piece of rectangular paper with the number "20" on it. "She told me to ask reception to call us a taxi."

"She gave you currency? Is that what this is? The paper version of money?" She shrugs in response. "That's weird, Kay. Why would she do that?"

"Whatever—let's just get there. I like the sounds of the Travelodge she mentioned. She said they include breakfast. Let's go there."

We arrive at the motel and pay the driver. He gives us back nine green monies he calls "change," and I shove it into the porcelain pig, through the hole on the bottom.

"This thing seems impractical," I tell Kay. "Why isn't anyone else carrying one?"

At the orientation, they told us everyone saved money this way. I'm having doubts about that.

The front-desk guy, Brad on his name tag, watches as we shake the money out of the pig to pay for three weeks at the hotel. He looked bored when we first got here, but now he seems entertained by the two crazy girls covered in sweat from the Las Vegas heat.

"You're gonna have to come up with more money than that," he says with a chuckle. "It's forty-five bucks a night. Whatever little girl you took that from only saved enough for one."

"Where do we get more, uh... bucks?" I ask.

Kay nudges me. That was obviously a dumb question.

"Guess you'd better try your luck at the casino." He laughs sarcastically. "Either pay up or be out by tomorrow, girls. Check-out time is noon."

He slides over a shiny metal thing I recognize as a key from our orientation, before he turns his attention back to the TV in front of a wall covered in pictures of busty ladies. "Room 221" is written on the attached plastic tag.

"What the hell are we going to do? Why would that assistant only give us enough for one night?" I shake the stupid pig, which only has a few coins and a bill or two left in it. Even most of the change from the taxi has gone into paying for the room.

I'm pacing back and forth. Kay is sitting on the dilapidated bed; nothing like the comforts of home.

When we first arrived at the motel, we thought we'd be checking into a palace, since it was an actual brick and mortar building. In our era, only the ultra-rich live in those. The majority of the population lives in converted trailers—or, if you're better off, converted shipping containers, which are larger than trailers. On the way to the motel, a truck passed us with a home on the back and pig snouts sticking out through the holes. In this era, our homes seem to be their method of transportation. It's weird to see houses on big wheels being used to transport goods, even livestock.

This new home of ours is dark and dingy and smells like the carpet has been wet and then dried with the windows closed, over and over. A flower-patterned, thinned-out comforter covers a small lump at the top, disguising the flattest pillows I've ever seen. There is a contraption on the dresser that must be a TV. It's big and boxy and covered by a layer of dust.

"Calm down, Grace. We'll just go make some more money at the casino like Brad said."

I stop pacing to look at her. Really look at her. She is incredible. She can't be serious. "You do know he was being sarcastic, right? A casino, Kay. Those are built to *take* your money, not pay you a salary. They didn't survive hundreds of years, right up to our own decade—even illegally—because they were charitable. A casino is a casino. A money-grab for the owners. You still work at one, no?"

"Yes, I know, but I don't see another choice, do you?" she replies harshly. "Look, we have three weeks. We need to get out of these stripper outfits, which means we need to shop or risk getting caught for stealing." She holds up her index finger as she continues. "Secondly, we need to pay for our accommodations or risk sleeping on the streets." Second finger. "Thirdly, we need to eat, Grace, or we starve." She looks me dead in the eye as she makes her last statement, without making it a point on her finger, with a seriousness I don't often hear from her. "And we need to save your son's life. We need to save Jordan."

I sit on the bed next to her, bury my face in my hands. We just got here, and I'm already feeling like we're not going to make it.

"Grace, I am just as nervous as you, just as scared."

It's nice to hear her admit it, after watching her confidence at that funeral.

"It hasn't escaped me that that stupid woman sent us here wearing suits that stand out like palm trees in the Arctic."

I laugh a little at her analogy. It certainly didn't seem like it bothered her. "Let's go play some slots. And if that doesn't work, we'll rob a bank."

We choose a casino that looks more like our time. It has a link-car track at the top, much like the transportation systems we're used to, minus the solar tube. Only it doesn't go anywhere, just around a track. We make our way to the gambling floors, laughing at the idea of two girls from the future, dressed as we are, carrying a ceramic pig and a pile of funeral sandwiches, robbing a bank. "Feed my pig, bitch!" We joke, getting giddier as we play out that scenario and other versions, including Brad and the cute funeral guy trying to stop us with the plane we rode in on from the future. The comic relief is welcomed. For a brief moment, it's like we're kids again, playing dress-up with elaborate stories. That's how it started for Kay and me. It was all innocent then before we took it a step further and brought our act to the casinos—except then the elaborate stories were to distract people to lose more of their money.

We look for just the right slot machine, choosing it like we used to as trouble-making kids. We used to like the sparkly ones with cute dogs or cats on them, and we giggle as we agree on one machine that reminds us of our childhood. We slide the last of our green bills in and spin away. The universe must be smiling on our positive attitudes, or maybe pitying us, making up for our homesickness. Whatever it is, the machine comes to life with bells and ringing and lights. Holy shit, we just won!

And that's when I catch someone staring at me: a man, turning his back and walking off in the other direction when I try to meet his eyes. I didn't get a good look at him, but I felt him getting a good look at me.

CHAPTER 6

Still giddy from our big win of $1,299.99, we sit in the booth of some diner with the theme "fifties American," whatever that means. The booths are made of old bucket seats from cars. Our booth says "Thunderbird." We order food that looks risky but smells good and joke about all the things we could buy. I push the thought of the man at the casino aside for now. I thought I was being paranoid and so I didn't pursue my gut feeling by following him, but now I wish I had. I should've made Kay wait at the machine while I went after him, but she told me I was being crazy. I regret listening to her, although I don't know what I would've said to him. "Hey, boy, we're from the future—come here often?"

On the way to the diner, Kay and I pretended the world was fine. Like the old girlfriends we had been in grade school, we even stopped in a few stores on the way and tried on some big hats. I bought a fun nail polish, which I now turn over in my hand, admiring the glittery bottle. We bought new outfits so we would blend in—jean shorts and a few tank tops—although we haven't changed into them yet. Ironically, they look much like the outfits we had on before Miss-No-Name made us change. I guess Dr. Messie knows more about fashion than his assistant gave him credit for.

Sitting across from each other now, it's pretty clear we haven't seen each other in a long time, and although it was awkward at first, we still manage to pick up where we left off, catching up on each other's lives. Kay is still living *la vida loca*, working at the casino. She still dates only older men who are witty enough to keep up with her, trying to find the right one to sweep her off her feet. She doesn't keep in contact with her parents much (no surprise there); she still lives in the same funky container home; and yes, she still changes the colours and decor based on her mood, the same way she does her hairstyle—sometimes weekly.

It's my fault we're not close anymore, and now here she is, helping me. I don't deserve her service and loyalty, but I make every effort to minimize the tension between us, so she doesn't question her decision to lend it to me.

There is a large TV on the wall behind the red and white counter of the diner, where some guests sit staring at it. It's very two-dimensional compared to our holograms, although not as boxy as the one in our room. But what catches my attention is the unfolding story on their news.

"Check it out." I nod toward the TV.

Kay looks just in time to see them replaying a scene shot from above the ocean waters. There is no volume, but the ticker at the bottom informs us about a tanker that has spilled oil in the oceans and the devastation it will cause. Then the camera comes back to a reporter, who talks about the effect this will have on the economy.

"Oil affected the economy," I state in awe, shaking my head.

"I don't get it; did they trade it? You can't eat that kind of oil," Kay says.

When the food arrives, we quiet down. I think about how life should be as simple as it once was for us, and yet it's not. Kay and I exchange a glance. These moments and small talk make me miss spending time with my friend. Why did I cut her off? And why didn't she try to avoid being cut off? When did I forget to have fun? Since Dad...

I push the thought away and breathe in the smell of the French fries I ordered, closing my eyes while taking in the aroma of the hamburger on my plate. The pickles tingle my nostrils. The meat is shiny, the fries too. When I reach for a fry, they burn my fingertips, which I instinctively put to my mouth to cool them down. My fingers taste extremely salty. I assemble my hamburger like I saw the other patrons doing, taking care to place each ringlet of red onion to have an equal amount on all sides of the glimmering meat. The lettuce doesn't stay on well, and so I swap it around, putting the lettuce first, then the onions last. I delicately place the top half of the bun, trying not to lose the seeds in the process. A few of them brush off, pinging the plate—argh. I examine my work of art before bringing the burger to my lips and taking a small, cautious bite.

When I look up at Kay, I giggle as I see how different we are. Her approach was much less careful than mine. Her cheeks are full of greasy hamburger goodness. She crams salty fries into her mouth and simultaneously slurps on her thick milkshake. Sesame seeds fall from her face, and the dill sauce has yet to be wiped off her full mouth.

"I'd be careful—you remember what they said about all this processed food," I warn.

Kay shoves a fry into her mouth in response. "If I died today..." she starts, wiping her face but missing half the mess on it. "I'd die a happy woman," Kay calls the waitress back and orders another milkshake. Where she finds room to put all that food is beyond me.

"Holy crap, this stuff is good. No wonder it's addictive." She talks with her mouth full, stuffing another bite into her mouth before finishing what's already in there.

I eat as slowly as she eats quickly. I silently savour every bite while Kay moans quietly, tasting each new mouthful, her eyes rolling back in her head. Kay finishes before I'm even half done and she gets on to business without waiting for me.

"We need to plot out how to make this money last the three weeks we're here," says Kay, not wasting any time taking charge. "So," she goes on, mouth still full, "not sure you realize, but making this money last the whole time we're here is impossible. You're either going to have to strip for money or gamble for it."

"Well, OK, then." I laugh out loud, stunned by her candour,

although I should be accustomed to it. "I think *you* should strip for it—you've got the bigger boobs, after all." I motion at her bosom, tucked into her low-cut shirt, which is far more revealing on her than on my frame. "You're already dressed for the occasion. Who wouldn't hire you?" I tease.

"Look," she responds, ignoring my joke. She swallows the rest of her food, dabbing her face with another paper napkin. I guess the jokes are done for now. "If we do nothing to earn any more money, we will have about sixty dollars a day. That has to feed us, pay for that grungy hotel, make phone calls to check and leave messages on the pager. This meal just cost us like..." She pauses as she does some quick math. "Maybe thirty bucks or so." She's already using the right lingo to fit in, but she can't do math worth a crap—it was twenty-two dollars. "And we haven't even done anything to look for David Williams. It's only day one. We need to spend money to find this guy, like transportation or whatever." She looks across the table at me.

I've stopped eating, wondering if she is serious or crazy or what. "I'm not stripping," I state, suddenly losing my appetite.

"I figured that," Kay replies, actual disappointment in her voice, and she slouches in her seat. "But let's be honest here. I'm a better people person. I'm better at talking to people, getting answers, a little more..." she looks for her words, "approachable. And you, well, you're really great at smart things like weighing odds, math, thinking things. Not people things."

"Where are you going with this?" I ask, knowing exactly where she is going with this.

"I think you should gamble, and I should do a preliminary search. I'll try to weed out the wrong matches with a name search, while you make us money. When you've made enough to keep us fed and housed for the duration, then you'll only need to sort through the potential matches, and not the duds. I'll do the groundwork, get it?"

"So, you want me to spend our money gambling? Or take my clothes off for it?"

"Well, when you put it that way, it sounds bad. Gosh, Grace, you sure know how to spin things. I'm just trying to put our strengths to good use. Divide and conquer. I don't want you to spend our money gambling—I want you to invest our money, make it grow. You're good at this! All those years your dad took you to those underground casinos before you got all righteous. What a shame if that went to waste." She folds her arms across her chest, looking satisfied with her shot at me. "Don't pretend like you're all perfect, Grace. You had a very interesting life, once upon a time."

I stuff a cold fry into my mouth—not because I'm hungry; my appetite is gone gone gone. I stuff it into my mouth to buy me time, in place of having to speak. I'm amazed at how horrible they taste when they're cold. They're oily, yet dry.

"So?" Kay persists.

I draw a deep breath, stuff another fry in my mouth, avoid her eyes. I nod yes rather than say it. Like saying yes out loud is going to bring it all back, my love and hatred for my father. I met Marc at that casino, on his eighteenth birthday, dressed in skydiving gear, getting himself pumped up for the plunge. He was a terrible gambler, but a sweet talker. I took his money in a poker game; in return, he took my heart. I think I miss him. I think I miss us.

I push those feelings down with another cold fry, but thankfully I'm saved by a jolt in my side. That thing is vibrating in my pocket. It reminds me of the repertoire in Marc's lap, receiving pamphlets about Jordan. Except this pager won't deliver medical alerts or pamphlets; this pager will notify me about updates on my son. I'm happy for the interruption from this conversation and where my thoughts were taking me about my feelings for Marc. I'm sure I'm just homesick, nothing more.

"Let's go—gotta check the message." I rise and rush out, leaving half a plate of uneaten food, not waiting for Kay's reply.

"Wait, Grace, wait! We have to pay!"

I ignore her and rush out to the street, looking for a phone booth, recalling the pictures they showed us of red booths. I see a similar-looking one, not red, across the street.

"You gonna be quick?" I ask the stranger on the phone when I get there.

He looks annoyed, bats me away. His reaction reinforces the fact of my not-so-tactful people skills Kay spoke of. I have no patience to wait.

Kay comes up behind me, ticked at me for leaving her.

"When you're done with that," she points at the casino entrance we're standing near, then hands me a wad of money, "double this or lose it trying. Meet me back at the motel when you're done. I'll start weeding out the duds, and we'll regroup this evening."

Kay being here with me is panning out well, and I'm going to remind myself of that each time I wonder why she was imposed on me. I need her. I love how she takes charge when I can't.

She doesn't say anything more, just leaves me behind and heads off toward wherever she's going to do her search.

"What are you going to do?" I ask behind her.

"Don't worry about it, I got this," she responds without looking back at me.

I look across the street at the casino hotel. There's a big sphinx guarding it. I decide I'll go back to that other one with the link track to nowhere—that's where our luck began. Don't walk away from a lucky streak: that's what my dad always said.

I turn the little black device around in my hand, examining it. In the orientation, the assistant called it a pager. She said they're not really used in the 2000s anymore, so we are not to show it around if we want to fit in. When I asked if I could have something more suited to the time period, she explained that pagers give off the least radiation. At first, they were just going to send us, with no way of communicating, but I wasn't having it. I told them I wouldn't go without some way of knowing Jordan was OK. Instead of calling my bluff, they provided me with this pager. I'll receive updates on Jordan, and in return, I'm expected to leave messages to let them know we're OK and to update them on our progress with finding the donor, David Williams. I guess it's a win-win situation—that's probably why they didn't call my bluff. They update me, and then they can follow me.

The little screen has come to life with a green light and blocky numbers on it, buzzing in my hand as a reminder to check. I'm anxious to hear the message, get an update on how Jordan is, and nervous at the same time, afraid that things are falling apart in my absence.

The guy on the phone covers the mouthpiece. "There's another one right there." He points impatiently. I give him a smile as thanks, cross over to where he's pointing.

I pick up the receiver and dial just as I was instructed to and listen to the mechanical voice telling me how to check the message. I have one message.

"Hi, it's me. Well, duh, obviously." It's Marc, and I'm surprised to hear his voice. For some reason, I assumed only Dr. Messie's personnel would be leaving messages. "Um, things are, well, you know. Jordan is holding up. He had one quick moment of unconsciousness, but the team at the clinic brought him right back. So, I hope you don't mind that Miss-No-Name told me I could leave the messages for you. Well, I kind of begged, a little bit..." He pauses. "Grace? Please leave me a message back? Just tell me you've arrived OK." He pauses again before hanging up, not saying anything more.

I replay the message and try to read between the lines, read into the silence and his pauses and his begging to communicate with me. Then I reply to his message.

"Hi Marc, all is good over here. Arrived safe and sound. Kay is doing a preliminary search while I..." I hesitate. I don't want to tell him about the deal Kay and I made. "We're just about to start our search now. Things are good. Thanks for the update. Please leave me more... updates. Umm, bye." My finger hovers over the pound key to send the message. I want to tell him I miss him. But that's probably a stupid idea. "Tell Jordan I love him." I hang up, allow my hand to linger on the receiver as I work up the nerve to hail a cab back to that other casino. I shouldn't be spending money on taxis. But something is drawing me back to that other place.

Deep breath. Here goes...

The sights and sounds of this casino are overwhelming in comparison to the memory of them from my childhood. When Charlie and I used to go with my dad, we had seats right next to him at the poker tables, saving him babysitting money. The rooms were dark, dingy, quiet so they wouldn't be noticed by the outside world.

This casino is loud and obnoxious, like my silver outfit—I'm glad I changed out of it in the taxi while the driver tried to pretend not to watch me. This casino is full of people; most of the stools are occupied. The bells ring, even the carpet seems loud if that's possible. So this is what it was like when gambling was still legal. The casinos we gambled or worked at were filled with quiet people trying not to see or be seen. One thing certainly hasn't changed, I think to myself as I watch an old, weathered man perform the rituals of rubbing at the screen, sweeping his fingertips along the cartoons, willing them to pay money before he slaps the spin button.

I walk through the slots and search for a card game. That's what I was good at. I learned by watching my dad. He was a terrible father, but a fantastic gambler. Blackjack, poker. Those were my strong suits. I smile at my own ironic joke as I approach the familiar sounds of clinking chips and shuffling cards.

First, I do what my dad taught me. Scope out the house, learn the rules. Every time a casino was closed down, we would search for a new one and would have to learn the rules all over again, as they differ from house to house. Adapting was key.

When I'm comfortable, I find a table I like, grab a stool, buy some chips, and place my first bet. It's awkward at first, and the feeling takes me right back to the first bet I ever placed without my dad. I was twelve; he was proud.

"I like your watch."

I look at the anchor for our table to acknowledge his compliment. Oh god, it's that guy from the funeral. He doesn't look at me and the "thank you" gets stuck in my throat.

"What's it gonna be, honey—are you gonna take a card?" the dealer asks me.

I bring my attention back to the game. I have eleven, against the dealer's five.

"I think you should double-down. Do you know what that is?" says the anchor guy with a smile on his face, still not looking at me.

I wonder if he recognizes me now that I'm not in that ridiculous outfit and I'm without my sidekick, Kay.

"It means you only get one more card and—"

"I know what it means, thanks." I hastily place a stack of chips next to my bet to double-down.

"Just trying to help." He puts his hands up in surrender. "You're obviously new here."

I sit up straighter, try to look confident, to contradict his comment about my looking new. I don't want to look new; I want to fit in.

I win the hand and double my initial bet. I'm in a hurry to either win or lose, meet with Kay, and get on to why we're here.

"So what kind of watch is it? It looks original."

I shake my wrist to hear the familiar sound the dull copper chain makes as it takes my vitals—or it used to, anyway, before the body scans were introduced in schools and automated alerts were sent home. Alerts I wished I had noticed when they went missing. Now I just wear the watch for the memory of my father.

"It was my dad's. He was an antique collector."

"Antique? That thing looks like it's from *The Jetsons*."

I don't know who the Jetsons are, but I recognize my mistake right away, from his emphasis on the word "antique." I make a conscious decision not to talk anymore. I don't think he has recognized me, and I don't want to give him a reason to remember me now.

I win the next few hands and quit while I'm ahead, something else my dad always said to do but never did. I tip the dealer and nod a friendly farewell to the anchor guy.

"Good luck with your audition," he says, catching me off guard. "That is why you were dressed in those silver outfits, right? You're auditioning for the new show?" Anchor guy nods to the giant sign advertising the first round of open auditions beginning tomorrow, August tenth.

"Ya, sure. Uh, thanks." I fake a smile and mentally kick myself as I walk in shame to cash out my winnings. Who would forget a couple of girls dressed as we were, in the midst of a sea of people wearing black—at a funeral, no less. Silver, stupid, shiny outfits, skin-tight, showing cleavage, at a funeral. Idiots!

The whole walk back to my dumpy motel, I think about the

rush I feel from the quick win and stress about being recognized by the guy at the funeral and what are the chances that I would sit right next to him at the blackjack table. Of all the tables I could've chosen.

When I arrive at our room, the door is ajar. It's strange, but maybe Kay just ran in to grab something. When I open the door all the way, I realize something is wrong and stop abruptly at the threshold. I step back to look at the room number, compare it with the number on my key in my hand. Yes, this is the right room number, 221, but this is not our room—it can't be. It's been ransacked, every piece of furniture overturned; the blankets are tossed about on the floor, baring a stained mattress and mismatched box spring. The mattress has been lifted and moved. The contents of the pack we brought have been dumped out on a pile, next to the dusty TV, which has been moved too.

I step inside to take it all in.

"Hello? Who's there?" I call out, against my better judgment. If someone is still here, that's a dumb thing to do, but I continue toward the bathroom, toward the sound of the shuffling I hear in there. Someone is here, cornered in that bathroom right now.

CHAPTER 7

I reach the bathroom door, which is closed. I don't know what I'll do now that I'm standing here. Should I open it? Call out again? Knock? Run out of the room altogether, because that's the smart thing a girl should do when there is an intruder cornered in her bathroom?

I can still hear the shuffling and try to imagine what they could be looking for in our bathroom.

"Hello?" I grab the handle, turn it quickly and slam the door open as fast as I can, banging it against the tub as I jump back to get a full view, startling whoever is there.

"*Ahhh!* What the hell?" It's Kay. She's gripping the phone book in her arms over her chest as she stumbles backward into the corner, away from the swinging door.

"Kay! Holy shit! I was calling out—didn't you hear me?"

"Obviously not! What are you, a church mouse? You scared the crap out of me!"

We stare at each other, each of us panting and relieved to see one another and not an intruder.

"What's going on here?" I ask.

"How the hell would I know? I just got here, a few minutes before you. I opened the door, saw the mess, then ran to the bathroom, which is where I had hidden the pig earlier." Her expression changes from surprise to puzzlement. "I don't understand. Nothing's been taken. It's like someone came in here just to turn the place upside down, and left. But whoever did this was obviously looking for something specific. They left it." She nods to the ceramic pig, smashed into pieces in the sink, with a wad of money in elastic bands, untouched. "Why would someone break into a room, and not steal anything? Not even money, the easiest thing to take."

We both look around the bathroom, then I examine the rest of the room. The few personal belongings we had are all around the room, but to her point, everything is accounted for, silver outfits and all. The only things I had on me were my father's watch, the pager, and syringe.

"Did you have that with you?" I look at the phone book.

"What? Oh, ya. I told you, I just got here, I didn't even have time to put it down." She sets the phone book on the chipped yellow counter. "Why do you ask?"

"You opened the door and found the place like this? Was it locked?"

"Are you accusing me of something, Grace? I didn't forget to lock the door if that's where you're going with your questions. I left you at the phone booth, came here to pick up the phone book, hide the money in the pig. I left with a pile of quarters to find my own phone booth, just outside the lobby of this dump." She waves her arm outward.

"No, I'm just wondering how they got in if the door was locked. And I wanted to know what you had on you, to figure out what someone might've been looking for. Your phone book, my watch, the pager, the syringe. Everything else is here, including money, which they went through the trouble to break the pig to get at. Unless they were after our snazzy new clothes." I tip my hat to her and wonder if I am accusing her of something, and if so, what? I think about the guy at the casino again, pissed off at myself for letting Kay convince me I was crazy, instead of making her wait at the machine while I looked for him.

"Grace, I think we're both over-analyzing this." She starts to clean up the mess, starting with the large pieces of the pig, careful not to touch the edges and cut herself. "Whoever came here was probably looking for something maybe from the last tenant. We're not exactly staying at the highest-end of places. Did you see our floor-mates? They look shady. The lady down the hall seems to have male visitors on the regular, and that dude..." She points to the wall, referring to the room next door, and lowers her voice. "I think he's a dealer, and I don't mean cards." She pricks her finger on the broken pig and puts it in her mouth instinctively. "I don't feel safe in this room. Let's talk to Brad and get assigned to a new room that's more out in the open, not a corner room right by a stairwell, perfect getaway."

"Ya, you're probably right." I stand and watch as Kay turns on the tap, runs water over her cut, her blood tinting the pieces of the pig in the sink from white to pink. "Kay?" She glances up at me. "I'm glad you're OK," I tell her.

She smiles. "Me too, Grace. Good thing neither of us was here. To think I was right there, in the lobby." She sighs with relief. "And you, next time, don't go looking for the creep in the bathroom. When you hear noises, you should run the other way." She shakes her head.

We clean up the mess as best we can, pack up our few belongings and pay a visit to the front desk. Brad is there, watching his small TV, looking annoyed that we're interrupting his telenovela.

"We'd like another room, please." I slide our keys to Brad.

He doesn't move to take them. "Is there a problem with yours?" he asks.

"No, we just want a room with a better view," Kay replies with a straight face.

Brad doesn't smile. I don't think Brad has a sense of humour. I also think he's a pig, based on the artwork around his office.

"Can we have that one?" Kay points at a room in plain sight, closest to the front entrance, right in front of a lamp post with a view from the phone booth Kay used all afternoon.

Brad takes the keys and switches them with another set from the pegboard behind him, without a word.

The new room is just as the first was: smelly carpet; ugly,

faded bedding; flat pillows. Kay opens the curtains to check out the new view she told Brad we wanted.

"This is much better—now we're in the spotlight," she says as she looks at the street light, just flickering to life as dusk approaches.

"And I can see the phone booth and, more importantly, the phone booth can see the room." She plops herself on the bed closest to the bathroom. "So? How'd you do?"

I tell her all about the funeral guy, how I ended up at the table next to him. And I tell her about the quick money I made us, feeling shy about talking about my gambling, something I haven't done in years.

"Gosh, what are the chances of that? Running into that guy, and he remembered you? That's hilarious!" She throws her head back in a laugh, making me feel silly about stressing over being recognized. Kay is always so easygoing, never letting things consume her. I should learn that trait. "Well, you'll need to go back for some more money while I continue my work."

"How about you? How'd you do? And what did you do?" I ask, trying to put aside my uneasy feeling that she is hiding something.

"I basically went through the phone book and called everyone with the right surname, crossed out the ones that don't have a David, highlighted the ones that do. Tomorrow, I'm going to head out to the addresses, go door to door and pretend to do a survey, see if anyone will participate."

"A survey?" I ask.

"Ya, I'll just say I'm a student working on some statistics and would love to ask a few questions." Kay seems super-proud of her idea. "You know, things like... is your household partial to Pepsi or Coke? Has anyone in your home ever broken a leg? Does anyone in your home suffer from food allergies? And I'll throw in some random other questions to look student-y." She tilts her head to one side, puckering her lips and batting her eyes innocently. I chuckle at her impersonation since Kay was never innocent nor student-y. "Well? What do you think? Do you like the idea or what?"

Even if I thought it was the dumbest idea ever, which I

don't, I couldn't tell her with that big, proud smile on her face.

It's weird—our past lives resemble our present-day lives. Our fears, likes and dislikes. Marc broke a leg once; it seems he is destined to do it in every life. And he's allergic to seafood. As for Pepsi or Coke, Marc had a taste test of the two sugary drinks and chose Pepsi. So, the profile of Marc's past life includes Pepsi.

"I love the survey idea," I tell her. "Just one question, though. Where am I in your plan? Are we tag-teaming with the surveys?" I just want to find the donor as fast as possible, then return home. The last shuttle is in three weeks, but if we find David Williams sooner, we can go home on any of the nightly shuttles before then. The sooner, the better, for Jordan's sake.

"While I go door to door, you call the other ones that I didn't get hold of. I got a lot of people who weren't home, and machines offering to take messages. And of course, try your luck again at the casino." She looks at the money I earned. "That's good, but not good enough. Anyway, if you call all the others, then it will help rule out the bad matches and leave us with more potential candidates. Once that's done, all that's left is surveying and then letting you see if you feel anything when you meet these people, whatever the hell that means." She rolls her eyes at the word "feels."

We still don't understand how I'm going to know when it's the right person. Apparently, I'm supposed to just know. I should feel something for the guy, as he is supposedly my soulmate. It seems that Marc and I meet in every life. You'd think I would've learned the first time around. But just like Marc breaking his leg in every life, we meet in every life, too.

"Sounds like a plan."

I'm so thankful that Kay came along. I tell her so, even though I can't help but wonder about her. I want to ask her why she agreed to come with me so quickly; it can't just be about Peter. There was something about the look on her face when I bulldozed into the bathroom. I'm not sure if she was stunned that I barged in, or if she was fumbling as if I was intruding. I need her, I remind myself.

The pager buzzes on the night table, putting an end to our

chat. Kay turns on the TV. I run out of the room just as she flips to the news channel, likely fascinated by the oil spill.

"Grace, it's Marc. Again. Um, I just wanted to let you know Jordan is doing OK today. He lost his soul for a few minutes, but he came back."

Marc's voice is comforting to me. After our room was tossed, our privacy invaded, it feels good to hear his familiar voice. But the news about Jordan's quick soul loss is scary. I'm not there to hold his hand through it. Marc is probably downplaying things, so I don't worry. It doesn't work—I'm worried.

I return to the room to find Kay snoring on top of the bedding, remote control in hand. I turn the TV off and try to sleep myself, but I toss and turn the whole night. I dream of Jordan dying, of Marc dying soon after him from a broken heart, and of me returning home to no one, alone. A lot can happen in three weeks.

CHAPTER 8

"It's been four days and nothing," I complain. "Out of all the people, you'd think a match would've been located by now. I just don't know what to do."

"There are more than a hundred and fifty people—you said so yourself. It's not going to be overnight. Stop worrying about what you can't control. Why don't you just worry about this," Wendy, today's dealer, sweeps her hand out along the table, "right now? Because if you don't take the face, I will," she says.

Wendy has an ace; I have twelve. I should take one for the team, but I don't.

"I'm not the anchor. You take it, Leo."

"Ya, boss-man-Leo, we could use a break here," Joe pipes up, slurring his words. He's had too much to drink, as usual.

"Grace, I'm sure you'll hear from them soon," Leo reassures me. "You auditioned and did your best—now you have to wait."

All four days while Kay relentlessly surveyed people, I've been making phone calls, and I even interviewed a few people myself. I've also been playing cards to make a few bucks, and I've made fake friends with the dealers, the waitress, and the regular card players. Leo, our anchor, is the funeral guy. Joe is his friend, who drinks too much, but you can't help but like him. They've been here every time I have, and I'm starting to feel like it's not just a coincidence, given that this is the cheap table and Joe seems comfortable throwing money around. He refers to his friend as "boss."

Leo, in particular, seems to have taken a liking to me, asking me out for a drink on more than one occasion. "You can wear your fancy audition outfit," he teased once, with a raised eyebrow. They all think I'm auditioning for the new show, and I have a hard time lying about it, so I don't deny it. Instead, I talk about the trials and tribulations of finding David—in an encrypted way, of course. The "auditions" are my secret code name for the surveys, the competition to find the right match. My fake friends encourage me to keep going, not to give up hope. And with all the messages going back and forth between Marc and me, I need the encouragement, even if it's falsely placed.

Jordan has been progressively getting sicker, and I am missing being home more than ever. I should be there, by Jordan's side. Marc is sweet in his messages, but I know he wants me there too, and frankly, I kind of wish I was by his side right now. Comfortable; Marc always made me feel comfortable.

"Bust. Sorry, Leo." Wendy takes his cards and his chips in two swift sweeps before flipping her own hand—not a face, thankfully—and eventually busting herself.

"Look at that, Grace. I took one for the team. Don't you think that deserves a thank-you drink?" asks Leo.

"You bet it does." I wink at him and flag down Polly, the waitress. "Polly, get Leo whatever he wants, on me." And I tip her for the free drinks. I still find it odd that gambling is legal, and they get you drunk for free to help you lose more.

Leo feigns a sad look at my turning him down, again, and then asks Polly for a rum and Coke. When Joe says, "Make it two," Leo shakes his head "no" behind his friend's head. Their dynamics make me laugh. I ask Polly for a water, but before she returns with it, my pager buzzes.

"The nineties called—they want their pager back!" jokes Leo, trying to make me laugh.

Dr. Messie's assistant was right, I don't fit in with this pager, but it doesn't make me the fraud from the future. It just makes me look unstylish.

Every time the outdated pager goes off, a lump in my throat appears, and I instantly feel homesick and anxious. It snaps me back to reality, reminds me of why I'm here and who I've left at home. It reminds me that Kay is running around, conducting interviews disguised as surveys, while I play a dumb game of cards.

"I'll walk you out," Leo offers.

"*No!*" I say, more firmly than intended. "No, sorry, I didn't mean to yell. I'm just a bit on edge. It might be the people calling to give me news. I'd rather hear it alone," I tell him. "Besides, I gotta meet up with my friend, so I should really just get going."

It's not a complete lie, at some point, I will be meeting Kay at our regular diner. The fifties American-flair restaurant has grown on us, and it's a good place to debrief.

"Sure, sure, I get it," Leo says coolly.

Joe pretends not to notice. But Leo can't hide his hurt expression from me, and I feel bad.

"I'll see you later?" he asks.

I nod yes, but don't know if I mean it. I never know if I mean it.

I leave the table, heading out to the phone booth without looking back. I flip my sunglasses from my head to my face, preparing for the overwhelming sunshine of Las Vegas.

Every time I leave, I hope that it will be the last. I hope to go home to our motel to find Kay there with a list of matches for me to check out. I hope to hear good messages and not to feel lonely when I hear Marc's voice on the pager. I want to hear that Jordan is doing better. I secretly hope that Marc will say that he loves me, put me on the spot to say it too. I wish I didn't hope that. I wish I'd stop feeling this way. I can't explain why he has such a grip on me. Why spending time in this casino—with funny Leo and his employee Joe, sarcastic Wendy, and Polly who looks like she hates her job yet likes our table—why this all reminds me of Marc, and how we met, and how much I really miss him, love him, miss him.

When I reach the phone booth, I take a deep breath, make a

silent wish that it's good news, as I always do.

"You have two mess—" I press "1" to skip over the machine voice and start listening right away.

"Grace, it's me, Marc. Today's a good day. Jordan's looking good, considering the episode he had in the middle of the night." What episode? He never left me a message about an episode. "He and Walt get along really well. Jordan's getting to be a real chess player. That Walt, he's like the brother Jordan never had. I've been bringing cooked meals, so Jordan doesn't have to eat that slop they feed them, and Walt's sort of invited himself." Marc's cooking? "Now I always bring enough for him, too." He pauses. "Sorry, I'm rambling. I just don't have anyone to talk to." He pauses. "Anyway... Let me know how you're doing? Please?"

I choose the option to replay the message before listening to the next. I love hearing the little updates about Jordan and how he's found such a good friend. I love that Marc is telling me about little mundane things, like cooking for Walt, the slop at the clinic, Jordan's chess skills. I play the message back a third time, paying attention to Marc's tone and his voice, the way he says my name, reading into the pauses. I just want to be home.

"*Next message.*"

"Grace, it's me, Marc. Come back."

His voice doesn't sound mundane anymore. He sounds panicked.

CHAPTER 9

"You need to come back, Grace! I don't know how much longer Jordan can hold off. Last night was bad, really, really... awful." He pauses; it sounds like he's catching his breath, while I hold onto mine. "Grace..." His voice comes through like a whisper. I press the receiver harder to my ear to ensure I catch each syllable of each word "We almost lost him last night." He pauses, his words sinking like battery acid into my brain. "He was gone for such a long time, much too long. They called a code 33. You know what that is, don't you?" He pauses as if engaged in an actual two-way conversation with me and expecting a response. Even if I knew what a code 33 was and he really was on the other side of this phone to respond to his rhetorical question, even if, I wouldn't be able to open my mouth to form a sentence. I feel as though I've been kicked in the gut; I'm winded, and a sour taste is fermenting in the grooves of the roof of my desert-dry mouth. And then I hear the click, signalling that the message is done.

I look at the phone in my hand and shake it before listening again.

"End of message," the mechanical woman says.

I panic and hit the button to play the next message, pressing the phone urgently against my ear.

"You have no more messages," she says.

"No!" I argue with the mechanical woman. "No!" I press and hold the button to play the next message, the tip of my fingernail turning white and purple from the weight of my whole body under my one finger.

"You have no more messages," she says again, taunting me through the sound of the flat note the number nine makes since I won't let up on holding it down.

I try to rewind, replay. Maybe there is more to the message? But it's the same, ending in Marc's desperate voice asking me if I know what a code 33 is. I listen again, and again, and again. It's the same message, but Marc's voice sounds more desperate somehow and scared—maybe hopeless. Is that possible? Or maybe I just hadn't noticed.

I hang the phone up and redial the number to the messaging service.

"You have two messages." This time I let her finish—maybe I made a mistake and messed something up. "Press 1 to listen to your messages; press 2 to change your personal greeting." I press "1", carefully, slowly—but not too slowly. I hear the happy "Grace, it's Marc," and skip that message to get to the other "Grace, it's Marc."

I listen again, to the message, to his voice, the tone, and his question. "...code 33. You know what that is, don't you?" and I hold my breath, squeezing the receiver as tight to my ear as I can, plugging my index finger in my other ear to block out street noise. And then I hear it. Marc was crying before he hung up.

"End of message. To replay this message, press—"

I slam the phone into the cradle. I've heard enough of that mechanical bitch. I whip off my sunglasses and spin around, my back to the phone.

"What the hell is a code 33?" I yell out at no one. Those brave enough to bear the late afternoon Vegas heat turn to look at me. I stare back at them like one of them might be the mechanical woman and can give me an answer. Some look away, shaking their heads. "Huh? Do you know?" I single in on some innocent young guy. "How's about you, kid? Ya, you! I'm talking to you! Do you know what that is? Code 33? Hello-o?"

The guy speeds up, hands in pockets, head down. Those who hadn't looked away the first time do so now and walk faster. I look around wildly at the crowd of people walking past me, quickly now despite the raging heat; rather than taking up the whole sidewalk, they walk in single file, avoiding me on the far side of the path. Some people change directions, turning around before they cross in front of me.

The crowd thins out enough for me to catch a glimpse of a homeless man in a dirty baseball cap; he sits in front of a rusty tin can, resting his back against the bus shelter and holding a beat-up cardboard sign that reads, "Ninja aliens kidnapped my wife for ransom." There is a Bible under the tin can. He's looking at me like I'm crazy. When I realize that he thinks I'm crazy, I do what any crazy person would do: I scream-laugh.

And then I leave the phone booth behind and start the long walk back to the diner to wait for Kay. She must know what a code 33 is. Her brother died from Metagenesis.

"Damn you, Marc!" I shout as I leave, angry at Marc for his half-message.

Some guy stops walking and turns all the way around, takes his glasses off to actually look at me. He has a burn scar on one cheek. I put my glasses on to avoid eye contact. Maybe his name is Marc, too. I laugh, feeling a little embarrassed, and walk faster.

CHAPTER 10

"You're early."

"Hi Camilla, how are you today?" I ask our waitress, distracting myself from code 33.

We know each other by name, thanks to Kay, who makes friends with everyone. Camilla is young, pudgy in all the right places, and wears clothing way too tight in all the wrong places. She's on a diet to lose fifteen pounds before her big wedding to Eddie. She tells us every day about how many calories she ate the day previous, and her exercise routine at the local gym. Kay and I have seen her sneaking fries off customers' plates while she thinks no one is looking before she serves them. We like Camilla. She's perfectly flawed.

"Eddie's here," she whispers to me, nodding her head for me to look toward the front counter.

I'm thankful that Camilla has a guest other than me while I wait for Kay. I look at my watch—it's only four o'clock. We usually meet around five, before the diner gets busy. Usually, Camilla talks our ear off, mostly with Kay who always seems interested in her and asks so many questions.

Meeting at this diner for a bite to eat every day has become routine. And we've become obsessed with the news on the TV. I always choose the same meal, the hamburger, but I change the flavour of the milkshake, just to keep it interesting. The diner brags about the 100-plus flavours. So far, mango-chocolate is my favourite. I can always rely on Kay to try something new from the menu, and she lets me sample her dish.

Instead of going back to see Eddie, Camilla slides into the seat across from me. Today, we're sitting in the Chevy Classic booth.

She lowers her voice, even more, leaning across the table, her big brown eyes darting around the restaurant as if to make sure no one can hear. "Someone came in here looking for you, some guy. Dartmouth—is that your last name?"

My blood runs cold at the mention of my surname, which I've not ever used or said aloud since our arrival in Vegas. I don't confirm my name but don't deny it either, which proves to be enough for Camilla.

"Some serious dude, the kind who wouldn't take off his sunglasses while talking. No smile. Wouldn't say his name when asked, or what he wanted." She looks around again. Eddie is looking her way. He's cute and scrawny. She smiles at him before returning her attention to the conversation. "Anyway, Manny told him he didn't know you."

Manny is one of the cooks—never smiles, never talks; the complete opposite of Camilla. I look over Camilla's shoulder, past the counter where Eddie sits, toward the kitchen. I can see Manny in the back. He nods knowingly at me when our eyes meet.

"Anyway, I just wanted to let you know. People come to Vegas for lots of reasons—to get lost is a big one, and you look like you want to stay lost. You don't have to tell me anything." Although she looks like she's hoping I'll tell her something.

"Did he say anything more? What'd he look like?" I'm unsure about how I feel that someone would know me and actually be looking for me. I think back to the guy at the casino when Kay and I won, turning his back when I caught him watching me.

Camilla shakes her head, reaches across to grab my hands. I hadn't noticed until then that I had been wringing them together.

"Before Eddie, I dated a guy like him," she confides. "I know the type. Mean bullies that always make un-kept promises not to hurt you again. You're safe here, Grace—don't worry." She winks, squeezes my hand and leaves me at the table.

I guess she thinks I know who is looking for me. But I don't. I sit in bewilderment, stomach sick over Marc's message and now stupidly stunned that someone knows who I am.

What else does someone know? Suddenly I feel exposed. I cross and rub my naked arms, wishing I had a sweater to help hide me from the world. Sitting in this window booth, I might as well be sitting on a stage with a spotlight in the middle of a crowd, with neon signs pointing at me. I look out the window, watching the people walk by, wondering if they're watching me. There are very few people walking the streets, it's too hot at this time of the day, but there are still small crowds, and they all seem like they could've just been looking at me until I turned around, every one of them.

I regret my crazy episode at the phone booth, calling attention to myself. Dr. Messie's no-name assistant wouldn't have liked that one bit. Who the hell is looking for me? What is a code 33?

Camilla brings me a glass of water with lemon. "I figure you'll want to wait for Kay to order. Just try not to think about that jerk. He won't come back looking for you again."

Our looted-looking motel room crosses my mind, sending a chill through me. Sure, the guy may not return to the diner, but he knows where I'm staying.

"Manny already told him we've never heard of you," she finishes.

As she turns to leave, I reach out for her, grabbing her by her apron a little more urgently than I'd intended. She looks back at me with questioning eyes, surprised. I decide to play the victim she thinks I am.

"Please, Camilla, how long ago? What if he's still in the area? When was he here?" I feign fear, some of it real. Fear over who is looking for me and why. Fear of failing and losing Jordan and even fear of losing Marc. "What'd he look like? I just need to be sure." I let go of her apron.

She looks relieved to have gotten some insider secret from me, confirmation of her suspicions. She looks around the diner again, as if new people have come in since we started talking, which they haven't. It's just the same few guests, along with Eddie at the counter, who is now minding his menu. When she's sure the coast is clear, she answers, still using a hushed voice.

"I was just starting my shift—maybe around two o'clock or so. He was average height and build, maybe like Eddie." I look at scrawny, cute Eddie and decide Camilla is an unreliable witness, but nod anyhow. "He had sunglasses on. I didn't get a look at this face. But like I said, he was mean-looking. But he's long gone and not coming back, hon." She rubs my shoulder and gives me a reassuring look before leaving to tend to Eddie.

At least an hour goes by. I don't touch the lemon water. The ice has long melted, probably from the heat of my eyeballs staring them down, watching them as they shrank and clinked, released small pockets of air and fizzled. The ice cubes have distracted me from the scary guy thing, which has distracted me from code 33. Nothing has distracted me from the obsession with checking my watch. I was early, but now Kay is running late.

Camilla has left me alone, spending her time with Eddie at the counter and tending to the few guests who have come and gone in the meantime. I almost wish she had sat and talked my ear off like she normally would have. It would've provided me with some sanity, listening to her babble about her weight and her struggle to fit into her fitted modern gown, which her curvy body has no business squeezing into.

At 5:45, finally, Kay walks in. I sit up straight in my Chevy Classic, both relieved and anxious to see her. But my relief turns into more anxiety when I see the look on her face. She looks like she's seen a ghost.

CHAPTER 11

Usually, Kay comes in and, rather than waiting for Camilla to greet her, she walks up to her, Kay style, embracing her, asking her about her day, her wedding, truly interested in everything she has to say. Even Manny's face brightens up when she comes in. It's funny how Kay is so friendly and outgoing, patient, loving and caring. All the things I'm not.

Today, Kay does none of that. She comes into the diner and beelines it right to our booth, where I've been sitting not so patiently, observing the various stages of ice-melting. She slouches into the booth across from me, shoving her bag in the corner against the window. She grabs my water and greedily sucks back half in a few long gulps. She's perspiring, but not with normal sweat from the Vegas summer heat. She's practically soaking wet. And she's completely out of breath, fogging the glass cup as she finishes gulping the rest of my water, leaving nothing but the lemon in the bottom of the glass.

"That drink wasn't cold enough. No ice?" Kay asks.

I roll my eyes. She licks the water and sweat combo off her lip, grabs a napkin and starts dabbing at herself. I wait for her to say something, tell me why she looks like she's just run a marathon in the desert. But she doesn't. She just sits there, catching her breath.

"So?" I ask.

"We need to get out of here. Something is wrong." My heart sinks into my stomach, and I feel my face redden with heat when she says, "Someone was following me."

I think about the mean guy looking for me, asking for me by my full name. There really was someone watching us at that casino—I'm not crazy! I run my hands through my hair, grabbing at the roots and tugging. I want to ask her what happened, who, what, and why. Why would she be followed?

But she doesn't leave time for questions. Kay abruptly grabs her bag and heads for the door, leaving me in the booth wondering what just happened. I guess when she said we need to get out of here she meant right now, right this very second.

"Wait! Kay, where are you going? You mean now?" I shout across the diner.

Camilla looks at me with concern, then at Kay, who is already at the door and looking back at me with eyes that seem to say let's go, now!

"Is everything OK?" I ignore Camilla's question. Up until then she had been leaning across the high counter next to the cash register, proudly displaying her cleavage for Eddie. Now she is coming around the counter, probably just noticing that Kay was even in the diner.

I brush past a few customers and follow Kay out onto the sidewalk. The heat hasn't budged, and it hits me in the face like a wall of fire.

"We can't meet there anymore. I think I was followed," Kay says in a hushed voice I can barely hear as I try to catch up to her.

"By whom?"

Kay shrugs in response, picking up her pace from fast to high speed, her eyes darting around at the passers-by. I examine the people we pass as well, but everyone looks suspicious to me—I don't know who I am looking for and everyone is wearing sunglasses on this bright, sunny day. "What did he look like?"

Kay stops in her tracks to look at me. "How did you know it was a 'he,' Grace?"

"You didn't give me two seconds to talk to you in the diner. You came in, drank my water, announced we had to leave and then ran." I pause, take a deep breath before continuing, as if confessing a sin. "A man came into the diner asking for me." I give her a few seconds to let that sink in. "By my last name."

Kay looks like I felt a few minutes ago at the diner when she told me she was followed.

"Come, on," she says, "let's go." And we walk without saying another word to each other.

Kay stays preoccupied with the growing crowd around us, making eye contact with everyone. The six o'clock sun is still strong, but the streets are coming alive. But all that is preoccupying me is code 33. I still don't know how I should feel about being looked for, and now Kay being followed. But I know how I should feel about Jordan's declining condition. And that is all that keeps running through my mind. Thoughts of Jordan. All I know for sure is that Jordan is at home, dying. And I'm eighty years back in time, looking for someone I don't know. And someone I don't know is looking for me.

When we're almost at the motel, instead of going directly to it, Kay leads us through a few casinos, zigzagging our way.

"Kay?"

"Yeah?" she responds without looking at me, concentrating on our surroundings.

"What is a code 33?"

Kay stops dead in her tracks, stopping in front of me with a look of horror on her face, her hand flying to her chest. "Why?" she asks, but she knows the answer. She grabs my hand and shakes her head, moulding her expression from horror to compassion before using her other hand to rub my upper arm. "Look, we can't talk about code 33 right this second. Let's just get back to our room. I have good news too, Grace—it's not all bad news today. The search is going really well. I've eliminated a lot of people from the list in the phone book. Things are going to work out. You'll be home to Jordan soon. Right now, someone is messing with us, and we need to make sure that this someone isn't following us back to our room. No more meeting at that diner where whoever that someone is knows your name, either."

That's all she tells me before she looks around again, presumably hunting for our stalker, then resumes the lead on zigzagging our way to our room through an imaginary maze. She's done nothing to calm my stomach from the fear growing inside me.

And when we make it back to our room, it's clear that whoever the someone is didn't follow us, but by the state of our room, they sure beat us there.

CHAPTER 12

"Again? Someone has come into our room *again?*" Kay steps out of the room, dumbfounded, much as I had done the first time an intruder ripped through our room.

This time, she is the one checking the room number, confusion on her face, making sure we are in the right room. But I'm sure we're in the right room because I'm the one who used the key to open it. The door was locked until I placed the faded brass key in the keyhole and turned it.

"What the hell does he want with us? And," she waves her arm to the outside dramatically, "we're right across from the office and in front of a huge spotlight! How could Brad let this happen? Why would someone break into *this* room? We're the only ones who were broken into last time; no one complained— I asked around. This is crazy!"

"You don't have to convince me, Kay. There is no way any of this is a coincidence." Anxiety pumps through me, my brain pulsing.

Kay steps right into the room now. I follow, taking it all in. Again, the mattress has been flipped over, the sheets ripped off, our few belongings thrown around the room.

I check out the bathroom and find that the venting grate has been removed. My heart skips beats as I imagine the money we need to sustain ourselves being taken. Last time, the intruder broke the porcelain pig but left the money. I peer into the vent reluctantly, holding my breath. I don't see anything, but it's dark, so maybe I just can't see it, even though I know I should be able to. I still stick my hand into the vent to confirm what I already know, nausea making my mouth salivate as I feel around the hole, my hand desperately searching for money that isn't there.

"Kay!" I shout. "Kay, Kay, this can't be, the money, it's gone!" I'm going to be sick, or cry, or both. "Kay! Did you hear me? It's gone." My voice is strained. My hand still whips around, my cheek brushing the dirty floor of this cheap motel. My arm is halfway down the vent, as far as I can go without crawling in myself. I feel nothing but grime. Kay appears in the doorway, her eyes locking on mine.

"No, it's not gone. It's right here." She's holding a stack of money in her hand, but she doesn't look happy about it, and I'm not sure if I should be relieved about the bucks in her hand or if I should be worried about why she's not happy about it.

I sit up and brush the dirt from my face, still crouched.

"They didn't take the money, but they took something else."

She keeps me in suspense. My expression and raised eyebrows insist on her continuing. What else can they possibly take of value? I have the vial in my pocket; I carry it with me at all times. I do a quick check by feeling my pocket and simultaneously shaking my wrist, reminding me that I'm still wearing Dad's watch. Nothing else matters in this room—it's all worthless.

"The money was tucked into the phone book," she says.

Just as she says it, I realize she's holding the phone book in the crook of her arm. I was so focused on the money that I hadn't noticed it.

"Okayyyy?" I ask.

"All the 'Williams' pages have been torn out of the book."

"What are you talking about? What do you mean, 'torn out'?" I ask, flabbergasted.

Her calm demeanour disappears in an instant.

"Gone, Grace! They're gone, ripped out, torn out, abracadabra, disappeared!" She dangles the book by the flap, and the binding starts to rip, other pages dropping out of it. I rush at it to save it, but I'm too late. She hurls the book across the room, half of it falling right at her feet.

"It's useless! This book is completely useless without that section!"

It's the first time I've seen Kay visibly upset since all this has started. Her eyes well up as if she might start crying.

"Kay, there are more phone books in the world," I say in an attempt to soothe her.

"But all my notes were in *that* phonebook! My list—all the names I'd crossed out and ones marked for follow-up!"

Instead of crying, she stomps on the remains of the book, twisting her foot into the few pages like she's putting out a giant cigarette. She looks like a child having a tantrum, and I do nothing to stop it. I almost want to laugh, not because it's funny, but because this is awkward, and I'm usually the one losing my cool, not Kay. I have to suppress the urge to laugh so much so that I fake a cough to do it.

Mid-tantrum, before I know what's happening, she leaves the room—stomps out, rather—and I start to follow her, only to see she is heading to the office. Instead, I back up to stay in the room and let her go alone to the lobby, where I can see Brad, not paying attention to his job but glued to the little television instead, as usual.

I hope she isn't going to complain, or say anything. We're not supposed to cause a fuss, raise any suspicions. I already feel guilty over letting loose on the crowd at the phone booth. We were warned to stay under the radar, not get noticed. That's why we didn't report anything happening the first time our room was broken into. I want to stop her, to run out after her and remind her, but I can't push my laughter away to do that.

So I just stand there, at the doorway of our room, and watch in horror as she barges into the office. I actually hear Brad's chair whip around, or I think I do. I can't see Brad's expression in detail, but I imagine it as utter surprise or maybe even fear. I flinch on his behalf as Kay leans over the counter and raises her finger in his face in an accusing way. I can't hear what's being said, but I finally let out my laughter fully; trying to tuck it away is useless. I back up further into the room and replay the image of her twisting her foot into the phone book, her hands in tight fists, her face reddening, and try to pair that with Brad's reaction as she barges into his office. I laugh and laugh and laugh, like the insane woman the homeless man had me pegged for. I let it all out, hoping to stop myself before her return, and every time I try to stop, it makes it worse.

I know this is horrible news. I know that I should be upset, and I am, I am upset—and scared too. Someone is following Kay, looking for me, knows my last name. And for the second time, someone has broken into our room. It is not a coincidence that once again, they left the money behind, but this time, they took something so specific, as if they know why we need this phone book. They know our mission somehow. And maybe my laughter is hiding my fear because I am definitely afraid now. Someone knows something. I don't know what or who or why or how. But someone knows.

And I laugh. The harder I laugh, the more the fear grows, and I push it away with more laughter until I'm wheezing.

When Kay returns, I am cleaning up the mess, putting things in their place, making the beds. I haven't touched the phone book yet. I wasn't sure what to do with it. But when I saw her coming, I quickly gathered up all the pages, thinking it would upset her to see it again.

"So, what'd you say to Brad?" I ask, trying to sound nonchalant.

My laughter is finally under control, and Kay appears calmer too.

"I just told him to watch our room from now on, that someone is harassing us."

She turns around and gives a little wave out the window. I get a side view of her narrowing her eyes at him. Brad waves back with a weak smile, his posture awake and alert. I wonder if he's afraid for his life. The thought almost brings back my nervous laughter. The TV glows behind him, but he is faced in our direction, not watching the little box at all. I doubt that's all Kay said to him, and I smirk at her downplaying it but don't push further.

"I asked Brad for an extra phone book. He gave me his." She hands it to me with a sad defeated face.

I leave the mess on the floor, brush my hands on my thighs and take the heavy book, trying to look optimistic. Kay worked so hard on calling all those people.

"Great, well, at least the names will look familiar. It's not the end of the world. We can just go through and—" As I flip through the book, it hits me why her expression is so down. It's not just her lost notes that have saddened her; this book is also missing a big chunk. No "Williams" section. I look up at Kay with my jaw dropped, no need for words. She already knows.

Her mouth draws into a straight line, the corners pulling into a knowing frown. I look back down at the book, smooth my hand over the jagged pieces that remain.

"I don't get it. Did Brad say anything? Did you ask?" Kay shakes her head. "What about the phone booth, the one right outside the office, where I check the messages from?" Kay shakes her head. "Gone too?" Kay nods yes.

What could all this mean? Who could possibly know why we're here? And they're not even trying to hide it. Leaving the money behind, stuffing it into the missing pages section and removing only the pages we need. That's deliberate. What are they after? Are they trying to stop us? Or trying to send a message?

"Why?" I ask.

Kay sits down on the floor, in the middle of the crumpled pages littering the room, and looks up to the ceiling as if the answer is written in the old nicotine stains. Then she turns her attention to the dingy carpet.

"Do you want to know what a code 33 is?" She is picking at the carpet, ignoring the larger mess in favour of the tiny snowflake-sized pieces of paper.

I don't respond. I don't move. I want to know, right? Don't I?

When I don't budge or respond, Kay looks up at me. "I assume that's what Marc's last message was about, right? Jordan experienced a code 33?"

"Does it have something to do with why we're being

followed?" I ask, and Kay shakes her head vigorously.

"No, no. Nothing like that. It's just that we're going to have to double our efforts to find the right match. I don't know why someone is interfering, but if Jordan is already at code 33, then we don't have much time. Finding a new phone book is the least of our concerns. Before we leave here and rip Vegas apart looking for a new phone book, I should answer your question. Because once we leave here, it's no stopping. We need to find a match, and we need to find it now."

I take a deep breath, force back tears. "OK, tell me. I'm ready." I join her on the old carpet, cross-legged.

She resumes her nitpicking at the specks of paper. I reach for the pager to give me comfort. I want to hold it in my hand for Marc's support, to feel connected to him. My stomach drops down to the floor. The pager is not in my pocket.

I jump up, pat my body down, searching in a complete panic. Kay gets up with me.

"What is it? What's wrong?" she asks, watching helplessly.

"The, the, the pager! It's *gone!*"

"You left it in the room?" Kay accuses, eyes wide. "It's stolen?"

"No! No, of course not, I just checked the messages." I'm scrambling, looking in the bathroom, ripping up the bed sheets I just made up. "Damnit!" I'm tearing the room apart, but I can't see through the tears of frustration fogging my vision. "Damnit! Damnit!"

"Maybe you left it at the diner," Kay suggests.

"No, no, no. I didn't even take it out of my pocket when I was—" Flashbacks of the phone booth. I must've set it down next to the phone at the booth when I was checking the messages. "Oh no." I stand completely still. "Shit!" and I cry.

"You left it at the phone booth," says Kay. She isn't asking me; she's stating a fact.

I nod yes. Kay embraces me and lets me cry on her shoulder.

"I'm such an idiot!" I allow myself to cry for just a minute. One minute only. And then I part from Kay. "Let's go get my pager. And while we're there, let's grab us a new phone book. And if someone is trying to find us and send a message, then maybe we need to go back to the diner and let them find us. Because maybe I have a message for them, too."

We head out of the room, and it doesn't slip my mind that we still haven't discussed code 33. But maybe I don't want to know right now because I just can't handle it. Maybe I want to be—no, I *need* to be angry instead of sad. Sad makes me homesick, makes me yearn for Marc, makes me weak and reminds me of my dad. Angry, on the other hand, works for me. Angry gets things done and will find my pager and the reason why someone is looking for us. Angry will find a match for Jordan while pushing feelings for Marc away. Angry will save Jordan's life. I need to find David Williams.

CHAPTER 13

"Camilla, what are you still doing here?" Kay asks Camilla when she brings us our menus. She is trying to sound upbeat for our waitress, who looked both relieved and worried to see us come back. "It's almost midnight, you must've been here all day, you poor girl."

"I'm working a double shift. I've got a wedding to pay for. Eddie's not getting enough shifts at the gym, so..." She fidgets with her ring. Given the clues Camilla leaked about her previous boyfriend, who made un-kept promises about not harming her, I'm glad for her that Eddie's problem is just bad luck getting jobs.

"Camilla, did that guy come back? The one who was looking for me?" I don't keep my voice down, and Camilla looks around nervously.

If someone is listening in, let them. I want them to think I'm not afraid. I won't whisper in fear. But it's almost midnight, and the diner is packed with people. There are even lines to get in. No one is listening to us anyhow.

Camilla shakes her head rather than saying no and leaves us to look over the menu. I don't open mine; I always order the same thing. But Kay, who usually spends ten minutes examining the menu, even though she practically knows it by heart, doesn't even open it tonight. We just sit across from each other, bewildered at the evening's events.

The pager wasn't at the phone booth, and neither was a complete phone book. In fact, we stopped at every single phone booth all the way up and down the Strip and did not find a phone book with a Williams section in any one of them. We took a bus to the old downtown and nothing. We even took a bus to the outskirts—some residential area—and stopped at a plaza, then a gas station. Nothing. Whoever did this went to great lengths to stop us from finding David Williams, or at least prolong our search; a phone book isn't the only way to locate a person, but it's just easy and doesn't leave a trail.

We're exhausted and starving. Not having the pager isn't the end of the world. I know the number to call off by heart. So I can still check messages. I just won't know when a message arrives. I'll have to make a point of checking periodically. Every morning, every afternoon, every evening.

"Do you want to talk about code 33?" Kay asks.

"No. When Camilla comes back, order me the usual. I'm going to check for messages." I get up and leave Kay at the booth; it's a Buick tonight. I call the number I know from memory.

"You have two new messages." But instead of listening to the messages, I hang up. I guess I might've been hoping there were no messages. No updates might be better than more bad news about Jordan. I don't want to hear it.

I wait outside a few minutes, saying a silent prayer before I head back inside that Kay will leave the subject of Jordan alone for now.

"Any messages?"

"No," I lie without making eye contact.

We don't speak to each other. Kay doesn't bring up code 33, and I'm grateful for it. Camilla brings us our meals in silence, which is unusual. She must sense the mood. I have an appetite—I'm starving, actually, thankfully. I want to sit here, and not think, and not feel. I scarf down my meal in silence, trying not to look at Kay or Camilla. I keep my eyes moving around. And then I notice something—or someone.

A young man, sitting quietly by himself in the corner. He's been staring at his menu for too long. He looks like he's just using it to blend in, but not reading it. There is something familiar about him. I think it's him…

"What is it?" Kay asks through a mouthful of food.

"That guy." I nod in his direction, "I think I've seen him before."

Kay turns to look at him.

"Does he look familiar to you?" I search my memory to place where I know him from.

"No, not at all." She looks again.

He folds up his menu, rises from his table and makes eye contact with me before walking casually to the exit.

"Oh ya, I've definitely seen him before." I get up as well, start to make my way toward him, not taking my eyes off him. I remember the guy at the phone booth who took his sunglasses off to look at me when I cursed Marc. I remember his burn scar. I recognize his body language too—same as the guy from the casino when we won that jackpot. I head toward the exit to intercept him.

But when I get close enough, suddenly, he darts.

"Hey!" I shout at him, pushing a woman out of my way. "Hey! Come back here!"

And I chase him past the lineup of people waiting for a table, out to the street. The streets are filled with tourists. I hear the direction he is headed in rather than see it: the people he is pushing through are not happy.

"Watch out, buddy!" and "What's your hurry—have another beer, man!"

I follow the sounds of outrage from the crowd as he bumps his way through them. The mob is slowing him down and clearing a path for me. He is fast, though, and I lose him for a second. I slow down and look around. Kay catches up with me.

"There!" She points, then gets ahead of me.

I run after her. The young man doesn't look back, not even for a second. I wish he would; I want to see his face again, memorize it. He runs across the street, out into the open where we can see him clearly. He doesn't cross to the sidewalk, though.

He stays on the street, which I find odd until I realize he has the advantage of not fighting the crowd or trying to get lost in it. He is much quicker than we are. And him being out in the open may give us a better view of him, but a clear path gives him the benefit to pick up his pace.

He runs without even checking whether we are on his tail, through the traffic; cars stop and honk. We run through behind him, dodging the stopped cars, angry drivers yelling obscenities out of their windows. He is too fast.

I run hard, my legs pumping, my lungs aching. I pass Kay, who is doubled over, apparently giving up, but not me. I keep at him, even with the distance widening between us. He's not even bothering to get back on the sidewalk. He must realize he is faster and his best shot is to outrun me.

"Stop that guy!" I yell out. "He stole my purse! Stop him! *Help!*"

The crowd reacts; people look at me, realize I'm chasing someone and start yelling ahead as well.

"Thief! Stop!"

Someone ahead jumps drunkenly out in front of him, but it's no use. The guy I'm chasing must be a professional football player, because he dodges the interception like a pro, without breaking stride. He fakes going in one direction and then the other before ducking under the stranger's arm and then flying out far ahead at the speed of a short-distance runner. He's practically gone.

"Damn you!" I yell at the top of my lungs with the bit of energy I have left, and I stop my chase. There is no use. He is so far ahead of me. There is no way I will ever catch up. I can't even keep up with him, so I have no hope of catching him.

I lean over with my hands on my knees to hold me up, trying to catch my breath, panting, seeing stars from abruptly stopping my run. Dizzily I get off the street to sit down on the curb. I'm trying to catch my breath when Kay joins me, still puffing herself, her face flushed.

"So, where do you know that guy from?" Kay asks.

"Huh?" I'm just trying to breathe.

Kay lets me catch my breath before asking again.

"I saw him at the phone booth earlier. Aw, shit! Do you think he has the pager?" Dread creeps up on me, but it shouldn't matter. Without the phone number and pin, you can't check the messages, and only I know that information. "At least now I know what the guy looks like," I say.

Kay looks at me, confusion on her face. "What guy?" she asks.

I state the obvious, "The guy, the one who was following you and looking for me."

"That's not the guy who was following me," Kay replies. I stare at her, not knowing what to say. "That's not him, Grace. I don't know what to tell you. That kid was not the guy who followed me today. And if that was who came into the diner looking for you, don't you think Camilla would've pointed him out to you in the diner when you asked if he'd been back?"

I just study her face, looking for an answer, not knowing what to say.

"What the hell are you talking about?" I ask, knowing her point is a good one.

Kay just shrugs apologetically.

CHAPTER 14

"Can we hop a cab?" Kay moans. "My feet hurt."

We ran in the complete opposite direction of the motel and are a good hour's walk from our cheap accommodations, but I don't care. I need to think. After midnight, the people of Vegas are loud and distracting, but in a good way. The sights and sound are just the buzz I need as background noise for my thoughts.

"You go ahead. I need to clear my head."

Kay sighs but doesn't hail a cab. She walks with me silently.

I actually just want her to leave me alone, though, so I step out into the street and hail a taxi. Kay, relieved that I've changed my mind, jumps into the yellow car first. The top of the taxi advertises helicopter sightseeing tours over the Grand Canyon.

"I'll see you back in the room," I tell her and, set on being left alone, I close the car door before she can respond. I hear the window roll down as the car inches up beside me.

"You know, Grace, ignoring the truth doesn't make it not true! I'm just as upset about Jordan as you are. I came here to help you! I did all that hard work going through the phone book, calling strangers, showing up at their homes to interview them. I've worked my butt off! Why are you shutting me out like a skunk in the garbage? How do you think I feel? I've lost all my hard work!"

I turn around, stunned. I didn't even know she was mad at me. And who does she think she is?

"A code 33 is serious!" she adds when I don't respond.

"Don't you think I know that?" I scream at her, in awe of her tone. "Am I supposed to feel bad about your hard work being wasted? And how can you possibly be as upset as I am about Jordan? He's *my* son!" A vision of Jordan gasping his way back from an episode of soul loss flashes before my eyes. I fiercely shake the image out of my head. "He's dying, and we can't find what we came here for because someone is getting in the way! I don't want to think about that right now! I don't want to think about a damn thing! I don't want to feel—I don't want to talk or be talked to! And I absolutely don't want to know what a fuckin' code 33 is! Now go the fuck back to the hotel room and leave me be!"

I stomp off, scrubbing the hot tears off my cheekbones.

The cab drives past me. I don't look into the back seat to see if Kay is watching me as it drives by. I don't check to see if she is hurt, like the last time I shut her out of my life when Dad died. I bet she is probably disappointed in me, again. But I don't care.

I walk for a bit, trying to fight off the urge to whip into a casino, play a quick hand and get my mind thinking about numbers instead of Jordan. Just a quick hand, maybe two. I shake my wrist, my habit when I'm nervous. Hearing my dad's watch jingle reminds me of why I need to stay away from that blackjack table. I am his daughter, and I might be just like him. The watch also comforts me. I miss him, my dad.

With each casino I pass, I feel stronger. I bet I could walk into one and just keep walking. I bet Dad couldn't do that. Any minute now, I won't have a choice. The one coming up forces guests to walk through it. You have to go up the escalator, through the casino, and then you will reach the other side. And I do it. No problem. I walk through the casino, all the way to the other side, and out again into safety.

But then I stop, turn back around. I take a deep breath, roll my eyes at myself and head back in. Not to play a hand, but to check those messages. There was a phone booth between the double doors.

"You have two new messages. First message."

"Grace..." Marc is super quiet, his voice just above a whisper. "Grace, I love you."

I'm taken aback by his message. I guess I was expecting more about code 33. I had my finger prepared on the hang-up button, just in case. My chest flutters, stirring up buried emotions. He hasn't said that to me in such a long time; I'd forgotten how good it feels to hear it. I decide to replay the message rather than listening to the second one. Maybe Kay is right. Maybe I am ignoring the truth. Maybe I've been ignoring it all along. My feelings for Marc, they won't go away no matter how hard I demand that they do. I'd rather face that truth than whatever the truth about code 33 is.

I listen to Marc tell me he loves me for a solid minute, replaying it over and over before I finally, delicately, place the receiver back in its cradle. Instead of playing the second message, I decide to go to the casino after all, just for a minute. I'll just play one hand. I can walk away after one hand; I've done it before.

I look around me. This casino is particularly sad, the clientele a little older, alone. Of all the casinos I could've chosen on a beautiful Vegas summer night, I choose the one that looks like it's going out of business if there is such a thing. An old man is sitting with a tank next to him and a little clear hose directing oxygen into his nostrils. He looks at me. I offer a meek smile, feeling awkward that I was caught staring, but he doesn't even seem to care. He just turns back to his machine and spins the reels.

And then I see a familiar face at another slot machine, watching me.

CHAPTER 15

The familiar face catches me looking and waves hello in response. I look around to see if there is someone behind me, returning her greeting, or if it's really meant for me. But no one behind me is waving in response or looking in this direction.

When I look back, she waves yet again, the familiar old woman from the funeral, sitting at the slot machine. I wave shyly at her. Not that I'm surprised to be recognized; I was wearing that stupid silver slut outfit when we first saw each other at the funeral. I'm just surprised to see her staring at me like she was waiting for me to turn around so she could grab my attention.

I walk away toward the gaming tables, but out of the corner of my eye, I see her coming toward me. What does she want? Kay was the one who made quick friends with her. I was the sidekick.

"Grace."

Her use of my name startles me. But I guess Kay must've mentioned our names when talking to her. So much for keeping a low profile. And what would be Kay's motive? I feel uncomfortable about where my thoughts are leading with Kay.

I smile as I nod at the old lady, my guard up. I don't want to make small talk. I turn my attention back to the direct path to the gaming tables.

"Grace, it's not just a syringe—it's also a tracker."

I look at her now, confused. I slow my pace down but don't stop walking.

"If you save Jordan, Marc dies."

Now I stop and look at her—I mean, really look at her. She's got my full attention.

"We can't be seen together. Were you followed?" she asks.

I don't answer, move or look away from her.

"Never mind," she says. "There is a late show starting at the Mirage. It's a 'Cirque-de-something.' I left you a ticket at the slot machine I was just sitting at. Lose a few bucks in the machine, in case anyone is watching us. Then meet me at the show." She leaves me standing there.

I look around, checking if anyone is watching me, as she implied they might be. People seem to look at me, but they all look serious or suspicious, which means they're probably not and I'm imagining it. Who isn't supposed to see us talking? Who the hell is this old woman? Obviously not just a nice lady from a funeral.

I sit down at the machine where I had first spotted her. An envelope rests on the ledge next to an ashtray. I hope it's a coincidence that the ashtray just happens to be next to the old guy with the oxygen tank. The tubes are no longer in his nostrils, and the ashtray contains a freshly put-out cigarette. I don't hide my disgust when he looks at me, but he doesn't seem to care.

I remove the show ticket from the envelope and examine it. It's for the 1:30 a.m. show: Cirque du Soleil, *Entre Ciel et Mer*. There is an image of acrobatics who seem to be floating in midair. It reminds me of my journey to get here, to this decade—only we didn't float. My seat is row H, seat 22. I look at my watch; it's almost 1:00 a.m. If I leave now, I'll make it just on time.

The old lady is gone when I look around for her. I guess she had a head start. I choose a machine away from oxygen man, in case he sets himself on fire, and lose $10 in two quick spins. I no longer have the urge to sit and gamble. I just want to find out what this old woman wants and what she knows. She must have answers about what is going on, who is following Kay and looking for me.

I sit there a minute longer before deciding I need to kill some more time. Even though the last thing I want to do right now is lose more money, I feed the greedy machine $20. I play slower, not even paying attention to whether I am up or down in my luck. I just press the re-set button, trying to focus on the sounds around me, the people, the conversations. I am suspicious of everyone, everything. I trust no one right now. I think I might not even trust Kay.

I know I'm the one who stopped talking to Kay after my dad died, avoiding the casino and anything that would trigger a thought about him. I'm aware that I was being unfair to her. But she seemed OK with letting me ignore her. And now here she is, with me on this journey, and she hasn't once brought up the subject of me cutting her out of my life, even though she has every right to do so. Why?

And now she's told that woman my name? Or did she? The woman seems to know me; it wasn't just what she said. It was the way she looked at me, confident like we've known each other from, from... I don't know. Another life, maybe?

I turn my attention back to my machine. Have I lost everything yet? I need to get out of here. I need to go to the show. I don't bother cashing out. I get up and leave.

CHAPTER 16

"Sorry, excuse me, sorry."

I make my way over people, stepping on some guy's toes on my way. He shoots me a dirty look. I shoot him one right back and stop right in front of him. "Get up then, if you don't want me stepping on your fat toes!"

He looks away from me then, pretending he doesn't see me, or that I wasn't talking to him. Jerk. I linger over him for an uncomfortable few moments before continuing down my row.

I reach my seat, but the old woman is not there. I check the ticket again, cross-check it with the number on the seat. Yup, this is the right spot. I sigh and shake my head in annoyance as I take my seat. I'm tired, and my patience level has exceeded any limit I might have for myself. My legs still ache from the chase. I rub my thigh where the bruise is still tender and visible, turning from purple-blue to yellow-brown. The old woman left the casino way before me, so there is no reason for her not to be here.

The show is about to start. Every seat in the row is full, except for the vacant one beside mine. I feel like a loser who got stood up on a date but decided to make the best of it. That's probably what the idiot down the row thinks explains my mood. I look down the row at him to shoot him another dirty look, just because. It feels good to direct my anger at someone.

But he's rising from his seat to let someone in. It's the old woman. I feel satisfied that the fat-toed jerk is now getting up to let someone in like I've won a small battle.

She sits next to me. She doesn't say hello; doesn't even look at me, actually.

"Who are you?" I demand.

"Whoa, one thing at a time, Grace," she replies without even looking at me. "I'll tell you what you need to know—a little patience."

The lights dim; the show is about to begin. We watch the introduction in silence. I'm not paying attention to the show—I'm nervous, anxious, and a knot is forming in my stomach.

"I know you're not supposed to go home for another two weeks, but I want you to leave now. There is a shuttle leaving tomorrow, and you need to be on it. You need to forget all this nonsense about soul searching and get the hell home." That's her opening line. I don't know what I was expecting when I ran into her, but it certainly wasn't this. Her voice isn't kind.

I don't respond right away. The audience is clapping, the old woman included. I can see she is smiling, but even in the dim theatre, I can tell it isn't genuine. I don't think she likes me.

"Are you the one trying to stop us?"

She looks at me now, confusion on her wrinkled face. "What? Well, yea, I guess," she replies, not convincingly. "What are you talking about?" she asks. "Did something happen?"

I shake my head vigorously. "Oh no, you don't. You don't get to ask me questions. Talk, old lady. Just talk. Tell me who you are, why you're here, what you know, and why you know it."

Some people behind us make shushing sounds. The old woman stares back at me, considering my questions for longer than I'm comfortable being stared at.

"Speak," I whisper-demand.

The woman turns her attention back to the performance. "I don't know if I can trust you, so I won't tell you my name. But you need to know you're being used, Grace. This whole Metagenesis pandemic..." She scoffs, shakes her head. Even through the glow of the low lights, I can tell she is wearing a face of disgust. "The syringe will insert the chip needed to clone the donor's soul. That part is true. But what you don't know is that it will also act as a tracker so they find him. And when they find him, they will kill him. To clone a soul, the donor has to die."

Another break in the performance. More applause. I look at the stage just in time to see some fancy flipping: a lady spiraling through the air with silky wings. I feel sick, as though I'm the one spinning around on stage. My mouth salivates.

"Grace, if you go through with it, go through with finding the donor and giving him that syringe, you'll essentially be responsible for his death. You will kill him."

I feel her look at me now, but I can't turn my head to look at her. I stare at the actors on stage. The music seems to be getting louder by the second. It's dizzying. My vision wavers.

"And not just him right now, but him later. You'll kill his future soul. You'll remove him. He—Marc—Marc won't be there when you go home. He will be snuffed out and vanish, your husband."

"Ex-husband," I mutter weakly under my breath.

The old woman furrows her bushy white brows. I can see her clearly in my peripheral vision, her expression, her brushing her hair off her face, leaning forward as if deliberately trying to get me to meet her eyes, which I can't seem to bring myself to do. It's as if looking at her might make what she's saying true, confirm that she is really sitting here, beside me, saying these terrible things. I'm like a child who hides their face on the premise that if I can't see you, then you can't see me, and therefore I'm not really here, and I can avoid consequences.

"Pardon?" she asks.

I don't repeat my stupid ex-husband comment. She rests back in her seat at last. We remain silent for I don't know how long, watching the performance—or at least pretending to. I don't clap at the right moments, nor does she.

The lights slowly turn on, the theatre comes to life, chatter from the guests starts up around us. It's intermission, but neither I nor the old woman moves to leave. The old woman rises, but only to let people by. I feel like if I stand, my legs may give out. The irony doesn't escape me that it's now my toes that are being trampled on as people crawl over me to get by. I do my best to tuck them in and curse under my breath.

A few minutes pass. I strike up the conversation again, asking her who she is, why she knows this information. But she ignores my questions and continues.

"The missing people are not just lost souls. They're not even missing—they've been murdered. That's why you were secretly sent back here. That's what the trial is: testing out the next big experiment, the doctor's newest miracle drug—which, by the way, was denied by the Ethics Review Board." She turns to face me again. I wish she wouldn't do that: look right at me. "It's abuse against humanity. Up until now, cloning souls from the past has resulted in future soul losses: Metagenesis. The doctor is hoping the new drug you hold in your syringe will work this time. He's hoping it's been tweaked just enough that you only have to kill the donor, and when you do, Marc, your husband, won't vanish as a consequence. You're not the first, you know."

I'm surprised to hear that, thinking back to Dr. Messie telling Marc and I over and over that we would be.

"They're using you," she repeats. "This has been tried so many times, there is almost no chance that Marc will survive. Do you really want to take that risk?" She inhales and exhales slowly. "If you go through with this, Jordan will be saved, but Marc will most likely die," she repeats.

It's troubling that she uses his name. I know that the other stuff should be shocking to me, and it is, but somehow, hearing her use Marc's name like she knows him makes it harder to deny that this woman is speaking the truth.

"I wanted to tell you before you left, but I didn't have the courage. I was afraid then, of him. But I'm not afraid anymore."

I don't even think she's talking to me now. She's facing forward again, eyes downcast, talking to her folded hands in her lap. Her eyelashes make perfect shadows on her face from the theatre lights. Her eyes look much older than she is. She must be an old soul.

"The doctor is a monster," she whispers, tucks a strand of

white hair behind her ear. "I don't even know you. We're all anonymous. I'm sorry, but I must protect my identity. You just have to trust me. Just trust me." She looks at me now, meeting my eyes. I swallow hard, trying to rid my throat of the lump, which is growing firmer. The no-name-assistant fed me those lines only a few days ago.

"Please. Do not kill this man. Do not kill your husband," she begs.

She's asking me to choose between killing my husband and letting my son die.

In response, I find the strength to get up. I force my rubbery legs to do what I need them to. I need to turn and walk away from her and not look back. She sits up straighter when she realizes I'm leaving. An announcement comes on, asking patrons to take their seat, the show is about to resume.

"I'm not killing anyone. What happened in the past doesn't affect the future," I quote Dr. Messie.

The old woman rolls her eyes at me. "Stupid girl," she says— but not to me, more to the air surrounding me. "You might not be the one pulling the trigger; whoever is following you will do that. Without you, they wouldn't know who the target is, and the donor would be safe, and Marc would be too. But you identifying your soulmate in this life for the doctor's hitman..." She trails off, shaking her head slowly without taking her eyes off me as if I might disappear if she does. The mention of someone following me, confirming that she knows more than she's letting on, forces me to sit back down, my legs weak again. I brush my sweaty hands off on the velvet material of the folding seat, my butt on the edge.

The audience begins filing back into their rows, carrying candies in disposable baggies, the smell of beer and wine coming from their plastic throwaway cups.

"Who is following me?" I demand, looking around to see if there is evidence of someone following me right now. I see fat-toe jerk down the row, avoiding my glare.

"Not anyone who is trying to stop you, dear. Whoever is in your shadow is just waiting to put a bullet in the head of whoever you poke with that syringe. It's all about timing. Once the drugs take effect, the donor must be killed instantly afterward. Otherwise, it's all for nothing."

"So, this, this murderer, they're not trying to stop me?"

She looks confused, doesn't answer my question. The lights start to dim again, but not before I see her nervously tuck her hair behind her ear. I don't repeat my question because I fear she doesn't have the answer. Something more is going on.

I rise and trip my way out of the row, grabbing onto chair backs to steady myself as I try to pick up momentum to get as far away from her as I can. Tears fall, and I wipe them away hard with the heel of my palm, my cheekbones raw from all the tears I've cried this week. I don't look back to see if she is following. I just concentrate on putting distance between us. I know this woman. She is not delusional, nor is she working with Kay. She's telling the truth, and I can't bear to face her any longer. Facing her would mean facing the truth.

The truth is that if I want to save Jordan, Marc must die.

CHAPTER 17

When I arrive back at the room, Kay is in bed. I can tell she isn't sleeping, though, because her breathing is shallow. I don't feel up to a possible interrogation as to my whereabouts, so I sneaked in, trying to be quiet, not to wake her. The red numbers on the clock read 3:10. I'm grateful that she is fake sleeping and I humour her by leaving the lights off and tiptoeing into the bathroom, where I hide.

Without even turning on the bathroom light, I close the lid gently on the toilet, so that the porcelain doesn't make any sound as it touches the seat, and I sit. I didn't come right back to the room after leaving the show. I made a quick stop at the blackjack tables (maybe not as quick as I thought, given the time). I had to think, or not think. What's there to think about, anyway?

I can't kill Marc. I'm no killer.

Now, as I sit here alone, without the distraction of the cards or clinking of chips, I can't stop replaying what the old woman said. Like a scene from a bad movie, I play back her telling me Marc will die, her begging me not to kill him. I imagine what it would be like to go home and find Marc gone. Had the woman not said anything, that is exactly what would've happened, and the thought sends sharp pains shooting from my gut, suffocating me.

I think and obsess over sweet, kind Marc. When my dad died, I went cold from the inside out, to keep from losing my mind. Rather than comforting me, it felt like Marc just pulled away. I took it as a lack of commitment on his part, and before long, all the things I used to love about him, I'd learned to hate. Instead of fighting, though, we skillfully ignored each other. His quietness and my edginess widened the gap between us like the ocean separating continents, and it was never going to close.

In my head, I replay his voice from his message, telling me he loves me now like he's reaching out from a sinking ship in that dark ocean and all I have to do is guide him in with the lighthouse. A shiver runs through me, picturing him saying it; what he must've looked like as he said it; the courage that it took him to say it. Marc loves me deeply.

I begin to sob.

Not over Marc, since he will live, but over Jordan. I sob over the realization that my son will die. His soul is dying. He can't be saved from Metagenesis.

"Why?" I sob, grabbing at my ears, trying to drown out the sound of my own pained voice, squeezing my eyes tight. I release my ears and ball my hands into firm fists, pound at my thighs, numbing them. All my frustrations and anger finally spill out of me. I just throw my head back, allow my body to go limp and my arms to dangle at my sides, and I weep, my chest heaving. I no longer care if I wake Kay from her pretend sleep, or the whole hotel from their real sleep, for that matter.

"Why, why, why, why," I wail to the ceiling, my voice catching and hoarse. I sit alone in the bathroom, unable to hold my grief inside of me any longer. I don't bother to mop the dragon-sized tears that fall and dampen my lap or wipe at my running nose. I lean on the tiles, humid from the rickety air conditioner, lose my balance and slip off the seat, crumpling in the corner between the wall and the toilet.

The light flickers on, forcing me to squint as I try to blink my eyes open into focus. Through my blurry vision, I can see Kay approaching me wearily. She seems unsure about what to do, hesitating at the door before finally making her way toward me.

She crouches in front of me and pulls my head to her shoulder. She's hushing me like a baby. I let her. For a minute. Before panic sets in.

I remember that it's after three in the morning; that shuttle the old woman wants us on is leaving at sunrise. We need to be in the desert by sunrise, the same place we landed, so we can get back home. I back off and push Kay away from me. She falls back on her bum, startled. I clamour and crawl my way past her and out of the bathroom, jolt up and rush to turn on the rest of the lights in the room.

Hastily, I gather our belongings, throwing them on the bed. Where is that bag, our knapsack?

"Grace!" Kay grabs my arm. "Grace! What the hell are you doing?"

"We have to get out of here." I shake her loose. My eyes are still trying to adjust to the light. I get on my hands and knees and check under the bed, run to the closet, check the drawers, the dresser, under the dresser...

"Grace, stop! Tell me what's going on. Where are we going? What's happening?"

"We have to go—the shuttle, the shuttle, we have to catch it! Where the hell is that backpack?" I don't tell her about the old woman. There is no time for that. "Forget it. We don't need any of this stuff. We just need to go."

I grab her by the arm like she's a naughty toddler and lead her to the door. Kay resists.

"C'mon!" I insist, tugging harder.

She twists out of my grip, refusing to follow. "I'm not going anywhere until you tell me what's going on! Wait, did Jordan take a turn for the worse?"

"No, no, it's not that," I tell her. He hasn't yet, but he will if we leave like we should.

"Well, then, what is it? Why are we catching the shuttle? Why do you want to go home? Did you find a match, or did something else happen?"

When I don't respond, her sad expression tells me she assumes the latter—and why wouldn't she, given the events thus far? We're being followed, possibly by more than one person.

Our room has been invaded and tossed, twice.

Kay tries to reason with me. "We can just move hotels completely. We can leave, Grace. Find another hideout. We'll be more careful now that we know something is going on."

I've got one hand on the doorknob, my heart pounding, my face still wet with tears for Jordan.

"We're too close to give up on Jordan," she says softly.

Terror rises in me with the sound of his name, in the form of heat that starts in my toes, then builds and spreads until it reaches my earlobes. The terror of knowing I will bury my only son.

I should explain about the old woman now. Explain that we're not here alone, we're being used. We're just instruments in a thicker plot. Dr. Messie is evil. I should tell her that Marc's life is at risk. I should tell her that for Jordan to live, someone will murder David Williams, and then Marc will lose his soul and die from Metagenesis. He will never be reincarnated again. But I don't tell her. For some reason, I decide to keep that to myself.

Why? Why would I keep that from Kay?

CHAPTER 18

"What's a code 33?" I ask, still gripping the handle. I'm out of breath from my rampage around the room. I'm so exhausted from lack of sleep that I'm seeing stars. My head hurts, I'm mentally worn down. And my heart aches for Marc. But my inner being, my existence, and my very soul are bleeding agony for my son. And so I don't tell Kay about the consequences of saving Jordan.

After all, the old woman said it's a trial. That they're hoping my syringe holds the right potion that will not result in Marc's death. What if they're right? Maybe I haven't made my decision yet. I should consider this longer. Leaving today is too harsh. What's the harm if I stay on? If I find my soulmate, David, Marc's past life—if I find him, I don't have to identify him with the syringe-tracker. If I don't identify him, they, whoever "they" are, won't know whom to kill.

"Tell me about code 33," I ask Kay again, turning around to face her now. "Does it mean that he's closer to...?" I trail off, not able to finish my sentence by saying the word "death." I release the door handle and let go of my intention to run home.

Kay stares back at me, her eyebrows knitted in concern. She looks up at the ceiling, sighs deeply and takes a seat on her bed before meeting my stare again. She looks like she's waiting for me to sit with her, so I do.

"Not everyone goes through that, a code 33. It doesn't mean that he's dying. It means that when they resuscitated his soul, he was experiencing flashbacks of his past lives."

That's all she says. I'm waiting for more. That doesn't sound so bad. It doesn't mean he's dying. It's just another symptom of his condition. Not everyone experiences Metagenesis the same way—I get it.

"Anything else?" I ask. I'd feel relieved if it wasn't for the look on her face, telling me there is more to say.

She takes my hand; hers is trembling. "The flashbacks he's experiencing, they are of the last few moments of his past thirty-three lives. He is suffering through the last thirty-three deaths, reliving them like he is dying all over again." She lets that sink in for a moment. "I'm so sorry, Grace." She squeezes my hand.

I go completely numb. Suddenly, I hear a loud buzzing in my head. I stare down at the carpet fibres. My hand goes limp in hers, and I retract it.

"Thank you for telling me," I hear myself say, much too calmly. My voice doesn't sound like my own. It's muffled like I'm fifty feet underwater. The buzzing is progressively becoming louder until it reaches ear-splitting. I think I hear Kay ask me if I'm OK. She says my name, I think. I run to the bathroom and vomit.

CHAPTER 19

"Kay?" I ask into the darkness. After telling her over and over again that I didn't want to talk about it, I've changed my mind now that I can't sleep. It's now 4 a.m.; the clock mocks me. My stomach churns, emptied of its contents but full of nervous energy.

"Mm...?" Kay sounds like she was just about to sleep.

"What was it like?" I know it's hard for her to talk about Peter. But I need to know. I need to hear what happened to him. I want to know what code 33 was like for her brother. Then I can prepare myself for what Jordan is facing without me. If he dies without me, I need to know what he will go through.

I'm lying on my back, staring at the ceiling, spotting imaginary shapes and faces in the imperfect texture highlighted by the shadows. Kay turns on her side to face me, props herself up on an elbow. I turn my head for a second to glance at her, see her figure through the dim light that filters through the thin, cheap drapes.

"Jordan won't go through that," she says firmly. "We're going to find a cure. We'll be the first ones. We're going to make history, do you understand? Don't you go getting sidetracked with things you can't change."

I can't stand it anymore. I don't want to hear fakeness,

especially from her.

"Just *tell* me, I want to know." I sob. "I need to hear it in case we don't. Please, Kay," I plead, tears streaming down into my ears, making soft drop sounds as they hit my pillow. I should tell her about the old woman, explain that Jordan won't be saved. "Tell me," my voice says, barely above a whisper.

"Peter didn't go through code 33. I'm sorry, but I can't tell you what I just don't know." I don't know if she's lying to spare my feelings or not. But she doesn't say anything else, and she lies back down, turns over in her bed, and adjusts her pillows. "Try to get some sleep, Grace. Things will be clearer in the morning. You'll check your messages; there will be something good from Marc, I'm sure."

I remember that there is a second message that I haven't listened to yet. There were two new messages. I only listened to the first one, of Marc telling me he loves me. I try to replay the message from memory, trying to make the memory of his voice soothe me to sleep. It doesn't work. Instead, I feel guilty.

Lying in bed, I toss and turn, flip and flop. I can hear Kay beside me in her own bed. For the longest time, she doesn't fall back to sleep. We don't speak again or anything. Both of us lie there, ignoring each other, lost in our own thoughts, exhausted and confused. For a good hour, I listen to her breathing lightly, until finally, she seems to succumb to sleep, her breathing pattern deeper. I envy her, sleeping.

I look at the clock; it's half past five. The skies are getting lighter, and the shuttle will leave soon, and we won't be on it.

I give up on the idea of sleeping and get up, pace the room. I run my hand through my hair, massaging my scalp to unburden my throbbing brain. I peek out through the blinds. The lights in the office are on, but Brad's gone. The office is closed. The parking lot is empty. I need to get out and do something.

I change quickly and quietly so as not to disturb Kay, take the key, a notepad and pen, and slip out of the room. I walk out, cross the parking lot to the phone booth. I pick up the dangling phone book and look through it, shaking my head in disbelief at the missing Williams pages. It's unbelievable the lengths that whoever did this has gone through to stop or stall us. I now feel confident that the old woman doesn't know that someone other than her wants us to halt our search.

I close up the phone book to use it as a writing surface, then pick up the phone and dial.

"Information—for what city?"

"Las Vegas," I tell her.

"For what name?"

"Williams," I say, and spell it out.

"I've got one hundred and fifty-two results for that name. Do you have an address or first name?"

"No, I don't. Can you give them all to me?"

We want to search all Williamses, not just Davids, in case the number is listed under another first name.

"No, ma'am, I'm afraid I can't. I can only give you one listing per call."

I sigh, annoyed. This is going to be a long process.

"Give me the first one, then. I guess I'll call back one hundred and fifty-one more times," I tell her, making sure she hears my snarkiness.

CHAPTER 20

I sneak back into the room. I've got a good list going, but the sun is up, and my eyes are scratchy and heavy. I've got forty-seven names, addresses, and corresponding phone numbers.

The shower is running, and Kay's bed is empty. Just a bundle of sheets remain. I don't know how she manages to ruffle the bed around like that.

I place the list on the dresser, where I know she'll see it, with a note that reads, *"I'll get the rest when I get up."*

I feel like I've done something productive. I still haven't listened to that second message, and you would think that the suspense of what Marc has to say would be eating at me—like maybe he is saying he regrets telling me that he loves me. That's what I pretend the message is about: regret over revealing his feelings for me. If I pretend that, then I don't have to think about the alternative: that it's more bad news about Jordan. And if he doesn't love me, then I don't have to feel such guilt over missing the early-morning departure on the shuttle.

I crawl under my blanket. It's a horribly thin blanket, made of unbreathable material, but after twenty-four hours of not sleeping a wink—and all that I've been through making it feel more like twenty-four years—the blanket feels like it was made in heaven, and perhaps even handwoven by the angels themselves. It feels like those angel wings are embracing me, tucking me in. The bed feels like a jumbo-sized, fluffy cloud welcoming me to heaven. My eyes, which moments ago had felt like burning sheets of sandpaper, blink shut before my head even sinks into the giant marshmallow pillow. I sleep. And I dream.

"Dad?"

His back is to me, but I recognize his posture, the way his shoulders always slump with sadness. His dark curls brush the collar of his blue work suit. We have the same hair. It's funny, that's the only way I ever remember him; dressed in his security guard uniform.

He doesn't turn when I call his name. It's early in the day. The sun blares through the slats in the partially closed blinds, creating shadows on the barn floor of our small container home. It's cold in here. A window must be open. I wonder why he's home, but don't ask. If he's not working to earn gambling money or sleeping to prepare for gambling, he's…well… gambling.

Something must be wrong. I grab at my wrist to comfort myself, to feel Dad's cool copper watch. It was the one thing I kept after he…

But I don't feel anything. My wrist is bare. I look down and confirm that it's gone. My watch is gone. Panicking, I look back at Dad. "Where's my watch?" I inquire, but I can't tell if I've said it out loud.

He's facing me now, and his face is blue as well, matching his suit. Is it the bit of sunlight reflecting off his suit? But the blinds dancing in the wind aren't open enough for that. His eyes are bloodshot. And what's wrong with his neck? Oh my god, his neck!

"Gracie-girl." He struggles to say my name. Why is he struggling? He looks scared. He's waving me off, swatting at me as if shooing away a fly.

I hear the familiar noise from the watch, my watch. It's on his wrist and clinks with the movement of his arm.

"Go away… Run." He forces it through his swollen lips.

And that's when I see the rope. The rope around his neck.

"Dad!" I scream in horror and run for him, stubbing my toe on the old green couch and knocking over the small lamp; it smashes to pieces.

"Daddy!" I try to grab him, but I can't, he's too high up. "Daddy!"

I jump at and take his hand, but he squirms out of my grip. He's pushing me away, and so I grab his wrist. The watch comes loose, falls to the ground, landing next to the tipped-over, splintered old stool. The watch, the last thing left of Dad.

I jolt up in a cold sweat. The blankets are suffocating me, the room is stuffy, the bed is hard, the pillows flat. I instinctively feel for my watch. It's here, safely on my wrist. I look at the clock; it's after 3 p.m. Kay's bed is still the same empty mess as when I went to sleep. The light in the room has changed from early morning to late afternoon. I can tell it must be an inferno outside. The note I left Kay on the dresser is gone. I get up from my bed, feeling drunk from bad sleep, and make my way to the window to peer through the curtains, blinking into the brightness of Las Vegas. Kay is at the phone booth with pen and paper in hand, chatting with someone, probably surveying them.

I recall last night. Code 33. Jordan. I pair that with the memory of watching my dad die, in agony. Even though Dad chose to end his life, he still looked like he was in torment. It didn't matter that it was his wish to die. Knowing that Jordan will go through his own death thirty-three times against his will, not by choice... He will suffer greatly on his way to his final death, and it is unacceptable. We need to find a match. We need to find David Williams, no matter the cost.

Maybe Dr. Messie's newest potion will work. I have to believe that we will make history and Marc will survive. Maybe. I jiggle my wrist to hear my watch. To remind me of my dad.

Kay looks over at me then, a big smile on her face. I move the curtain out of the way and smile back. She gives a thumbs-up so eagerly that she drops the paper and highlighter on the ground. She awkwardly tries to bend over to pick them up while keeping the phone tucked between her cheek and crook of her neck. It makes me laugh.

I should tell Kay about the old woman and what she told me. But I don't think she would understand. I wish I could trust that she would have my back while I decide, but Kay wouldn't hurt a spider, literally. She makes a habit of running around with a container on cleaning day, saving all the spiders first. She sings to her plants, she rescues lost animals. She would do what's right, and that means we would be on the next shuttle home without question. She wouldn't ponder the information as I am.

I watch Kay clumsily hang up the phone; with her arms full of the phone book, paper, pens, highlighters and her disposable bottle of water, she makes her way excitedly back to the room. She looks so pleased with herself. I open the door for her and take some of the stuff out of her overflowing hands. She trips her way through the door and wraps her arms around my neck, squeezing me.

"Grace, thank you for doing that! You must've been up all night getting those numbers! You're just like a bat-eared fox on the hunt!"

I love Kay and her weird analogies.

"What's a bat-eared fox?" I ask, not that I really want to know, but her enthusiasm is welcoming. I want to humour her and soak in her good mood to help improve my own.

She releases her hold on me and starts rifling through the papers. "A cute fox with button eyes like yours. Stays up all night, holds onto its internal temperature, been around for close to a million years. They're known for—oh, just look it up!" She laughs, probably realizing that I don't care.

She hands me a paper with a name and address, studying me for my reaction. "This might be the one," she tells me with a proud expression, like a child showing off a perfect test score.

David Williams, formerly of Las Vegas
Prefers Pepsi over Coke.
Broke a leg as a kid.
Allergic to shellfish.

The profile of Marc's past life. The profile of a man who must be killed to save Jordan. I gulp the sour guilt back and force a smile.

"We better go find him, then. See if I feel a connection to him as my soulmate. Let's go meet Marc's past life." I'm feigning the enthusiasm.

Kay doesn't seem to notice my hesitation. She's too excited about her find.

"Should we call a taxi?" I ask.

CHAPTER 21

Baker, Nevada: that's where David Williams lives. His dear old mama still lives in Las Vegas. That's who Kay spoke with. She was only too pleased to help Kay find her long-lost high school friend. Apparently, David didn't have many of those.

Getting to Baker, Nevada, is going to be a long journey—a five-hour drive, to be exact. It turns out David is a Park Ranger who gives tours through the Lehman Caves in Great Basin National Park, near the Utah border. Dear Old Mama was hesitant about giving out a home address for her precious only child, David, but was happy to tell Kay where she could find him at his workplace. She even offered to call him ahead of time, but Kay insisted on surprising him.

A taxi ride would cost us more than a thousand dollars each way. But the better plan is to take a tour bus anyway, as we want to visit the park and have David as our guide. Either way, Kay doesn't know about my dreadful decision to spend (lose) a bit of cash at the casino last night on my way back from the show. But she doesn't argue when I tell her I should go make a little money for us, which tells me she suspects.

"Poker is better suited to your skills, Grace," she says. "I'll look for a tour departing first thing tomorrow. Go make us enough to pay for it."

But when I walk by and see Leo smiling at me, I decide to join him at my usual blackjack table. Leo has a way of taking my mind off the stress.

"Forget something, Grace?" he asks with an impish grin as I take my usual seat beside him. "You left this here yesterday, so I held on to it for you, kept it safe."

I look down at his outstretched hand and see my beautiful little black pager.

"Oh wow!" I yelp. My hand covers my mouth rather than grabbing for the pager, afraid it might disappear if I reach for it, like a mirage in the desert.

Leo seems pleased to present this lost item to me. He knows how much it means to me, although he thinks it's for auditions and not for receiving messages from Marc eighty years in the future.

I gently take the pager from his palm. He seems sheepish when I do.

"You're welcome?" He phrases it like a question with a raised eyebrow, and I am so happy I can't even describe it. I wrap my arms around him, clutching the pager, squeezing him with delight.

"Thank you thank you thank you," I whisper gratefully as I cling to him.

He doesn't hug me back right away. I guess I've caught him off guard. But eventually, I feel his warm hand on the small of my back, awkward at first, but then he brings me in tight for an embrace, gentle, yet strong. He runs his hand up and down my back, his fingers catching on my bra strap. It gives me shivers and I back away quickly. His hand lingers on my waist, his finger tangled in the belt loop of my jeans. I know he has feelings for me. I don't want to embarrass him.

When I look at him to say thanks again, his smile is different. Like a guy with more than just a crush. I feel a bit guilty. I don't want to give him the wrong idea.

I give him a friendly punch on the shoulder to break the mood I didn't mean to create. "Thanks, Leo, you're the best anchor ever!" I tease.

"Ya, for sure," he replies, retrieving his hand while uncomfortably averting his eyes away from me and back to the cards in front of him. "How about you take me to dinner later, you know, as a reward," he says, trying to get back to our usual banter about him asking me out and me turning him down.

But I can tell he's half-serious and covering up his real feelings with his usual joke. He looks self-conscious and even takes it further. "This seat isn't just called the anchor, it's also known as third base. If you won't reward me with dinner, maybe…" He winks to make a point that this is all just for laughs.

Without missing a beat I play my part and reject him. "No, I don't want to go to third base with you, Leo." I want to get up and leave the table, go play poker instead; the odds are better. But I don't want Leo to think it's because of him. So I stay and instead make small talk with the young couple seated to my right, hoping Leo will go back to being Leo and we can all move on. Even the dealer seems to deal the cards a bit slower, probably noticing the delicate moment in front of her.

It takes a bit of time, but it works. Within a few minutes, Leo and the sweet young couple are talking the usual table-game talk. I back out of the conversation with relief, satisfied with myself because I don't think either Leo or the couple noticed my slyness. I wish Kay was here to see that! Who says I'm not a people person? I can do this.

I tune back into the conversation and even add to it. I'm so proud of me. Gwen and Stan are their names. They are getting married at the end of the weekend. They seem too young to be married. "Wow, you must be, what, twenty-two? Twenty-three?" I ask.

"These two? They're barely legal," the dealer answers on their behalf. "Young Gwen, I hope you know men don't turn into men in their twenties."

I roll my eyes at the dealer, who looks to be about a hundred years old. I used to hate when grumpy old people said stuff like that to Marc and me when we were a new couple.

"It's OK," quiet, big-blue-eyed Gwen speaks up. "Stan's an old soul."

She says it so passively and calmly. Poor thing. This young couple, just starting out, and he has an old soul. I'm devastated for her because she will lose him. I'm horrified for him because he suffers from this disease. Now I understand their rush to be married so young before he dies from Metagenesis. I want to smack the dealer for her rude comment about this young man.

"Oh no, that's devastating, Gwen. Stan." I place my hand on her shoulder. "I'm so, so sorry," I tell her in the most sincere tone. "How long have you known about his condition?" I can empathize with her. I remember when I'd only just found out about Jordan. The denial, grief, anger, and loneliness.

The table has gone completely silent. And of course it has. This poor couple in love and already destined to lose each other to a terrible disease. Only the table isn't looking at them with pity or sorrow, they're focused on me. The hundred-year-old dealer, Leo, and even Gwen and Stan are all looking at me with confused expressions.

Finally, Leo bursts out laughing. "I guess you must like your men young and dumb? Grace doesn't date old souls, they're too wise for her. Is that it?"

I feel my face redden with embarrassment.

"Now *that* explains why you don't want to let me take you to dinner!" he goes on. "I'm a CEO with a real job and education!"

The rest of the table joins in laughing. I am such an idiot. Metagenesis doesn't exist yet. Any proud moment I felt earlier over holding a conversation and being a people person is gone, as quickly as the hand I just lost.

"Busted!" the stupid old dealer declares as she swipes away my cards and chips in two swift motions.

I know she's referring to my twenty-three against her face card, but I feel like a cat who's swallowed a yellow canary. Guilty. Caught. Stupid. At least Leo seems to be back to his old self.

I pretend my pager is vibrating and use it as an opportunity to excuse myself. "Oh! Gotta go!" I say and make a show of wagging the pager around as proof of my urgent need to leave.

"Good luck!" Leo says and waves bye.

I'm relieved that he is so engaged in the cards and Gwen and

Stan that he doesn't offer to walk me out like usual, and I don't have to turn him down, like usual.

When I pretend-check the pager on my way out of the casino, I notice that it's flashing. I check it for real. Five messages. That's four more on top of the one message I hope is Marc telling me to forget about his "I love you" message. I stop in my tracks, let out a deep sigh and turn around to head back inside, toward the phone booth. I need to hear these messages.

CHAPTER 22

"*You have one saved message and four new messages.*"
I skip the "I love you" message that I saved. Listening to that would be like a child refusing medicine they need simply because it tastes bad. And right now, my guilt feels and tastes bad, and I prefer to avoid it.

"*First new message...*"

"Hi, Grace. It's me, Marc..."

Here it comes. I hold my breath and brace myself.

"Please respond?" He pauses before hanging up.

That's it? End of the message? Well, that was only message number one. There are three more. I wait for the next message to start playing, rather than skipping to it, letting my anticipation build as punishment.

"Gracie!" It's my brother, Charlie. I'm surprised to hear his voice and even look at the receiver in my hand as if to confirm it's really him. "Gracie, how long did you think you could keep this from me?!" He sounds mad. "And why? Why would you keep this from me? I knew you weren't off earning money for Jordan's clinic bills—I'm not an idiot. But I never thought..." He pauses. I hear him sigh. "How do you think I felt, learning the truth from the press? Some reporter dude shows up at my door and asks me how I feel about my little sister on a hero's mission to save mankind from Metagenesis! If I'm proud of you, or scared you may not make it back!" His voice catches. "Gracie! This is huge! You're making headline news! Dr. Messie is taking all the credit. Everyone is worshipping him like some kind of god."

He says "god" like he doesn't like Dr. Messie. I don't blame him. Dr. Messie has the personality of a wet rag, just like the one he uses to wipe his sweaty face with all the time. But I now know he is a manipulator and a liar, and I'm being used by him for dirty work.

"But you're out there, my baby sister, risking everything, risking losing Jordan, risking getting stuck there, and I find out through some geeky reporter? Like a second-hand citizen! And then—"

"*End of message,*" says mechanical pager woman. "*Next message.*"

The rest of the messages are more of my brother's rant. Nothing more from Marc about anything. Not about his loving me, not loving me, or even updates on Jordan. Just Charlie. I'm not sure how I feel about not hearing more from Marc. But hearing from Charlie...

His messages go on to explain how Dr. Messie was granted strict approval to begin the trials and then it was leaked to the press (by an unknown party) that he had already sent someone (me) to clone a soul.

The "leak" thought it would bring negative attention to Dr. Messie, but it seems to be having the opposite effect. He is being worshipped. Everyone is hopeful that his trials and research will prove fruitful. Rallies have started, showing support. Vigils at cemeteries for those who lost their souls to Metagenesis. Crowds gathering at lost soul clinics. It seems people have their hopes up, wanting me to succeed so much that they've ignored the fact that Dr. Messie took the liberty of sending me back despite the Ethics Review Board's initial rejection of the trial. It also seems they are not aware of the fact that I'm not the first one. And based on Charlie's messages, it also seems as if no one is aware of the interference I am encountering here. The old woman, the young guy we chased down, the mean man looking for me. They don't seem to know that the good doctor is using me.

The fact that Charlie has no idea that I'm supposed to murder my husband means a big chunk of the story is conveniently being withheld. I consider leaving him a message to tell him the truth so he can advise me on what course of action to take. My brother has always been my voice of reason.

I dismiss the idea as quickly as it came to me, not knowing who else might hear the message—or maybe I just don't want to hear Charlie's reasonable opinion. The world is waiting for my successful return. They *need* me to succeed. They need us to get to Great Basin National Park to find David.

I head back to the casino, detouring, so I don't pass Leo at the blackjack tables and make my way directly to the poker room. In here, no one knows me. I made a point of not making conversation with anyone every time I was here, treating my visit as strictly business. I just need to win enough to get us on that tour bus in the morning. I need to revert to my old ways, not my dad's. I need to win.

CHAPTER 23

When I get back to the room, the sun is well on its way to heating Vegas up like hell. And that's exactly how I feel. I sneak into the room, hoping beyond hope that Kay is still sleeping, even though at nine in the morning, it's very unlikely. My suspicions are quickly confirmed by her voice attacking me when the door creaks open.

"Where the hell have you been?"

It's funny that she includes hell in her accusation, given that I've just compared both my mood and Vegas to hell. It seems to sum up everything nicely.

I come inside and close the door gently behind me. Maybe she'll calm down if I tiptoe and speak in a whisper. "Sorry, things didn't quite work out like I planned," I begin to explain, thinking about the bad hand I played, losing most of our money, money that was meant to pay for our trip this morning. I have a back-up plan, but before I can even begin to divulge it—

"The bus tour left at 7 a.m. sharp!" Kay yells. "I signed us up, waited for you at our regular meeting time at the diner to tell you, but you no-showed—"

Damn, I'd been so caught up in blackjack with Leo that I forgot to meet up with her. In fact, I don't remember the last time I ate. I open my mouth, ready to tell her my plan, but then she goes on…

"—and we were supposed to be on that bus at 7 a.m., on our way to a tour that is being given by *David Williams!*" She uses his name like a weapon, leaning forward as she yells it at my face. I actually flinch. "And what did you do? What 'didn't go as planned,' Grace?" She rolls her eyes and wobbles her head as she mimics me.

I don't think I look like that when I talk. I want to tell her about the car I got us, but she's angry, and I can't get a word in edgewise.

"Did you lose the rest of our money?" she continues. She's not done yet.

I put on a stone face and decide to let her finish before trying to explain that we're driving. She knows I lost the money. The question is redundant. She knows I don't have anything left (well, I do have *some* left—maybe $100). She knows I'm my father's child. What she doesn't know is that I have a plan, if she'd just let me talk. But I deserve the lecture, and so I let her get the rest out of her system.

"What do we do now? Do we walk to the national park? And I suppose we should take our belongings with us since we can't pay stupid pig-face Brad for our room. Tie our stuff up on a stick like hobos on the run!" She throws her hands up in the air, turns around, plops herself on the bed.

"Are you done?" I ask, cautiously.

"All this negative energy… it's not good, not good…" She's shaking her head and seems to be talking to herself now. "Great Basin National Park is *far*. It's not like we can just walk there…"

"We're not walking, we're driving," I tell her proudly, seizing an opening in her rant. "I got us a car, Kay." I remove Brad's keys from my pocket and dangle them by the naked woman at the end of the chain.

Kay's expression changes from angry to suspicious.

"Do you want to know how I got Brad's car?" I ask with a smirk. I start explaining but don't get two words in before Kay interrupts with her hand up to halt me.

"Why do I get the feeling that if I know how I won't want to participate because I might be a co-conspirator? Grace, you know me like a dog knows his own asshole. Do I really want to know how?" she asks.

I try not to laugh at her comparison. I think she just called herself an asshole, and I want to point it out, but she doesn't look up for a joke.

"Probably not," I admit with a shrug. I offered Brad a blow job, sort of. "We just have to get it back before midnight, or the police may come looking for it."

She makes a show of shoving her index fingers deep in her ears to block me out.

CHAPTER 24

We finally leave the city, and I'm relieved. We pass a sign that reads "Drive carefully, come back soon," and I wave at it, finally releasing my death grip from the steering wheel.

Getting the car going was quite the task. Not only was Kay still mad at me, but I had to learn how to drive, on the spot. I couldn't quite figure it out.

"My head is going to detach from my neck if you keep that up! How the hell does phlegmatic Brad drive this thing?" Kay had expressed, bracing herself with her hands on the dashboard.

"What is 'phlegmatic'?" I dared ask.

"Look it up!" she yelled back.

We exchanged words then. She was very upset over missing the organized tour and was not ready to let me off the hook for it. So I guess since I was the one who had screwed up the excursion, then I was the one responsible for getting us out of the city, even though I hadn't slept yet.

Brad's car is very different from my simple link-car, the one I had sold to pay for Jordan's medical exams. My link-car practically drove itself. When I touch the pedal in this car, it jolts forward, giving us whiplash, and then comes to an abrupt stop when I slam my foot down on the other pedal, causing the seat belt to dig into my collarbone. How those straps are supposed to save you in the event of an accident is a complete mystery to me. Without links, a driver is completely on their own out here, forced to weave in and out of traffic. Transportation is so disorganized. Everyone is honking at us.

"Finally!" Kay exclaims. "Peace!" She blows an exaggerated kiss at the sign I just waved at.

I can feel Kay loosen up, her shoulders relaxing and dropping down to normal height, away from her ears. I hope she's on her way to forgiving me.

The rest of the ride up to the Utah border is relatively tranquil. We switch about halfway through so I can catch some sleep. Two nights in a row of staying up to greet the sunrise is getting to me, but I don't fall asleep right away. I recline my seat and enjoy the desert scenery. There is nothing ahead of us but empty roads. I'm thankful that the sun is now hiding behind some angry clouds, promising rain, allowing us to keep the windows open and smell the air of a storm brewing.

Kay doesn't ask me how I got the car, and I don't tell her. She is too honest, too good. That's why I really know I cannot tell her about the old woman until I'm sure I'm ready to go home.

Anyway, Marc's death is not fact. I don't know what that old woman's motives are. I don't know if what she says is true or if I can trust her. And even if she is being truthful, even she admits that Dr. Messie hopes the new mix in my syringe will work. That means there is more than just a chance that I can save Jordan without harming Marc.

I stick my hand out the window. The feeling reminds me simultaneously of my childhood and of the pain of losing my father three years ago. For a moment, I am transported to the day before my dad died. He had taken Charlie and me out driving through the country. Not in our link-car, but in one of those old cars, much like this one we're in now, along the deserted ancient back roads. Thinking back on that now, it would've come in handy if he had taught us how to drive that old thing. Dad had asked us to come out with him, like old times when we were little. I had left Jordan and Marc at home and let Dad take us out like kids, Charlie up front, me in the back.

The drive resembled the way we lived our lives then: alone, illegal, thrilling yet peaceful. Dad always kept a low profile, even though the only crime we were guilty of was gambling. I kept letting the wind catch my hand, then spreading my fingers, cupping the air and dragging it through. I caught Dad watching me in the rear-view and held eye contact with him. He smiled, probably remembering his own childhood. Or maybe he was remembering our mother. They say except for my tight curls and her curvy figure, I look like her, and I was about the same age as she was when she left us.

The last conversation we had with Dad had been in that car. Or actually, it was the last conversation Dad had with Charlie. I was always an afterthought he tried to include.

"Gracie, did you hear what I said to Charlie? This is important."

I had heard, but I shook my head no and let him repeat it because I didn't understand what he was talking about. Maybe he would offer up more of an explanation. He didn't.

"Don't let society determine what is right or wrong," he said. "Society is wrong. Don't be another casualty to society. Do you understand?"

I didn't.

"Where are you?" Kay asks, bringing me back from my memories.

I look around for a road sign, suddenly panicked that we've missed an exit or something. I am not driving and should be sleeping, but I still feel responsible for ensuring we make it there.

"I mean, in your head, Grace. Where are you in your head? You seem to be in some distant, faraway land."

I relax. We're not lost. I'm lost in thought, but we're still on our way to find David Williams.

Dr. Messie is what's wrong with society. David Williams will be a casualty of that, as will Marc... maybe.

Sorry, Dad.

The skies open and release the rain. It patters on the roof of the car and soothes me to sleep.

CHAPTER 25

We arrive at Great Basin National Park a little before five. The rain has stopped, but the clouds haven't parted, suggesting more rain is to come. We would've gotten here quicker had it not been for the small detail about running out of gas. Kay woke me up in a panic. She thought she'd broken something. We had no idea what to do when the car slowed down and stopped without warning. OK, maybe it did warn us. There was a blinking light, but we had no idea what it was for. Were it not for the nice people who stopped to help us out, we never would've figured it out. Link-cars are powered by the links and solar tubes, not by fuel. Even Dad's old car had been converted to solar power. What a wasteful era.

Now, here we are. We approach the office and purchase tickets to tour the caves with our guide. We confirm that David Williams is, in fact, working. My heart flutters at the thought. I hope it means that we are in close proximity to Marc's soul and that's why it flutters. I'm anxious about how I will feel when we meet or touch as if he's my blind date. Maybe being in the same vicinity as he is will be enough. I jiggle my wrist to hear my watch and pat at the pocket of my jeans, to feel the outline of the syringe representing my son's life.

We wait our turn at the post where the guide is supposed to

meet us. My stomach is rumbling with hunger pains. I haven't eaten since the day before, except for granola bars and a boring apple we took with us for the ride up. Kay hands me another dry granola bar before unwrapping one for herself. The wrapper says "cranberry almond." I doubt that, I think to myself as I examine the small bits of what is supposed to be the cranberry. It tastes like the throwaway cardboard box it came in. We exchange looks of displeasure.

There is a small crowd gathering with us to wait for the next tour of the caves to start. And that's when I see him.

Mister. Dark sunglasses, unsmiling, alone.

He looks mean. This must be who Camilla was describing. He is not a tourist, although he is dressed like one. To blend in, he is wearing an obnoxious tee-shirt with some tacky Las Vegas slogan written on it, tucked into baggy brown shorts. Instead of a belt, a fanny pack holds them up. His baseball cap shields his dark face, but I don't mistake him for a tourist at all. I wonder if he always wears sunglasses in the rain, or if it's a coincidence that both times I've seen him, it's raining and he's wearing sunglasses. Through his shades, I can't tell if he is looking at me or not, but I actually think that he is. His head seems deliberately turned in my direction, and he doesn't appear to care that I am looking right at him. I guess Mister is not just a driver for Dr. Messie, as he told me the day he showed up at my front door to escort me to the doctor's home office. I suppose Mister is most probably also the hitman the old woman spoke of, and likely the guy in the diner who inquired about me by last name.

"It's really beautiful here," Kay says, probably trying to calm my nerves by taking my mind off my task.

If she knew my task is not only to recognize the love of all my lives but that I must stab him with a tracker so Mister can put a bullet in his head, she might be trying to stop me, not calm me.

When I don't respond, Kay looks around. "What is it? Do you see him? Is he already here?" Kay asks with excitement I should feel but don't.

She doesn't seem to recognize Mister. I guess she had a

different driver.

"No, no." I shake my head. "I don't see anyone at all." I look away from Mister.

Kay's face brightens. She is looking over my shoulder and then she lets out a snicker. "Wow, Grace! What a prize Marc was in this life!"

She is being sarcastic, and before I can figure out what she's being sarcastic about, I hear his pinched voice.

"Welcome, ladies and gentlemen, to Great Basin National Park. I will be your tour guide today, through the Lehman Caves. My name is—"

I hold my breath and turn toward our guide. David Williams?

"—Melvin." Not David? "Your regular tour guide had to leave for an emergency, but the show must go on, and you are in very good hands with me."

Melvin takes a bow by way of introduction. He is short and nerdy and is dressed in a brown Ranger-looking outfit. I look to Kay for her reaction.

"I'm relieved that geek isn't your soulmate." She looks disappointed, not relieved.

I'm both relieved and disappointed that Melvin isn't David. I look for Mister and spot him walking away from the group. I guess there is no need for him to be joining this tour.

"Maybe we can get a refund. We're going to need the money to stay the night somewhere near here so we can do this tour again tomorrow. It's way too far to drive back and forth."

She heads off without waiting for a response, leaving me standing there with the rest of the tour group. I examine my own ticket, which clearly states in bold red: "NON-REFUNDABLE." I get the feeling we'll be doing this tour with Melvin.

CHAPTER 26

"It's getting dark, and you need a stupid guide to get in there. What were we thinking? Coming out here with no money..." Kay looks like I feel, beaten.

All the patrons have gone, even employees. We're almost alone in the park as we wander around with no place to go. And I think we're both mad at me for losing our money. Now we'll have to stay here overnight to meet David tomorrow. We don't have enough money to pay for a hotel room *and* for another guided tour *and* for more gas to get back to the desert to meet the shuttle.

Let's hope David even comes to work tomorrow. An emergency could mean anything. Tomorrow, we need to buy tickets again to join yet another guided tour through the caves, led by the real David. I will stick him with the syringe as discreetly as someone can stab someone, and we make a run for it. I try not to think about Mister, the driver-hitman.

I'm also a tiny bit concerned that I might've promised Brad I would have his car back at the stroke of midnight, and that if I didn't, I might've given him permission to report it stolen. It's already twilight; the sky is darkening by the second. If we drive really fast, we might make it in four hours. We could be back around midnight, as promised. I'm sure Brad won't do anything right away. Especially given the circumstances of how I got him to lend me his car in the first place.

"Let's just find out where David lives—scope it out," I suggest. "If we find David now, we don't have to stay overnight. We can still go back tonight."

Kay bats a hand in response. "I told you, his mom wouldn't give up his home address. And when I tried your trick of calling the operator for information, they came back empty. He's not even listed. There is no David Williams in this town, according to the operator."

"Try calling his old mom again—persuade her. You're good at that, Kay."

"You mean, harass his mom? She'll think we're stalkers and warn David not to come to work. That's the last thing we need." Kay makes a good point.

"Ladies, ladies, you need to clear the area now. The caves are closed now—time to go home now." An older man appears. He's wearing a faded green uniform, presumably the security guard, although he doesn't look like he could secure a hat on a hook, with his thin, feeble, shaky hands and squinty eyes behind thick glasses. He looks to be in his seventies or eighties, and I don't like his use of the word "now" or his accent when he says it.

"Yes sir, just waiting for our ride," Kay replies with a quick lie.

We have no ride. We're walking to wherever we go, somewhere, anywhere. I had suggested that we sleep in the car, but after I told Kay about the possibility of Brad reporting it stolen... Getting caught and then arrested for car theft goes against the discreet behaviour we're supposed to be maintaining. We'll have to sleep someplace out in this park.

Kay's response satisfies the old man. He nods and saunters away, clearly not concerned about two lone ladies waiting for a ride. What else would we do? Head back to the creepy caves? Although it did seem like a good place to sleep, and that's kind of what we are hoping for.

"Let's do this," Kay whispers.

We climb over the fence and feel our way along the wall, Kay first, me behind her, holding her shirt, so we don't lose each other. It's almost completely dark, but we can still see the outlines of the caves, the edges of the stones. They appear different in this low light, more jagged somehow. It's amazing how the scenery changes when day turns to dusk, twilight, and finally into the night.

Sneaking around with Kay brings me right back to being fourteen and boy crazy. "Kay, remember that time we snuck into that party with those older guys?" I whisper-ask as I nervously follow my best friend while she ploughs ahead, much like that night. We were a group of four or five girls, who all lied to our parents about our whereabouts.

"Oh yes, I remember perfectly," she says, louder than she should when one is sneaking around forbidden caves in the dark.

"I still can't believe we got away with that," I say, a smile on my lips.

That night, Kay and I both said we were sleeping over at each other's homes. For Kay, it was easier. Her parents worked so much they barely noticed her absence on a good day. But had it not been for Charlie reluctantly sneaking us back into the home, we would've gotten caught and grounded for life, like the rest of our group did. Poor Charlie was not keen on his little sister being out with boys his age but knew Dad would've killed me. Charlie always looked out for me. I wish I could talk to him now.

"That was the night that Vanessa lost her virginity," Kay says and we both laugh. "A little lamb she was no longer."

I'd forgotten all about that. That party was full of booze, horny guys, and stupid boy-crazy girls. Vanessa was an older girl we met at the casinos. We were tagging along with her friends. She talked about that night for months after that.

"What ever happened to her? Vanessa?" I ask.

Kay doesn't answer right away. We reach a little cove, and we nod in agreement that we're far enough inside the caves.

"I heard she lost her soul," she says, and even though she said it quietly like anyone does when speaking of the dead, her voice seems louder now than it did just a few seconds ago.

Even breathing seems louder in here; I hear nothing except hers and mine. We sit back to back, leaning against each other for support. It reminds me of sitting back to back with my brother, Charlie, at Dad's funeral. I don't ever want to sit at a funeral like that again. We remain still a little while, to respect Vanessa's memory.

"At least we're out of the wilderness. Who knows what kind of animals hang around here," I say, changing the subject.

"Well, Grace," Kay puts on a whiny, pinched-nose voice, imitating Melvin. "There are several important species in this park, some even dangerous, such as the Utah Mountain Kingsnake or Yellow-Bellied What-Cha-Ma-Call-It. Those are poisonous and should be avoided if encountered..."

I laugh at her impersonation. I'm relieved she isn't letting Metagenesis dominate our conversation, after bringing up Vanessa.

When we first met Melvin, Kay teased that I've moved on up in the lives I've lived to have gone from him to Marc, or that I had changed Marc for the better. Even after Melvin introduced himself, the jokes continued. Melvin was so boring that making fun of him was all we could do to keep awake during the tour. We even got shushed by others in the crowd, who were trying to enjoy his long-winded explanations. We disturbed them so much so that at one point, Melvin pulled us aside and reprimanded us for talking over him, threatening to kick us out. We behaved from then on. Marginally.

I was relieved to not have to make the decision to put the tracker in David, and we poked fun at Melvin all throughout the tour. And now the fun-poking continues... and I miss Marc, at the idea of having been in his past lives and him in mine. It's a strange feeling to know that you've known someone through so many lives.

"Grace, I'm so hot for you, you're the woman of my dreams, my soulmate." Kay snorts—poor Melvin. We laugh together, taking turns with the jokes.

"Hey, Grace?"

"Ya."

"How'd you get Brad's car?" she finally asks.

Although I've told her about the whole deal to report it stolen at midnight, I haven't told her about how I got Brad to agree to lend us his car in the first place. I didn't want to tell her, because I figured she wouldn't approve. But her mood seems so light, and we're laughing like the girlfriends we've been forever, so I confess.

"I offered him a blow job."

"*What?*" Kay turns right around. I almost fall backward and have to brace myself against hitting the cool cave ground, scraping my hand, then elbow. "You gave that nasty guy a blow job!"

"*No!* Of course not! I just offered him one. And when he agreed and got ready—and when I say ready, I mean exactly what you're thinking—" Kay makes exaggerated gagging noises, "—I pulled out a cheap camera I picked up at one of those pawn shops for like five bucks and snapped a photo."

Kay relaxes a bit, but she's waiting for me to continue. "Annnnd? What'd you do?"

"Well, it turns out that Brad really doesn't want his fiancée to find out about the picture I took of him, stiff as a carrot. And while the camera was in my pocket, it was recording his voice, begging. I only kissed him, I swear! And not even with my tongue!"

Kay laughs and laughs. We both laugh. From Melvin to Brad.

"Oh my gosh, Grace! I didn't think you had it in you!" Kay exclaims.

"But you thought I had it in me to actually go through with a blow job?" I jokingly accuse.

We're laughing so hard I'm literally snorting like a pig.

"That guy has a fiancée? Is she a blow-up doll? Who would ever—?"

Snort snort snort.

Suddenly, I feel her back stiffen against mine. She stops laughing instantly and grabs my hand, taking me by surprise.

"What?" I ask, and she shushes me, squeezing my hand harder.

It's completely dark now. I can't see a thing. Just like Melvin promised, the night skies are the darkest we will ever experience in the solitude only a desert can bring.

But I see it, what has stopped Kay's laughter. A beam of light from a flashlight. It must be that old guard doing a round. Our breathing seems loud. I try to quiet mine by releasing my breath in slow, controlled patterns. The beam flashes a few times, in and out of the cave, and we don't move. Just like when Dad almost caught us sneaking back into the house on the night of the big party, before Charlie intercepted him.

We wait it out. The guard will be gone soon when he realizes the cave is empty. For a solid five minutes, we sit in complete silence. I'm afraid to even move my hand to tuck a loose curl behind my ears, which is tickling my cheek. It's the only thing I can think about. Every movement in this cave is amplified.

And then, to my horror, I hear, rather than feel, the buzzing of my pager.

CHAPTER 27

Slow footsteps turn into fast-shuffling feet coming toward the sound of the pager. Stupid pager! I didn't think that old guard could move that fast, and I wonder if it's a different one who might actually catch us and throw us out of here.

The running feet are heading toward us.

"Shit!" I whisper and jump up, grabbing Kay by the arm. We've got to get out of here, fast. "If we get split up," I tell her, "meet back at the car."

I see the beams of light on the cave walls, illuminating the space for a few seconds only, but enough to see Kay nod in agreement. Her eyes are wide.

I spin and lead us deeper into the caves, feeling the way with my hands as I tiptoe-run. It's useless, though—every sound in here seems to be broadcasted on a megaphone announcing our whereabouts.

I turn to tell Kay that we've got to run, but she's gone! What the hell? Did she misunderstand me? Does she think I actually told her to split up and meet back at the car?

I don't have time to look for her. I've got to get out of here. But I don't have anywhere to go other than deeper into the caves. I run blindly into the darkness, not knowing if there is a way out of here. I fear I could collide with a wall. And whichever guard is behind me, he's closing the gap that separates us, fast. His flashlight brightens the caves around me, which should be showing me a path and way out, but to my dismay, there is no ground ahead of me. There's a body of water and no way around it. I have nowhere to run.

I glance over my shoulder. He is coming at me. Now I'm sure it's not the security guard we thought was doing his rounds; he's too quick and nimble. It's a man with a gun. I can't see his face, but I immediately assume it's Mister, and I don't understand why he's after us. I look down again, stare into the dark pool of water, not knowing how deep or how far, remembering Melvin's stories, but what am I to do?

Oh, shit. I draw in a long breath to hold, and I dive in.

Bullets pelt past me, and I swim deeper, afraid to look back or up; afraid to stay near the surface and get shot, and equally afraid to continue swimming deeper into what could be a bottomless cave. I hear a splash and know that someone has jumped in after me. It's strange, but I think I still hear gunshots, which makes no sense if the shooter is in the water. Can you even shoot a gun underwater? Unless it's at Kay.

I chance a quick look behind, hoping to see my best friend at my back, but she's not. It's a man, flashlight in hand, his hair floating around him and then not as he pushes the water behind, closing the gap between us with each stride to catch me.

I stop looking back. There's no time for that. I just need to swim harder, faster, deeper.

It's getting darker down here, which is a good sign that I'm swimming fast enough to get away from his flashlight, but the bad part about that is not being able to see where I'm going. I don't know if there is another side to this water hole, or if this is one of the spots that Melvin spoke about where one can dive for an eternity and never emerge. I pray for a way out as my fears start to convince me that I am swimming to a dead end. What then? I've come this far, and that's it? Is this where my story ends?

Absolute death is what runs through my brain as my lungs scream for air and I don't see, feel or imagine a way out.

I'm at such a depth and distance now that even if I turned

back, I don't know that I could hold my stale air without gasping for breath before reaching the surface.

I'm at the point of no return.

So I swim harder.

And faster.

If I'm going to swim toward a dead end, I'm going to do it with everything I have left, just in case I'm wrong. I wonder if in my next life I will have a fear of drowning. Or fear of water, or of dark spaces and caves. I wonder if this is the new scar I will leave on my soul. Am I going to make it? Please, let me make it, I beg inside my pounding head.

Air escapes through my nostrils, bubbles rising, at first involuntarily, but then I deliberately let out more. I feel like if I just give a few more bubbles away, maybe it will relieve the pressure in my tightening chest. I was wrong. Deflating my lungs even that little bit is making them crave air, fresh, stale, any kind of air. The fit within me to suck in is dizzying.

I'd love to turn around and swim back, but it doesn't matter—I can't turn around anymore, I'm too far. My only hope is making it to the... *Swim, Grace!* Other... *swimmmm...* side. *Just a few more kicks...* I can do this, I can do this, I can do thissss!

I kick hard, with my whole body. I'm swimming in complete darkness, so either the man is gone, or his flashlight is off. Either way, I'm dead, or we both are, so it won't matter what happens from here on in.

I change direction and swim upward, hoping to reach the surface and not bang my head on the ceiling of the cave while still underwater. I don't even try to protect my head from hitting anything. I think I'd rather die of a broken neck than drowning, which right now is a real possibility. I'm this close to sucking water into my lungs. The urge is overwhelming. The pocket of air left inside me might actually be weighing me down, sinking me, and in a final effort, I push the rest of it out, pushing with my arms, my legs like egg-beaters on high.

And then I break through the surface, and I don't hit my head, but the air on my face hits me like a vortex. It's cold and warm at the same time, I'm drinking it up, gasping as I inhale sweet oxygen into my aching lungs, coughing, gulping in the air until I'm drunk on it, and choke on it.

I go under again, involuntarily, but bob right back up to continue overdosing on air. I float on my back for a moment, eyes shut. Actually, wait a second... my eyes are open, wide open, but I'm in complete and utter darkness. There are no lights in this section, and the few seconds of relief at indulging in new air to breathe is quickly replaced by panic when I realize I'm probably cornered, in a dead end. The thought of possibly having to go back where I came from makes me cry with frustration. I can't see anything around me and fear I'm treading water with nowhere to go, expending what's left of my energy.

Maybe there's a ledge. I wave my arms around, feeling for one or for something to grab onto, but there's nothing. I widen my eyes, squeeze them shut, open them again, trying to adjust to the darkness, but it's no use. I can't see a thing; the dark is too thick.

I need to calm down, so I try to focus on listening to the sounds around me. Am I alone? Yes, I think I'm alone. I can't hear anything or anyone else, not even an echo, which strikes me as odd if I'm in a cave. But the lack of echo could be a good thing. That can mean I'm not closed in—maybe there's no roof, an opening over my head. Or even better, there may be an exit; a way for me to get out of here. I need to find my way back to the car and Kay. I'm not sure how I feel that we were separated. It happened so quickly, I have to wonder if she left me on purpose.

I ignore my doubts about Kay and instead focus on getting out of here. I try to calm myself by floating on my back with my ears underwater, listening to my internal breathing, thinking. I come out from under the water, will myself to calmly swim in one direction, as leisurely as possible, so as not to waste what's left of my strength in case I have to keep going. My legs are already burning from my rigorous swim to get to wherever I am.

When I finally reach a ledge and drag my limp body out, I say a silent thank you that the lack of echo led me to believe that there was no roof over my head and a way out. Not that this cave would go on for so long that I would have to swim forever to get to the other side, which is the real reason there is no echo.

If I had understood the sheer size of this cave, I might not have had the willpower to continue. If I'd known my destination was twenty minutes away and not mere seconds, I don't think I would've pushed as I pushed. OK, maybe it wasn't twenty minutes, but it sure felt like swimming the length of two of those old-fashioned, Olympic-sized pools they used to use in competition when the world was divided into countries.

Now I just lie on the ground, soaked and exhausted, my eyes barely open, slowing my breathing and allowing my rubbery muscles to recover. I replay the image of the man swimming toward me. His hair swooshing around him. It was dark, so I could only make out his shape and not his skin colour or anything like that, but I'm quite sure Mister's kinky hair wouldn't flow around even if it was long enough. And he needs me to identify the donor, so why would he be after me? I think about what that might suggest, but I don't come up with any ideas. My brain is too tired.

But I need to find my way back to the car, and at least now I see a light at the end of the tunnel—literally. The cave does have an exit; the stars and moonshine create shadows at the hole leading to the outside. Two minutes. That is the recovery time I will allow myself. I count back slowly in my head from one hundred.

Eighty-four, eighty-three, eighty-two... ah, screw it! I force my eyes open, stand up and fake it. When I reach the exit, I peer out slowly, my heart racing. I'm paranoid, and why wouldn't I be? I've just been shot at, chased to the brink of drowning.

I cautiously make my way out of the death-trap cave, but not before removing my wet jean shorts and sopping wet shoes. The shorts were chafing my inner thighs and making rubbing noises when I walked, and the shoes were making swishing sounds, doing me no favours if I want to remain unseen. I carry them and feel weird about tiptoeing around half naked in the desert. But my panties and tank top are quiet, allowing me to dart around the bushes and behind cacti without disturbing anything. I try not to think of the snakes or other animals lurking in the dark, especially since I'm barefoot. I just head back in the direction I think I came from.

When I arrive at the car, my stomach sinks to the soles of my feet. The car is wide open, but Kay is nowhere to be seen. She must've gotten here before me, but something chased her away. Or someone.

"Kay," I speak out, against my better judgment.

I hear a rustling behind me. Shit! Someone is here.

CHAPTER 28

"It's me! It's me!"
I hear Kay before I see her, her voice coming from the same direction as the rustling in the bushes behind me.

"Shit! I thought you might've been that guy!" I let out a sigh of relief.

"Ya, and once again, when you think there is an intruder, you call out instead of running? You're a slow learner, Grace," Kay says angrily. I notice she is panting like a marathon runner.

"You're the one who snuck up on me—why are you hiding in the bushes?" I accuse.

"I heard you coming, but didn't know it was you, so I just hid. Luckily for me, you called my name out," she spits back.

She coughs, and I notice she's struggling to talk. I notice she's trying to catch her breath, likely around the same time she notices I'm in underwear and soaking wet.

"What happened to you? Why are you naked, wet and shivering?" Kay asks with envy in her voice.

She is dripping with sweat and, in the dim light from the open car door, I can see her flushed, red face. Her hair, which earlier was in a tidy bun, is mostly undone, loose baby hairs completely frizzed out. I smooth my hair as I look at hers, assuming it's a big knotted ball resembling a crazed lion mane compared to hers, which is usually naturally straight.

I don't reply to her question. My voice is stuck in my throat. I am trying to process what just happened. Kay and I just stare at each other. But even she can't ignore gunshots. I take a seat on the passenger side. Kay circles the car and joins me on the driver side.

"Was that popping sound what I think it was?" she asks after a few minutes of silence, probably realizing I'm not offering explanations without prodding.

I nod my head in response. She shakes hers with bewilderment.

"Why?" she asks.

I shrug my shoulders. I have no idea why. I have a good idea of who, however. Mister. Why would Mister want to kill us? Maybe he is working with the old woman and not with Dr. Messie? I don't share my thoughts with Kay. I haven't told her about seeing Mister earlier, and if I confess now, she will be furious and want to know why I kept that from her. I kept it from her because I kept from her the old woman and everything that the old woman told me, too.

I touch my pocket to check that I didn't lose the syringe. Nope. It's still here. But the pager is gone, again. Damnit.

"We've got to get out of here," Kay says as she reaches into the glove compartment for the naked lady keychain.

"No!" I grab her arm and slam my hand on the glove compartment to keep her from opening it. "We came all this way. I need to know if that is David Williams, and I'm not going anywhere until I stick this tracker in him!"

"Tracker?" Kay asks.

"Syringe, whatever..." I correct myself.

"Someone is trying to kill us, Grace!"

I'm glad she doesn't interrogate me about the "tracker" slip-up. She backs off the glove compartment and slouches into the driver's seat, rests her head back on the headrest. I do the same in my seat. I feel defeated, but I know I am not going anywhere until I meet David tomorrow.

"All right." Kay gives in. "But we're not sleeping in the caves. We're not sleeping in the park. We're driving to a truck stop with lots of lights and people and activity, and we're sleeping in the car. In shifts."

I reach into the glove compartment and hand Kay the keys.

"I have to tell you something, but not until we get the hell out of here," she says, then takes the keys from me and we drive off to find our sleeping place.

After gaining some distance from Great Basin National Park, Kay relaxes and takes a deep breath before dropping a bomb.

"I saw that guy from the diner—he pointed a gun at my face." She starts to sob.

"What?" I reply, in shock. Mister?

"When you took off running, I went in the other direction toward the main office building, hoping to find the security guard and call for help. I couldn't get in. The building was locked up, and there was no one there either, so I just hid, not knowing what else to do." Tears stream freely, and every so often she blinks hard when trucks whip past us from the other direction, their lights too bright.

"Anyway, I heard the gunshots, and I thought..." Kay pauses to sob. "I thought maybe you were..."

She bites her lip and doesn't complete her sentence, but she doesn't have to, and I feel guilty about the doubts I was having right around the same time she feared me dead. More trucks pass us at high speed; our car wobbles as they whoosh by.

"So, I broke into the office and hid under the counter, but it wasn't long after that that he came in and flicked on the light like he wasn't afraid of being seen. He just rampaged through the room, looking through papers and throwing things to the ground, and then he found me. He just put the gun up to my face and stared at me—I didn't know what to do or say. I kind of just closed my eyes and waited for what was coming for what seemed like an eternity. When I opened my eyes again, he was gone." Kay is so caught up in retelling the horror she just experienced that I don't think she notices she's slowed the car down to a crawling pace.

I point at the dash to remind her to give the car some gas, and she obeys.

"I'm sorry I dragged you into this" is all I can manage to say.

I feel guilty that I don't set her mind at ease by telling her Mister is here to kill David and not us. That's probably why he was looking for us at the diner, just to put a tail on us. Although I'm not clear on what is happening, that much I'm sure of.

"Oh, Grace, you didn't drag me into this. I was ready to come with you. You know that," she says.

And it makes me wonder again why she agreed to come with me so quickly, but as usual, it's a bad time to ask.

When we reach the truck stop, I go right to the phone booth to check the message that almost got us killed. I no longer have the pager. It's lost for good after I dived into the water with it. But at least I know the number by heart.

"Grace. It's me, Marc." Finally.

"You didn't return my message..." Marc's voice is quiet and unsure. I picture him shuffling his feet, hands in pockets, his hazel eyes darting around. "I, I... I hope I didn't scare you off. I mean, with my last message. You know, I was just feeling..." He takes a deep breath in. "...With everything that's been going on and all... I didn't really mean to..." He pauses for a few long seconds. He's going to recant his last message. I close my eyes, waiting for the blow. I'm thankful I didn't return his message and say something stupid in response, like admit my own feelings. "What am I saying?" he asks, but not to me. It sounds like the receiver is a mile away from his face when he says it like I'm not meant to hear him second-guessing himself.

"I was calling you to take back my last message," he states, with renewed confidence in his tone. "That was my plan." Pause, deep breath. "But I'm not taking it back. I'm not. Grace, I. Love. You," he states firmly, enunciating my name and his declaration. "Please return my message. Please," still sounding firm. Then another pause. "Please?" Not so firm.

A sad smile creeps up onto my face.

There are no more messages from him. He's putting himself out there, waiting for me to say something. This is not at all what I expected. I expected him to take back his message professing his love for me. I thought he would tell me exactly what he started to say in this message now; that he got caught up in all the commotion and confused his feelings. That's how I think I feel. I feel as though the fight to save Jordan has made me feel somehow closer to Marc, as if holding on to him may preserve the best thing between us: our son. I suppose the fact that we've been told we're soulmates has made me wonder if I'm confused now in this life, or if I have been confused in every life prior.

He can't feel this way for me. It's not right. He needs to forget it. We're not going to be together when I get back—*if* I get back. David has to die, and Marc might die. He can't have these feelings for me. And I can't have these feelings for him, or I may never go through with what I unknowingly came here to do.

I decide to leave him a message. What I want to say in my message is that I think I love him too. I want to tell him that it's probably because of what we're going through, losing our child, and nothing more. I also want to tell him that I miss him. But I should definitely demand that he leave me alone so I can do what I need to do without hearing his voice in my head, disguised as my guilty subconscious. That's what I want to say in my message.

Instead, I say, "Marc, please leave me alone." I press the pound key to send the message right away before I change my mind.

"*Message sent.*"

I linger and listen to the mechanical voice, thinking about torturing myself by replaying the saved message of Marc telling me he loves me earlier.

"*You have one new message.*"

That's strange. I just checked all my messages. Without prompting, the newest message plays.

"No way, Grace. I'm not falling for that again."

I look at the receiver in my hand with confusion. Did he already get my message? Was he on the other end receiving it as I left it? I put the phone back to my ear to hear more.

"I'm not leaving you alone this time." He sounds very confident, empowered. "Before, when I pushed, you resisted, so I pushed more, and you went cold. Then I backed off. And look where that got us! So I'm not backing off this time! I won't leave you alone! I love you—we're soulmates! It says so right in the research! Every life we find each other!" His voice is going up an octave with each point he makes. "And even if it didn't say so in that research, it says so on our hearts! I know it, and you know it! So stop fighting me. Stop resisting. I know you feel the same—I know you love me too, Grace!"

"*End of message.*"

I look at the receiver, think about leaving another message. Will he get it right away? Is he waiting for me to respond?

I leave another message.

"I don't, Marc. I don't feel the same," I lie in a monotone, trying to remain calm to counter his high-energy message. "I only want updates on Jordan. Don't leave me messages unless it's about him."

It actually hurts to say those words. I reluctantly press the pound key to send the message. I wait to hear if there is another new message if he will reply right away. I hold my breath, half-hoping he doesn't.

"I don't believe you." He doesn't believe me. Well, what I can't believe is that he isn't backing away. Marc isn't a pushy guy. "I think you're scared," he says, his voice back to a normal level.

It surprises me to hear him say these things. *Me?* Scared? Guilty, maybe. But not scared. I shake my head.

"I think you're scared about actually losing me, or that I'm going to leave you, just like your dad did." His mentioning my dad feels like a dirty kick in the face. "Well, I'm not going anywhere, Grace," Marc proclaims with calm confidence I don't usually hear from him.

"*End of message.*"

"You know what, Marc?" I try to sound like I don't care, even though he's touched a sore spot bringing up my dad. He should know better. "If you're so 'in love' with me..." I say 'in love' like I'm scorning the whole concept of it, "...then who did those red high heels belong to? I saw them at your place that day I came with Mister to pick you up," I accuse him, thinking back to that day. I press the pound button with distaste to send the message right away. I'll bet he doesn't even know that I noticed the presence of another woman in his home.

"Are you serious right now?" His voice is back up to the volume of frustration. "The only reason you're bringing that up is to make yourself angry at me, detach yourself, so you don't have to feel bad," he accuses, and he's partially right—but it's because of the whole killing him thing, not my fears of abandonment. "*Yes,* I had someone over. Have you forgotten that you left me? You *left me,* Grace! You sent divorce papers to my home. You hadn't spoken to me in months, other than to scream at me for no real reason! You kicked me out one day while Jordan was at school, with no explanation! You wouldn't even let me take the dog! Lucy was my birthday gift! She was my dog! And it wasn't only a few months of being alone, wondering what I ever did to lose your love. Grace, you left me way before you actually put me out! You retracted your feelings toward the world the day you buried your dad. You built an impenetrable wall around you to protect yourself from feeling anything, including feelings for me. Everything just shut off! You're getting mad at me now because that's what you do best when I try to get close to you. When I try to tell you I love you! When I look at you, try to hug you, kiss you..." His voice catches. "Fuck you, Grace!" He hangs up.

His anger surprises me. He has never spoken to me like that before. And he's never brought up my dad, or how he felt about the whole situation. I guess I might've closed myself in a bit after Dad died. OK, maybe I know I did—a lot.

I don't return Marc's message right away. I don't really have a defence. I don't know what to say. I should say that I'm sorry. I want to tell him that finding my dad half alive, hanging from a rope, and hearing my name escape his blue lips with his last breath—I want to tell him that was... it was the worst damn day of my life. I want him to know that I never want to hurt like that again, and I don't want to feel what it would be like to lose anyone else.

But I don't say those things.

I place the receiver back carefully and hang out at the phone booth a while. I think about what Marc said. Is he right?

I call to leave one more message. When I do, there is another message waiting for me. I punish myself and listen to Marc continue his venting. But his tone is back to normal again.

"Why did you leave me, Grace?" He doesn't hang up. He remains silent on the other end, except for his shaky breath.

I listen to the rest of the message, waiting to see if he says anything more. He doesn't. I listen to the rhythm of his breathing, which seems to calm down throughout the remainder of the message. I remember what it was like to be in his arms, resting on his chest, feeling it rise and fall with the motion of his breathing. It felt so good to be in his embrace. I love him. Listening to him being silent on the other end feels like I'm right there, with him. I close my eyes, and I can see him in front of me. I can almost reach out and touch him.

Tap tap tap. I jump at the sound and open my eyes. Kay is knocking on the side of the phone booth. She leaps back, startled at me fumbling the phone, placing it back in the cradle. I change my mind about leaving Marc another message. I have nothing to say. No reasoning or explanation to offer him. Maybe I never explained anything to him about why I deserted him in the first place because I myself don't know exactly why.

"Everything all right?" Kay asks, cautiously.

I nod yes and lead the way back to the car.

"We need to try and catch some sleep," I say as Kay follows me. I feel tears burning the back of my eyeballs, and I try to swallow the hard lump growing in my throat. But when I make it to the car, my will to hold everything back betrays me. I viciously wipe away hot tears.

Kay joins me in the car, puts her seat back to the upright position. "Do you want to talk about it? Is it Jordan?" she asks.

I shake my head no. "It's Marc," I confess. "Marc telling me he loves me." I sob. "Marc asking me why I left him."

Kay hands me napkins she stole from our diner. I use them to blow my nose. They're not the right absorbency or fabric for that purpose. Kay digs in her bag for more. Why didn't I think of reaching for those napkins when Kay was bawling over having a gun in her face? Because I'm selfish. I'm a bad friend and a bad wife.

"Why *did* you leave him, Grace?" Kay asks.

That's the million-dollar question.

"I don't really know," I say, defeated, shaking my head and shrugging my shoulders. "I guess I was just trying to protect myself?" I frame my response as a question.

"Do you still love him?" she asks, but I can't even say it out loud.

How can I say that I love him and at the same time be responsible for his upcoming death? I don't answer Kay's question, and she doesn't push me. She comforts me until I'm done having a good cry over Marc. I have never cried over Marc before. Not when I left him; not when he kept pleading with me to let him come home, to explain, to tell him what he did wrong, to ask me what he could do to win me back. I have never mourned him. I was too heartbroken over my dad and keeping myself busy, trying to be perfect after he died. How am I going to go through with my mission of finding David, now that I can finally admit to myself that I'm still in love with Marc?

CHAPTER 29

"No one is going to shoot at us in broad daylight," I reason as we get out of the car.

The whole drive back here, Kay has been like a nervous Chihuahua on its way to face a pitbull at a ballroom dance. That was her comparison, not mine. I'm nervous too, but one of us needs to appear confident—I guess it's my turn. I stretch my sore body from our achy sleep in the small car as a way of stalling while I build my fake courage.

We parked far enough away to avoid hitting all the parked cars, but close enough not to look suspicious. Even though I'm trying to convince Kay that we are safe in a crowded place, I look around anyway, search for Mister in dark sunglasses. Today the sun is out in full force, not a cloud in sight, and everyone is wearing sunglasses. But Mister has a very distinct look to him, and I would recognize him even if everyone was dressed identically.

The scene today is very different from yesterday. It's not just the clouds swapped out for the hellish blazing sun. What really stand out are all the police vehicles. At least five, I count, plus a few more black sedans which, to my guess, are unmarked law enforcement.

"Oh no!" Kay exclaims and starts to get back into the car.

"Brad must've reported the car stolen."

"I don't think that's what's happening here," I say to her.

I don't get back in the car. I walk away from it, in slow motion, without closing the door behind me. There is yellow tape all over the place, as well as equipment belonging to the police and likely the reporters who have emerged from news vans parked nearby.

I approach the crowd of employees and tourists gathered on this side of the yellow tape. People are talking to each other in hushed voices, suggesting gossip. I join the group and try to listen.

"What's going on?" I ask a gentleman wearing a brown Ranger uniform. He must be a park employee. They all dress the same.

"Someone got killed here last night," he responds in a low voice without looking at me. "They found a pager at the scene. Should be an open and shut case. No one carries a pager anymore," he scoffs.

I back off quickly, stepping on Kay's toes behind me.

"Ouch!" she yelps.

"Hey, you all right?" the gentleman asks Kay as he turns around. He unfolds his arms and reaches to steady her from being knocked down, exposing his name tag: *David Williams— Tour Guide.*

CHAPTER 30

Kay must notice the name tag at the same moment I do. She disguises her excitement by feigning excruciating toe pain.

"I can't feel my toes!" she exclaims, but she's looking right at David, bewildered. "You know what I mean? Like when you run into someone, and you should *feel* something? Grace? Do you know what I mean?"

I guess she doesn't realize that I too saw his name tag. David, the tour guide, is a handsome man with mysterious deep-set eyes and a jawline so ridged a hammer couldn't break it. I can't take my eyes off him. Do I feel anything? I squirm for my syringe, but then stop and look around for Mister. I don't see him. If I stab David with the syringe, who will ensure he dies at the right moment? And I need to be sure—do I feel sure?

I look at David, staring into his eyes.

There is no spark.

"*Grace?*" Kay says my name loudly.

David giggles and the sound of his laugh doesn't faze me—should it? He must think we're both nuts; Kay with her yelling and me staring into his eyes, trying to get a sense of his soul. I sense nothing.

The crowd starts to part, and I feel like the centre of attention for a moment. There is a finger pointing at us.

"There," says Melvin. "The pager belongs to those girls there."

My heart picks up its pace, beating hard against my chest. I look from David to Melvin, then to the police officer who is heading in our direction. I suppress the urge to run.

"Oh my! There it is! We came back here to report it missing from yesterday!" Kay to the rescue.

"I'm Officer Drexel. May we have a few words?" asks a plainclothes officer who holds the yellow tape over his head as a way of inviting us to the other side.

Kay and I duck underneath it.

"Do you recognize this man?" The officer shows us a picture of Mister, his eyes unnaturally closed, his mouth forming a thin, awkward line. It is just a headshot, but I can see the gray collar of his tacky tee-shirt. His skin is a dull brown—not the lustrous brown of his Caribbean heritage, but pale like it's been lightly dusted in chalk.

"No," Kay responds with honest big blue eyes.

I shake my head no as well: a lie. Confusion comes over me. How is he dead? Wasn't he the shooter?

"What was your pager doing here?" the officer asks.

"We drove up from Vegas yesterday for a tour of the caves, led by Melvin there." Kay nods in his direction. Her tone is sombre, respectful of the dead man.

I can't speak. I suddenly feel like I've swallowed gravel, my mouth is so dry.

"Can we have our pager back?" Kay asks.

"What time did you leave the caves last night?"

I guess we're not quite off the hook, but Officer Drexel doesn't look overly suspicious. And why would he be? Why would anyone be suspicious? We were running from gunfire ourselves. We were not the cause of it.

"I don't know," Kay says, and I think about the old security guard. I wonder if he would recognize us with his thick, bottle-like glasses. "We stuck around to look for the pager, but gave up when the sun went down. So I guess we left whenever the sun went down, whatever time that was."

Officer Drexel looks from me to Kay and back to me,

holding my gaze longer than Kay's. I try to smile, look innocent, *which I am.*

He hands the pager to Kay. I try not to release the sigh of relief I was holding.

"We're interviewing anyone who was here last night. Officer Gordon will take your information and contact you at a later time to come make a statement if necessary."

Officer Drexel leads us back under the yellow tape and a uniformed officer, I assume Gordon, takes our contact info. Kay hands me the pager and then rhymes off her real home address, eighty years from now. I love how quickly she always thinks.

I glance at the pager: three new messages.

"Where is that?" asks Officer Gordon.

"Up north," Kay replies smoothly. She's not lying, we do live up north in Toronto. Just not in this decade.

We head back through the crowd, Kay looking for David, but I'm not. He's not the donor. Right this very second, my mind is made up about him. I feel absolutely nothing. I'm inexplicably confident that he's just a Ranger with a model's face. And no, it's not because I'm shocked over Mister's death, or that I'm afraid of stabbing this David and killing Marc, Marc whom I love. I just know. This is not Marc's past life.

I lead the way back to the car. Kay catches the hint and follows.

"Are you sure?" she asks from behind me.

"Yes," I reply. "I don't know why I'm sure, but I'm sure." I can't hide the disappointment in my voice, but it's more than disappointment. It's confusion. Mister is dead. Why? What does that mean for me? For Jordan? What does all of this mean?

"I noticed there were some messages. Do you want me to wait in the car while you check them?"

"No, I'll check them at a pit stop along the way." As much as I want to hear the messages immediately, I want to get as far away from the murder of Mister as I can before I do.

When we're safely on our way, I ask Kay if she's OK. She hesitates before answering.

"That dead guy was the one who was following me, before.

Remember when I told you I was being followed?" she says.

"The guy who pointed the gun in your face," I state what I think is obvious.

"No, not the kid," she responds, her eyes focused on the road so she can't see my face scrunch with confusion.

"Do you think that dead guy is who Camilla was talking about? The guy who came in looking for you in the diner?" That's exactly what I am thinking. The hitman was following us. But who was following him? "Who pointed the gun at your face, Kay?" I ask. I'm completely confused.

"The speed runner we chased down Las Vegas Boulevard. The one with the burn mark on his face—that's who pointed the gun at me last night. The young guy, remember?" she answers like I'm supposed to understand. "Who the hell did you think I was talking about?"

Uh, the hitman, I want to reply. But obviously, there is a disconnect. She doesn't know Mister was my driver, or that I saw him here yesterday.

"Ya, of course. Sorry."

We drop the subject, but we're both in deep thought. The young kid must've killed Mister. Why? What the hell is going on? Who's the kid with the burn mark on his face?

I look at Kay. "Kay, why did you come with me? You were really eager," I say, trying to keep the accusatory tone to a bare minimum, but it doesn't go unnoticed.

"Are you accusing me of something?" Kay asks, taking her eyes off the road and staring hard at me.

CHAPTER 31

We stop about halfway back to Las Vegas. Kay has been driving the speed limit the whole way, so as not to give the State Troopers reason to stop us—other than the stolen vehicle thing, of course. I splash cold water on my face in the small, dirty bathroom of a gas station that looks abandoned but is not. A weathered-looking old guy greeted me with an uninterested grin on my way to the restroom. We're the only patrons. We've learned that running the air conditioner to keep us cool drains the fuel, and so we've been driving with the windows open and the air conditioner on low. The faucet doesn't have hot water, even if that was what I wanted, but it isn't as icy as I'd like it to be. I look in the mirror and hardly recognize myself. Bags under my eyes; my hair frizzier and curlier than usual. I never thought I'd be as excited to get back to our motel as I am right now.

I pass Kay on the way to the phone booth. She is picking up some snacks and cold water, paying for gas.

"I'll meet you in the car," I tell her.

She ignores me. She's pissed off at my questioning her motives for being here. She ripped my head off, using one of her weird words to describe me: "Eusociality." I have no idea what that means, but based on the rest of her rant, I gather she thinks I'm selfish and I've lost my ability to see good in people. She came here to help me find a cure to save Jordan. She came here to honour her brother, Peter, and she said I should just accept that.

I take a deep breath before picking up the phone and dialling the pager number to hear those three messages. Here goes nothing...

"*First message.*"

"It's me, Marc."

The fact that he is introducing himself tells me this was not a message he left back to back right after last night's message, asking me why I left him. His voice is quiet, subdued, sad.

"Tell me something... You know the way we are—I mean, not now. The way we used to be. Was it real? I like to think it was. And if it was real, was it right? Were we right? The research, maybe it was wrong. But I really don't think so, and I wondered what you thought. I'm not asking because of Jordan. I'm asking because... because of us."

"*End of message.*"

My heart twitches as I try to imagine the feel of his hand holding mine. It had certainly felt real before I pulled it away out of fear. Afraid of... of what? He felt right, but maybe I still feared to lose him; being left by him. Dad loved me, too. He left.

I press the option to hear the next message.

"Grace! It's Marc." His voice is full of alarm, snapping me out of my daydream. "Look. You need to come back. Jordan is really bad. Dr. Messie is trying to convince me he has time, but honestly, I think it's just for the media. No one cares if Jordan dies without you. They're just hoping you want to be the start of this new cure bad enough to risk it. Come back. He doesn't have much time."

I hear a ruffling on the phone.

"Hey, Gracie." It's Charlie. I guess Marc handed him the phone. "If you haven't found the donor yet, I think you should come back. Jordan is really bad. When he's alert enough, he keeps asking for you. Marc's right. It's not looking good. Come home."

There is one more message, which I'm now afraid to listen to. But I force myself.

"It's Marc." He sniffles. "It's so awful, so awful." Is he crying? "That kid, Walt. No, no, no. Oh, Grace."

Now he is freely crying, and it hurts to hear.

"Just come home, OK?"

"*End of message.*"

CHAPTER 32

"Hi Leo," I respond to his friendly greeting as I take my usual seat next to him, putting a few twenties down in front of me for the dealer to change.

He is looking at me like he feels sorry for me. I must look like I've aged years since the last time we saw each other, two days ago, before my trip to the caves with Kay.

The rest of the drive back from the caves was silent between Kay and me (meaning, she continued to ignore me), but my head was far from silent. I was plagued by thoughts of Jordan, memories of my dad, guilt over Marc, confusion over Mister and the old woman, and wonder as to why I hadn't yet confided in Kay about any of these thoughts. Is it because I don't trust her, or is it because I don't trust me?

We got back pretty late and then had to deal with a distraught Brad, who insisted on watching me delete the video and picture of him in exchange for not calling the cops on us and kicking us out. I had a long shower and let the water beat those thoughts out of my head. I kept turning the faucet colder and colder, and once I had gotten accustomed to the level of coldness, I would turn it even more until finally, it was as frigid as it was going to get without shooting icicles. I stared down at my toes and watched as the flesh beneath my nails turned a purplish shade of blue. I wanted to numb all feelings from my heart and conscience, both heavy with burden.

"Did you hear back from the auditions?" Leo asks carefully, ignoring the cards in front of him.

"No, no answer yet. But I'm worried about what will happen when I get the call. What if it's not what I really want? What if I get the part, and then I find out it's the wrong part for me? I think that's what's frustrating me. Not knowing what to do if I don't get the part, but also not knowing what to do if I *do* get the part. Am I making sense?" Somehow, speaking in code to Leo helps. He is always empathetic and finds the best time to say something funny, and since he has no idea what I'm actually talking about...

"Happy birthday, Leo!"

My fake counsel from Leo ends abruptly when his buddy Joe shows up and slaps Leo on the back. Joe has one of those noise-makers in his mouth and wears a birthday party hat made for a child. He pulls out a pile of glittery hats and hands one out to everyone at the table. He saves a Spiderman hat for Leo, which he places on his head for him, snapping the elastic under Leo's chin, causing him to flinch.

"Thanks, Joe!" Leo exclaims without taking his eyes off me.

I smile at Leo. He is too nice a guy. It's his birthday, and he is so concerned about my mood he doesn't seem like he wants to partake in whatever Joe is doing unless he's sure I'm OK. And so I make sure he thinks I am. I put my birthday hat on and plant a toothy smile on my face, liberating Leo from feeling like he shouldn't be happy that it's his birthday.

"Leo! Why didn't you tell me it's your birthday? I'm going on about my usual complaints, and meanwhile, we should be celebrating!" I say as enthusiastically as I can. Leo deserves at least that from me.

"We?" Leo asks, hopeful. "All I want for my birthday is you, wearing only that hat," he says with a wink and playful grin.

"In your dreams," I reply and wink back.

"I dream about you every night. I'm ready for the real thing, Grace. I'm the birthday boy, after all," Leo jokes with a naughty tone.

I laugh. I know he's joking. I'm glad he's back to normal. I'm grateful he changes the direction of my thoughts.

"So, what are you doing to celebrate?" I start a normal conversation as Joe takes his seat and the rest of us get back to the card game.

"Today's my actual birthday, but I'm celebrating on the weekend—having some friends over at my place. Do you want to come?" he asks. He's serious about the invite, no longer joking about the date or taking me to bed.

"Sorry, Leo."

He looks let down, but not surprised. Poor Leo.

"Hey, how about your friend, Kay? What if you both come? Then it wouldn't be like a date, but just a night out for a couple of girlfriends." I open my mouth to reject, and he puts his hand up to my face to stop me. "Don't answer. Don't say no yet. The party's not for two days yet. Just think about it." He stops a passing waitress for a pen, reaches into his pocket and pulls out a crumpled-up receipt, scribbles something on the back and hands it to me. "It's my address and phone number. Don't give me an answer at all. If I see you there, I'll be the happiest birthday boy in Vegas. If not, I'll assume the worst; that you were tragically kidnapped by a UFO." I take the paper from him, fold it neatly and put it in my pocket, next to the syringe. "Bring your bathing suits and appetites."

"OK," I tell Leo. "I'll think about it," which I won't, of course. Under different circumstances, a younger, freer version of Kay and I would've jumped at a chance to meet new people and hang out in some cute guy's swimming pool with his friends. I remember that version of Kay and myself. We did things like that all the time; that night when we snuck out with Vanessa and her crew was the start of a beautiful party era.

"Hey, I gotta go. I'm meeting Kay for dinner. I'll tell her about your birthday get-together." I'm lying about telling Kay, but not lying about the fact that I need to meet her for dinner. I hope she's done ignoring me.

CHAPTER 33

I walk instead of taking a taxi to the diner. I need to conserve our money. Kay went back to the phone booth, picking up where I left off, calling Information to ask for David Williams. She had ten dollars in quarters to use. I took the rest to the casino. I managed to cash out with marginally more than the sixty I walked in with. Slow and steady. I just need to make enough to keep us fed. I still don't know what to make of the events of the past days, and I think I will have to come clean and tell Kay we may need to go home. Not only because of the whole murdering-Marc thing, but because of Jordan. I think I should go home. Although I want to be his hero, the reality is that I need to be his mom.

I turn the corner and spot Kay in front of our diner, beside the giant plastic milkshake advertisement. It's odd that she is waiting outside. Usually, if one of us get there before the other, we just go ahead and take a booth, chat with Camilla about more and more wedding plans. Besides, it's way too hot out here. Why would Kay be outside? And she's not just waiting out here; she's pacing, with her hands clenched.

As I approach, she sees me and folds her arms across her bust. Her face is flushed red and her eyes narrow as she glares at me with fuming anger. I have no idea what has come over her, but she looks angrier than I have ever seen her, *ever*.

Rather than waiting for me to get close, she makes her way toward me, stomping through the tourists on the sidewalk. Apparently, she is unable to put off whatever it is for even the few seconds it would take for me to reach her.

"How *dare* you!" she yells. I stop in my tracks, not sure what I'm being accused of. "How *dare* you!" she repeats. "How long were you going to keep this from me?"

Keep what from her? I run through a quick list of the things I've kept from her. It's a long and troubling list. Losing most of our money; knowing the murder victim, Mister; Marc's request for me to come home early; the meeting with the old woman, deciding to murder David—I mean Marc—I mean *David* (Marc might *live*, I remind myself).

"We are going to the desert, *tonight!*" That's when I notice she has a pack on her back and another at her side—mine, I presume. "We are catching the shuttle to go home, *tomorrow!*" That statement takes a few things off my list of possible lies I've been caught in. "We are *not! Killing! Anyone!*"

OK, that clears it all up now. The old woman must've gotten to her, told her all about the whole killing-my-husband thing. I wish she'd keep her voice down, though. People are glancing at us as they walk past, and it doesn't help that she's screaming about murdering people.

"Listen." She takes a breath and looks me square in the eye. She's spitfire angry but seems like she's preparing to reason with me, bringing her voice back to a normal octave. "I know how you feel. I, too, was forced into a direction I would never have chosen for myself," she admits, but to what I don't know.

We are staring at each other, facing off like two pawns in an ancient game of chess, neither of us able to make a move.

"Kay?" I cautiously break the silence first. "What direction were you forced into?"

She doesn't respond or break eye contact. My pulse picks up. I feel myself heat up with anticipation. I take a deep breath and find the nerve to ask what's been gnawing away at my paranoia. This time, I don't care how I come across, or what my tone implies.

"What are you admitting to? Tell me why you've come with me, and don't feed me some bullshit about Peter." She doesn't answer, and so I persist. "We hadn't spoken in a long time, and yes, I know that it was my fault, I admit it. I avoided the casino and everything associated with it when my dad passed away. But you didn't try to keep in contact with me, either. You let our friendship dwindle away, too. So why were you so willing to drop everything and risk your life to travel with me across space and time, when you wouldn't even stop by my home to try and talk to me when I stopped coming to the casino?" I couldn't put my finger on what it had been that was making me question her motives until now. Her hinting that her intentions were not as pure as she's been letting on all this time has finally given me the guts to face my hesitation about her.

"I came with you..." Kay starts, then stops. She looks like she's reconsidering.

"Are you working with the old woman?" I accuse.

Kay shakes her head vigorously, appalled that I would even suggest a thing.

"*No!*" she shouts at me with disgust. "I had no idea who the hell she was when she approached me that day at the funeral." She looks away, tugs at the bag on her back. "I came with you to find a soul for Jordan, and..."

"And *what?*" I am becoming very impatient with her. I know she doesn't owe me an explanation—it's not like I've been honest with her—but I'm tired of not being able to trust her, either.

"Peter's not dead."

CHAPTER 34

"What the hell are you talking about?" My vision blurs with the pressure bursting in my head from my outrage. I no longer care if we're making a scene on the streets of Vegas.

"His soul is gone. But Dr. Messie kept his body alive. My parents donated my brother to science in exchange for a small retirement fund!" Kay tears up but then regains her composure.

"So what were you going to do? Steal David's soul for Peter or something?" I can't believe this is a conversation I am having with Kay.

"Is that what you think of me? I tell you my parents sold my brother while he was still alive and that he is being used for research like a lab rat, and you accuse me of wanting to steal your beloved David's soul?" she screams at me. "Why does your brain always go to the worst place on the trust spectrum? Stop fishing—save your bait, Grace! There is no double meaning here, I am not double-crossing you, I came here to honour Peter, just as I said!" She's screaming and crying at the same time. "It's pretty simple, actually. If Jordan lives, there is no need to continue to research on Peter, and they will finally let him go! His soul has been gone for so long there is no hope for him! I want my brother to finally *rest in peace!*" Tears are running freely down her face. "I love Peter, but I won't be part of the murder plot that old woman told you and me about—it's wrong! We're not killing innocent people! We have to go home!" Kay concludes.

She has pleaded her case, and now it's my move. She waits, hiccupping from crying. And I can honestly say that right up until I got here and stood in front of Kay, I had decided that I was going to go home. I had decided that there is no way I am going to allow David to be killed by Dr. Messie's hitman. Right up until now, I was going to go home to Jordan, tell Marc that I'm sorry and I love him. So I don't know why Kay's revelation has changed my mind.

"I'm not going anywhere," I say with a calmness that almost scares me.

It certainly shakes up Kay. Her blue eyes, still wet with her tears, grow three times their size with crazy madness. Her face turns a deeper shade of red than the tomato it already resembled. She starts to tremble like a volcano right before an eruption. All the negative energy building up inside her must be on the verge of explosion via the smoke that may burst out of her ears.

"What is *wrong* with you?" she sputters as she yells at me, finally letting go of the negative energy she hates to hold on to. "You would risk Marc's life? You would *kill* someone?" she accuses.

"You don't understand what I'm going through," I tell her plainly.

"*Yes, I do.*" Kay's eyes look like they may bulge right out of their sockets. "*I am losing Peter!*"

"What am I supposed to do, Kay? Let Jordan die like your brother?" I ask her calmly, knowing I sound insensitive about Peter.

"*Yes!*" She shouts it at me like it's so obvious even a toddler would know. "Just like everyone else who suffers from Metagenesis! Accept that answer! Accept that you can't save him, just like I can't save Peter! You might go through with this, and it may not even work! It's just a trial, Grace! A trial! You may kill an innocent someone over something that hasn't even been proven yet! And then Jordan will die, too! Then you'll really be alone! No Marc, because you killed his soul. No Jordan, because he died. No friends or family because you're a *killer*!" She pauses, dramatically turning her back to me and pumping her fists in the air, making sounds like a gorilla.

"Grace! *Rrrraaaa!*" She turns back to face me. I think *she* might kill *me*.

"I'm leaving now." She tries to steady herself, not so eloquently. "I'm leaving to catch that shuttle, with or without you. If I go home and Marc is dead or missing, I'll know why, and I'll make sure everyone else does too. I suggest you accept that and come with me. There is still time for you to be with your son."

We glare at each other for a few moments. She is waiting for me to say something, and I am going to say something. I just need to make up my mind and coherently gather my thoughts.

"Peter is your brother, not your son. It's not the same. There is no love that compares with the love a mother feels for her child." I don't care that I'm coming across as being heartless about Peter.

"But you're talking about committing *murder*!" Kay seethes.

"Your parents, siblings, friends, soulmate... You may love these people, even risk your life or die for them as you have for Peter. But your own child? Kay, there is no price I wouldn't pay. I would kill for Jordan." I'm trying to convince myself as much as I'm trying to convince her. In saying this out loud, in the universe, maybe I'm committing to finding David, inserting the syringe-tracker and letting the rest fall where it may.

"Your own husband? You would kill Marc?" Kay tries to match my calm tone with this question, probably hoping it will be more impactful. But her face is still on fire, and she looks like she's still ready to blow.

"My *ex*-husband," I correct her. "Kay, I would like you to leave on that shuttle and don't look back to see if I'm behind you, because I won't be. I'm not coming with you."

"*You! You! You!*" she stammers, struggling for the right idiom, I'm sure. "*Hamartia!*" she finally spits out, literally spits it out.

I blink at the spit to avoid it, turn my face, close my eyes and mouth, puckering my lips.

"What the hell is a 'Hamartia'?" I taunt. I don't know why I'm so calm. Maybe I'm finally at peace, knowing why Kay came with me, and that I can finally start trusting my instincts again. Or maybe because I've come to the realization that I'm determined to save Jordan and I don't need her to do it. I can make those phone calls myself. I don't even need to survey anyone. I can just go to their homes and walk up to them and see if I feel something and walk away if I don't. I'm still not sure what will happen when I do find the right donor. When the right David Williams is in my presence, and I feel something, will I have the guts to risk everything and stab him with the syringe-tracker? Will I have the guts to risk Jordan's life if I *don't*?

"*Look it up!*" she screeches at me, invading my personal space, her face two inches from my own, her voice cracking and hoarse. She spins around and stomps off.

I collect my knapsack off the ground. I guess she's checked out of the room. Do I go back and try to talk Brad into giving me a couple of free nights? I consider that option for all of two seconds before I head back in the direction I came from, the casino.

CHAPTER 35

The scene when I get back to the casino is considerably livelier than when I'd left it. But Leo is gone. Joe and a few other regulars are there, throwing back drinks, laughing, joking.

"Hey Joe," I say, disappointed that Leo is not there, but happy enough to see the others. "Whatcha drinking?" I could use one of whatever he's having.

Joe looks happy that I've asked. "Now that your boyfriend's gone, you decide to loosen up?" Joe kids as he calls the waitress over and orders another round.

I've got a few dollars left. I'll just play one hand or something, while I find the courage to go back to the motel, alone, without Kay, and hope that Brad will let me back in.

I win the first hand, and I shouldn't have. Why anyone would split two face cards against the dealer's ace is anyone's guess. But I was feeling lucky, or invincible, or like I had nothing to lose. The whole table hoots and hollers at my brave (stupid) bet, which pays off. That prompts Joe to order another round, and then another round, and then another.

By the time I leave the table, I'm slurring my words, but desperately trying to look sober. I walk as straight as a drunkard can toward the phone to check the message on the pager, which just vibrated. I can handle it, whatever Marc or Charlie have to say. I've made up my mind, anyway. I'm not going home. I'm not leaving until that last shuttle, a week from now. And in that time, I will find David and kill him myself if I have to.

Even with all my bravado, I still miss my family immensely. Marc and Jordan. A tender part of me wants to go home, jump into Marc's arms, let him hold and love me forever like he used to promise me all the time. I want to be by Jordan's side. He might not make it, and I won't be there with him, or for him. I should. I should be by his side. I know all of this. Deep down. But that's not going to happen.

I have to repeat the message I'm listening to; Marc is talking too quickly. Or maybe I'm half-listening, half-talking to myself, half-drunk. OK, totally drunk.

"Grace, *listen*," I say to myself. And I obey me. Obey me, that's funny. I let out a small burp. I restart the message and try to focus.

"Grace, you need to come back *right now!*" OK, it's Marc, and he's angry. I'd prefer a message about his love for me, not another message about Jordan getting worse. Jordan needs to remain stable until I get back. "He is dying, Grace."

"End of message."

That message shocks me sober. I push thoughts aside about what Metagenesis does to a person and is doing to my son. Laboured breathing, your soul not coming back, your body starting to give up, code 33.

"Come home!" Marc screams.

That's the next message. He must be on the other end again, leaving messages back to back.

I grip the phone, my knuckles locking the device firmly in my hand, which is now shaking. Bile rises in the back of my throat. I stubbornly punch at the keypad, turning up the volume, replaying and rewinding the first message. I hadn't really listened to it fully before I heard him say that Jordan is dying.

"...He is hanging on by a thread; it's a miracle he has held on this long! Even Walt isn't sleeping a wink, keeping vigil at his bedside. It's like he's afraid to let go, so he doesn't get in trouble and disappoint you. It's like he's waiting for his mother. The doctors are giving me the 'any minute now' speech. It's over,

Grace. He is dying. His soul is gone more than it's with him."

I skip the message from Marc commanding me to come home and go to the next message that is waiting to be heard.

"...And I've just about had enough of you trying to make things perfect. Life isn't perfect! You can't make us all perfect. I love Jordan, and watching him this way..." Marc's voice cracks. I hear his breath catch. He slows his pace down, steadies his tone.

"...You just need to come home. It's OK to give up and let Jordan give up too—he is suffering. We need to allow him to give up. I won't let him suffer. If you don't come ba—"

The message ends; it's too long. I skip to the next message to hear more.

"Grace, you can't control life or death." This message is not as angry. He is no longer yelling, but he is crying, talking between sobs. "If you don't come back, I'll be forced to sign the euthanization papers without you. I won't let him suffer like this, waiting for you to come back, pretending to be a hero. We were both with him to witness his first breaths, but if you don't come back, only one of us will be with him when he takes his last." He doesn't speak for the rest of the message, but he doesn't hang up either. He lets the gravity of that last phrase sit heavy in the rest of the message, backed up with the sound of him quietly sobbing.

I cry with him until the message declares it's done recording and the computerized lady asks if I want to delete this message, or if I want to replay it. I choose the option to leave a message in response.

"Marcus Dartmouth," I declare, "don't you *dare* sign any papers to authorize anything without me! Don't you *dare* give up on me or Jordan! Don't you *dare* let him give up! If he is waiting for his mother to die, then let him *wait*! Because I am coming back when I have found what I came here to get, and not one second sooner! You let him *wait*! You *make him wait for me!*" I am seething into the phone. "You are a *coward!*" I'm holding the handset away from my face, staring into it, shouting at it like it's the very thing that is causing all my pain. "Don't you *daaarre!* Do you hear me? You will *not* euthanize him! You will *not do a damn thing about my son without me, you cowarrrd!*"

"*Press pound to send your message now. Press 1 to send it urgently.*"

I slam the phone into the cradle; smash it against the keypad, screaming at it. I smash it over and over again. Pieces of the black plastic chip off the handset.

"DON'T" smash "YOU" smash "DARE" smash, smash smash "COWARRRD."

"*Ahhh!*" I give it one final slam, throwing the receiver into the phone, my energy expended. I collapse into a sobbing heap. My arm is vibrating from banging the receiver into the hard metal phone. It now swings and dangles from its cord, bouncing off the painted brick wall behind it. It's telling me to "*Please hang up and try (my) call again.*" People are looking in my direction, but no one stops. They hurry past, boyfriends protectively pulling girlfriends closer as they pick up the pace to get away from me.

The feeling and scene around me are very déjà-vu. I look around for the homeless man with his cardboard box and kidnapped wife sign. I don't see him.

But who I do see surprises me. And he's standing over me, holding a hand out, waiting for me to take it.

"Come with me," he says.

I must still be drunk.

CHAPTER 36

I rub my eyes and blink hard, looking again at the young man with his outstretched hand. I've seen this man before. Only the last time I saw him, Kay and I were chasing him down Las Vegas Boulevard. And the time before that, he was passing me at a phone booth, much like now. The first time I saw him was at the casino, right when we arrived and won that jackpot. This is the young guy from the diner, with the burn scar. The man who pointed a gun at my best friend in the caves.

"Please," he repeats. He has a kind face, although he does not smile.

I don't know why, but I trust him, even though so many things are pointing at me not to. I usually trust no one.

We walk in silence to the Canadiana Hotel & Casino and take a seat on a park bench in the Rocky Mountains. Although littered with tourists, this area still feels private. There are gondola rides up the mountains to artificial ski hills, and a tall tower in the background, which I recognize. But in my time, it looks ancient, not so new and fresh or located near the Rocky Mountains.

"Mom, it's me."

I turn right around in my seat to square my shoulders with the young man's and look right at him. I don't know what to say

186

or think or do. Who is this man calling me "Mom"?

"Look at me. Don't I look familiar to you?"

And I do, I look at him carefully. His soft curls are cut short now, but I can tell those are my curls. His eyes are hazel, just like Marc's. His pronounced chin, the dimple in his cheek. All Marc. He does resemble Jordan, an older version of him; even his body language. I remember sensing that when he passed me on the street, although I didn't give it much thought. I kept seeing Jordan in everyone, everywhere, in my dreams, on the street. Seeing Jordan was nothing out of the ordinary.

"My name is Jordan Dartmouth, son of Marcus and you, Grace."

I gasp at hearing all our names.

"Who are you?" I ask. My voice sounds like it does when I'm dreaming, slow and inside my head.

"Who are you?" I demand more firmly, clearing my throat, so my voice is awake. I rise out of my seat. "Is this some sort of sick joke?" I can feel my voice start to shake with nerves.

"I know this sounds crazy, but you have to hear me out—please just listen," he begs with pleading eyes, hazel eyes, Jordan's hazel eyes, like Marc's.

Can this really be my son? I don't move, I'm frozen, every bone in my body still, joints locked. He waves a hand at the spot I vacated beside him on the bench, for me to sit back down. I obey without taking my eyes off him as if he is a ghost that may fade away if I do.

"You've been following me, turning up in places, getting in my way. And at the caves..." I say.

"Mom, I came here to stop you. I came here to ask you, to *beg* you, please, go home on the next shuttle."

I start to get up to leave—who is this crazy guy?

"Wait, Mom, let me expl—"

"I don't know who you are," I threaten, my voice rising, "but you need to just just—"

"—MOM, do you remember me petting Lucy before I told you I was dying? And right after that, I took her out for a walk. Then you made me an ice cream sundae with brownies, my favourite. Did you tell anyone about that? How would I know that? My friend at the clinic, his name was Walt, do you remember him? How would I know about Walt? No one knew who Walt was. *Sit down!*"

"Oh shit," I reply, shocked.

"Mom, listen," he reasons, momentarily closing his eyes and taking a deep breath before continuing. "When Dr. Claudio found a cure for Metagenesis and saved my life, I was so grateful that I spent years studying in the field of reincarnation. I was the doctor's first success story, and I owed my life to Dr. Claudio."

It's odd that he uses Dr. Messie's first name. No one does that back home.

"I wanted to give back, help other families save their loved ones from the fate I almost faced. Dr. Claudio took a liking to me. I was like some pet he had saved or rescued. When I graduated, he even let me intern at his company, Recycled Souls." He pauses to let it sink in.

I mouth the company name, let it roll off my tongue: Recycled Souls.

"So, it worked, you're alive—I found the right match then, the donor, right? That's why you're here? To encourage me to keep going? You've got a funny way of showing it. Do you know who Dad's past life is? David? Can you tell me how to find him?" I know I'm rambling and grasping at straws. Jordan's expression doesn't show encouragement. It shows worry, angst, desperation and deep sadness.

"I don't know who Dad is in this life. I didn't even know his name was David until I went rummaging through your room and found your phone book, loaded with notes. I only knew who you were because I still remember what you looked like. I knew how to find you because of the milkshakes you used to go on about when I was a kid. Can I continue?"

I nod. I'm sitting on the edge of my seat—floating, rather.

"I stumbled across something, something huge, something that confirms that this, everything," his hands wave at an imaginary everything in the air, his eyes wide, "all of this, this reincarnation stuff." He spits the word "reincarnation" out like it's a virus he needs to rid himself of, like the very word itself is venomous. "The Messie family, Dr. Claudio's family, they are responsible for soul loss. They are the reason the disease exists in the first place. They life travel, and by doing that, they *invented* the Metagenesis disease. Of course they didn't mean to. They probably didn't realize that when people travelled back to observe," he makes quoting motions with his hands at the word "observe", "they interfered with people's lives, people's souls. Somehow, the people they observed," quoting motions again, "were the ones who started to lose their souls and died."

He pauses again, shuffles closer to me.

"Dr. Claudio knows. He knows and is trying to protect his family name, or more likely his family fortune. If this gets out..." Jordan shakes his head. "The worst part," he continues with true sadness in his voice, "the worst part, Mom, is that after I was cured, there was a huge increase in the number of lost souls. They called Metagenesis nature's holocaust. Millions of people became infected. They said that humans were becoming extinct. And Dr. Claudio? That guy? He just cashed in on it, became a rich hero. He sent more and more people back, and then more and more people lost souls, and then more and more people would go back... and it just went on and on. Are you getting me?"

I don't respond right away. I am not sure what to say. Holocaust? Human extinction? This is too much to take in. It's like he is that child letting me in on a terrible secret, groping Lucy's ears again, the moment before our lives changed forever. I have a million questions again, except this time I can't whisper lies about how it's going to be OK into his soft hair. This time, I want him to whisper lies to me, tell me there is a way all of this works out. I want a happy ending. But his face says otherwise, and so I ask the obvious questions.

"Jordan," I say to my adult son—so weird, addressing this adult as my son weeks after leaving him as a nine-year-old boy back home, "Jordan, what do you want me to do? Why are you trying to stop me from saving your life? What will happen if I don't?" I ask.

"I was the last trial," he says. "Dr. Claudio was too close to getting caught at carrying out experiments on humans, and his research would've been denied, as it was unethical. They were catching on that people were travelling back and messing around with reincarnated lives. If I hadn't been a success, he would've had to stop. But when I was cured, the excitement was all everyone focused on. They didn't know it would trigger a human extinction. Soul cloning was the biggest breakthrough in medical science since they eradicated cancer back in the 2040s."

He stops then, giving me time to think about this. I can't look away from him, and he isn't looking away from me, either. We stare at each other for a few uncomfortable moments.

"I wasn't even the first experiment. You were not the first mom to go back to clone a soul."

He leaves that between us for another few moments.

"Why don't you look surprised to hear that?" he asks.

"Are you here alone?" I inquire.

He looks around nervously, then back at me. Confusion shows on his face for a split second but then clears, like he just realized something.

"You mean the hitman?" he asks with amusement. His grin is menacing. "I took care of him."

"Pardon?" I ask, shocked at what he is implying. "You pointed a gun at my best friend!" I accuse.

"I didn't realize Auntie Kay was in that room. She startled me. I would never hurt her," he says with genuine regret.

"You killed Mister?" I ask directly.

Jordan ignores my question and continues with his explanation.

"I want you to stop looking for David," he says. "As I said, if Dr. Claudio hadn't succeeded with me, I would've been the last failed experiment. So if it never began with me, all those other souls after me, those millions and millions of souls, they wouldn't have to die. No holocaust, no extinction. The gates to travel back were going to be closed for good. No more meddling with past lives."

"I don't understand. What do you actually want me to do?" I ask weakly, with a sickening feeling creeping up on me, as I predict his response. This can only mean that he wants me to...

"Let me die, Mom. Stop looking for Dad's past life. I don't know who he is. If I did, I would just whisk him off to safety from you—you're so stubborn. Even with the hitman gone, I can't trust you won't do it yourself. I'm an apple that didn't fall far from your tree." He looks me straight in the eye. "I want you to let me die, Mom. Forget David and let me die."

"That's crazy," I argue, angry tears threatening to break my composure. "If I let you die, you're, you're *dead,* got it? D-E-A-D! Why? Why would I do that? What kind of a mother..." The words catch in my throat as the tears spill over, my lips quivering.

"Mom, I'm dead anyway. I'm already dead."

"What are you talking about?" I'm shouting now.

"I didn't just sneak out through some portal, or buy a ticket aboard some shuttle. Dr. Claudio chased me out. I must've tripped a security alarm or something when I snooped in his files. I was being chased and hunted. Coming back here was my only way out. If I go back, I'm dead."

"By Dr. *Messie*?" I demand, picturing an older version of that fat man, sweating, dressed in white, dabbing his forehead, chasing after Jordan, in his twenties, fit, young. I couldn't even catch him, and I'm pretty fit myself.

Jordan lets out a sarcastic laugh. "Are you kidding? Dr. Claudio has a whole army of followers, believers. I doubt he even wipes his own ass! People will do anything when they're controlled by the world's richest, most popular man, who claims to hold the key to cure the disease that is driving the human race to extinction. He'll have one of his lackeys after me—someone I'm sure will be paid handsomely to kill me dead. D-E-A-D," he mimics me spelling out the word, saucy boy.

Jordan is visibly upset, and I sense there is more to the story about Dr. Messie and this lackey.

"What about Dad—is he..." I want to ask if he survived. Is he alive? Did I kill him? Was he sacrificed? I stop myself from finishing the question. "What happened to your face?" I ask instead, not sure if I'm ready to know the answer about Marc. I touch my own cheek in the same spot as the scar on his.

His eyes water at my question. He doesn't answer me, and he looks as though he may break down. I guess I've hit a soft spot, so I change course.

"What happened to Walt?" I ask. He takes a deep breath and his lips quiver. I guess I've hit another soft spot. I mentally kick myself. That's two for two. But at least he answers me about his friend Walt—sort of.

"Like I said, you weren't the first mom to try to save your kid. Didn't you ever find it odd that no one ever visited him?" he asks in reply, then gets back on track with his purpose for finding me. "Look, back to my point—I barely made it here in the first place. I knew the year and location you were in because you used to talk about it so much. You'd go on for hours about the legal casinos, the good food, and the wasteful napkins. I obviously remember what you looked like." He smiles then, although it's a sad smile, it's gone as quick as it appeared. "I am hoping beyond all hope to stop you, so more souls don't die from Metagenesis. Dr. Claudio will have his men at the gate, ready to kill me if I try to go back. I'm dead already. Don't let me die in vain. Promise me, Mom."

"Promise you?" I ask, incredulously. "Promise I'll let you die? I can't promise anything yet," I say, shaking my head slowly.

Exasperated, Jordan abruptly rises to leave.

"Wait! Wait!" I have to know about Marc. "How's Dad?" I ask hurriedly before I change my mind.

Jordan looks down at me, his expression dejected. "Metagenesis is taking everyone." He swallows hard, shakes his head slowly back and forth and wipes a tear away.

No! I scream in my head, but not from my mouth. My words lodge in my throat as my tongue becomes suddenly as thick as a brick. Jordan kisses me on the cheek as he always did when he was a little boy and turns to walk away. "I love you, Mommy," he says with his back to me.

He leaves me on the bench, alone, scared, confused.

CHAPTER 37

I sit on the bench for what feels like hours, surrounded by the fake mountains. The tourists evolve from stylish couples and groups of travelling friends to loud and obnoxious animals who have had too much to drink. Girlfriends who were previously arm in arm with boyfriends now hang from their partners' arms for stability, intoxicated. Crowds of friends yell over each other, laughing at everything and nothing, sloppily making their way to the next club or bar. Girls who previously resembled ladies in pretty heels now carry them, walking barefoot on the dirty sidewalks, their hair out of place, their makeup smudged. I envy them. I wish that were Kay and me right now.

The little syringe in my hand has warmed up from my holding it the whole time, rubbing at it, thinking, processing, obsessing. I remember the determination I felt the first time I held the small vial before I stepped into the glass room at the back of the plane. Protecting it like it was my son's delicate soul. The fragile pinkish liquid would save his life. That's what I remember. And now, Jordan tells me it will merely prolong his life, at the cost of millions of others. The human race is counting on me to let my son die.

I jingle my watch and peek at the time. It's one in the morning. Prime Vegas night time. I decide it's time to pack it in, find a place to sleep. I wouldn't make it to the shuttle if I left right now, anyway. I wonder if Brad will let me back in. I wouldn't if I were him. But with not much money left and no one else to rely on, I see no other option but to beg Brad the pervert.

I brace myself and tighten the bag on my back. With a deep draw of cigarette-and-beer Vegas air, I rise from my bench, my butt sore from the faux wood slates, and tuck the syringe back into my pocket. For a second, I don't recognize the folded paper in the way, but then I remember, and it brings a welcome smile to my lips. I retrieve my hand with the familiar paper between my fingers and unfold it to see a receipt from the sex shop. I laugh out loud at the fact that Leo wrote his address and number on the back of a sex shop receipt, and wonder if he even noticed.

I head to the phone booth, but not to check any messages on the pager. Instead, I call Leo.

CHAPTER 38

I guzzle back the cheap whisky, wiping the excess off my lips as it burns my throat, coating its way down to my empty stomach while buzzing my brain.

"Classy, real classy!"

I look up to see Leo in the driver's seat of a beautiful silver car, window half down. It's far shinier than Brad's car. People stop to look. I get in on the passenger side and pull my belt across my lap, noting that the inside of the vehicle is far fancier than Brad's as well. It smells of leather. There are so many fancy-looking knobs and dials and gauges. The seats are smooth against my thighs, and I curiously run my hand along the dashboard: high-end leather. It's cool in here like the air is on full blast, yet there is no air blowing into my face.

"Nice car. What is it that you actually do for a living?" I ask, aware my tone is implying that I want to know how much money he makes, and not where he works.

"I'm the CEO of an engineering enterprise. One of our current projects is at the Grand Canyon, actually. You ever been?" he asks, steering the conversation in another direction.

But I'm curious about him. He mentioned a house with a pool. He seems to be on a permanent vacation—always at the casino when I am. And I'm sitting in his very fancy car. Passers-by stop and point as we drive down the strip as if Leo is a celebrity. I know he's not, as no one does this when he's playing anchorman at the blackjack table.

"Grand Canyon? No, no, I haven't been there." I think I'm a bit buzzed because I decide to pry a bit more, even though I get the feeling that Leo would rather that I didn't. He never really talks about himself, and he certainly doesn't dress or behave like a CEO or like he belongs in this car.

"So why are you playing small change at the casino and betting like a little girl?" I joke, but I am intrigued. People with big money gamble big—when I worked the casinos, I was a pro at recognizing big spenders. They don't sit at blackjack tables where the max bet is twenty dollars.

"I only play there because I keep hoping to run into you," he replies in an even tone, nervously gripping his steering wheel.

He's not joking, and I'm not drunk enough to keep prying. I take another long draw of the whisky. The smell stings my eyes, causing them to water a bit. This stuff, which tastes like rubbing alcohol, cost a few dollars at the corner store where I waited for Leo to pick me up. And I'm embarrassed that I'm drinking from a bottle out of a paper bag next to a guy who can afford this car.

"Oh," I respond.

The rest of the ride is quiet and awkward. So I drink a bit more until I don't care that it's quiet and awkward.

We enter a gated community and pass front lawns larger than any I've ever seen, adorned with fountains and cacti. We reach a long driveway, which leads us through another gate. It reminds me of Dr. Messie's home, minus the DNA scanner. I feel uncomfortable.

Everything changes when we step inside, though. His home is massive and elaborate on the outside, but inside, it's sparsely furnished, and the pieces in his home are modest. Leo himself seems a bit shy and modest about me being here. The loud and playful Leo of the casino seems to have gone into hiding now that he's a bit exposed.

"Nice home," I say, trying to break the ice with a light tone and careful smile.

On the phone, I told him I had had a fight with Kay and just needed a place for the night—and he wasn't to take advantage and come on to me. He had joked that it would be me who wouldn't be able to keep my hands off him, the birthday boy.

"Thanks. It's in need of a woman's touch, I'm sure," he says sheepishly as he leads me through a large room with nothing but a saggy leather couch that looks too small for the room and the TV in front of it.

The ginormous TV is flanked by equally ginormous built-in bookcases, but they are empty except for a few mismatched framed photos and a book or two. The other wall is completely floor-to-ceiling windows, with striking views of his backyard and vistas of the Vegas valleys below.

"Outside?" he suggests, but I'm already making my way toward the sliding door. He rushes ahead to open it for me and then takes the brown paper bag from my hands. "Let me pour us some real drinks," Leo says, leaving me on his back patio, poolside, while he runs back inside.

I'm not sure I can handle another drink—I'm already struggling not to trip over my own feet, and my eyelids feel heavy from drinking all night, but I take the fishbowl-sized wine glass he hands me, anyhow, and sip from it, trying to appear dainty, rather than drunk and tired. The wine is dry and full-bodied. If I were a real wine connoisseur, I might compliment Leo on his impeccable choice of wine. I sit on the outdoor furniture, which doesn't look like it belongs with the type of pool next to which it resides, and we clink glasses. I wish him a happy birthday, and he smiles. He has a nice smile.

"So, what was your big fight about?" Leo asks, taking a seat beside me, but not too close, honouring the promise he made me on the phone not to hit on me. He seems genuinely concerned.

"Oh, you know. Girl stuff." But my shaky voice betrays my downplaying it. I didn't realize until now that I was upset about Kay leaving. So I gulp more wine and talk in code.

"She and I, we don't see eye to eye. But to be honest, it's my fault. I lied about something I knew she'd disapprove of and she found out." There, I said it.

"What'd you lie about?" he asks.

"I'd rather not say..."

He tries another angle. "OK. So... *why'd* you lie about it?"

"To protect her," I say, and Leo's eyebrows knit together.

His expression says "bullshit," but he keeps quiet, allowing me to reconsider my answer and continue.

"To protect *me*," I admit to him, and probably to myself for the first time as well.

I look away from Leo, gulp at my wine. He refills my glass before I can object. My head spins, telling me to stop drinking, but I ignore it and greedily slurp it back. Leo chuckles and refills.

"Kay is really... she's really, um... I don't know how to explain it, other than to call her a tree-hugger. In a good way— she's a good person, a good soul. She wouldn't harm a spider, you know? I also found out her true intentions for helping me with something, and I was a jerk about it. She deserved my understanding. So if I'm not perfect like she is, then..." I let my thoughts trail away from me and gulp more wine. I should be sipping it, lady-like. It's so tasty it probably cost a fortune. I think I taste a hint of jostaberry, which is refreshing to me. Charlie and I used to pick them as kids alongside the ancient roads on our drives with Dad. Jostaberries grow wild in the summer back home.

Leo refills my glass with every sip I take. It's like the endless glass of wine. I'm not sure if he's keeping up with me, but the bottle is empty. He rises from his seat.

"Hold that thought—I'll just grab another bottle," he announces and heads back inside.

I hear music playing in the background, and the pool lights up in front of me as I'm waiting. I guess he's doing more than just grabbing a bottle. I feel guilty being here, knowing he has a crush on me. So far, he's been very gentlemanly, and I hope me being at his home doesn't change our friendship at the tables. I know that everything is telling me I should go home to Jordan and Marc, but I can't bring myself to commit to doing that quite yet. So I add "feeling guilty about leading Leo on" to my long list of things to feel bad about.

Leo returns with another bottle in hand and refills my glass. I hadn't noticed it was already empty.

"Leo, do you know what a 'hamartia' is?" I ask, still thinking about Kay.

"A what?"

"Hamartia. It was something Kay said." He looks at me before heading back inside. He returns a minute later, thumbing through a small book. He takes his seat before stopping on a page, shrugs his shoulders then shows it to me, the dictionary definition of Hamartia.

Hamartia: A hero or heroine who possesses a fatal character flaw, leading to their tragic downfall.

I read it over and over again. I feel a bit ill. "May I use your restroom?"

"Of course."

Leo shows me the way. I can hardly walk straight. He holds my elbow and guides me.

"Whoa," he says. I can smell the jostaberry from the wine on his breath too, and I realize that he is also on the tipsy side. He leaves my bag at the bathroom door with a "Just in case you need it." He is being a complete gentleman.

I stare at myself in the mirror, leaning over the marble sink, not sure what to think of myself. *Hamartia.* My drunk brain tries to rationalize all that has happened as I turn the syringe around in my hand, examining it. Meeting Jordan tonight was troubling at best. I wish I had asked him more questions, not about his scar and Walt. Then I clammed up when he told me about Marc. I keep thinking about how he had spoken about me in the past tense. "I still remember what you looked like" and "you used to go on about it when I was a kid." Like I used to do these things but didn't anymore. It's like I'm no longer part of his life in his twenties. Did something happen to me? *Tragic downfall.*

What's more troubling is Marc. "Metagenesis takes everyone," Jordan said. So it took him. He will lose his soul. But something is bothering me about Jordan's abstract answer.

These thoughts, along with too much cheap whisky and good wine mixing in my empty stomach, bring me to my knees in front of the toilet bowl. The cool tiles beneath me feel good.

My breathing is anxious. My mouth starts to salivate, and I break out in a cold sweat. Nausea kicks in, and I heave, but nothing comes up, not even bile. I don't remember what I ate last, or even *if* I have eaten.

"You OK?" I hear Leo through the door.

Oh no! Is he just standing there, waiting for me?

"Yes, yes, I'll be out in a minute. You got anything to nibble on?"

Go away.

"Of course! How rude of me! I'll fix us up something."

I hear his footsteps leaving the hallway. But the sensation of wanting to throw up is gone. My head is still spinning with thoughts and buzzing with alcohol, but at least the nausea has subsided enough for me to pick myself up off this floor and make my way back to my seat without Leo watching me stumble and trip over my own shadow. I mustn't drink anymore, I promise myself and tuck the syringe into the backpack instead of my shorts, wrapping it in the few belongings I own.

I'm simultaneously hot and cold and clammy, and I feel terrible. I wish I could've just thrown up—it would probably have made me feel better. When I make it back outside, rather than sitting down, I make a run for the pool, jumping in the deep end. That should sober me. The cool water isn't as cold as I would've liked it, but it's refreshing nonetheless. I allow myself to stay at the bottom for a bit, close my eyes and float slowly. The sensation reminds me of the few seconds of the journey to get to Vegas with Kay, letting the darkness take me.

Before I make it to the surface, I hear Leo splash into the water, and my eyes pop open when he grabs at my waist and pulls me into him from behind. His chest is bare, and I realize he has removed his shirt and even his jeans before diving in. My legs weave around his. I didn't bother removing my cut-off shorts and tank top, and they now seem heavy on my body. My tank is rising; his arm is around my naked waist.

He pulls me to the shallow end and releases me once we reach a point where we can both sit still in the water. I crawl the rest of the way to the side of the pool. It must be zero depth entry because when I turn and sit, the water is only a few inches high at most.

"What the hell are you doing!?" Leo demands, agitated. He's panting to catch his breath.

I look at him. He is sitting beside me in nothing but boxer shorts, water dripping from his hair and eyelashes. Cute guy— that was what Kay called him before. She was right. Leo is a cutie. I admit it was nice being saved from drowning by him.

"You can't just jump into the deep end of a pool fully clothed and completely intoxicated." He is staring at me incredulously, not joking, not even flirty. I've upset him. "You'll drown!"

"Sorry," I tell him. "Next time I'll jump in intoxicated and half-naked, like you," I smirk, trying to change the mood. I didn't mean to upset him. My gosh, my head is spinning.

"You're crazy, Grace," Leo exclaims, exasperated, but he manages a half-giggle as he shakes his head.

Fatal flaw.

"If I were really drowning, why'd you take the time to strip first?" I tease, looking him up and down, making him uneasy. "Leo, did you know you wrote your name and address on the back of a sales receipt from a sex shop?" I ask, still trying to make him laugh.

He looks at me and his eyes grow big first with embarrassment, but when he realizes I think it's hilarious, he laughs. And we both laugh. It feels good to laugh. But dizzy... it feels good and dizzy to laugh.

I lie back on the ground, letting my head touch the bottom of the pool and the water fill my ears, leaving my chin, nose, and forehead exposed. With my eyes closed, the world is spinning, and I fear getting sick in Leo's pool. I feel water drops on my face, and when I open my eyes, Leo is bending over me, his eyes searching my face. His smile is nervous. He comes in for a kiss... I may be drunk and craving his kiss, but I'm not drunk enough to betray Marc, so I turn my head and push at his naked chest. His firm, naked chest. We awkwardly bump noses, and Leo backs away from me abruptly. I sit up on my elbows, and Leo sits up as well, his back to me, bringing his knees to his chest.

"Sorry," he says meekly. "I know I promised... it's just that whenever you're around... I just can't seem to leave you alone. You're so... so..." He doesn't finish his sentence.

We sit in silence for a few minutes.

"I'm really drunk," I admit.

CHAPTER 39

My head is spinning pretty badly, and the bright sun in my eyes doesn't help my pounding head, but I need to get up and get moving. I do a check on the time; it's already seven in the morning. For a few brief seconds, I can't remember where I am. I squint through the brightness and look at my surroundings, trying to place myself, and then remember. Kay left me, and I'm at Leo's. The room is empty of furniture except for this bed and a dresser that looks dwarfed in a room with twelve-foot ceilings, emphasized by the equally tall curtain-less wall-to-wall windows.

I don't remember how I got into this room or bed, but I'm so comfortable, I'd love to just sink into it and drift back to sleep. For the first time in a long time, I slept peacefully through the whole night, no nightmares, not about my dad nor Jordan. I did dream about Marc, though. About a happier time and how we used to be. It breaks my heart. I really miss him.

"Metagenesis takes everyone," I say it out loud, finally pinpointing the trouble with Jordan's answer. When? Metagenesis might take him, but it doesn't mean it's because I find David. It could be years from now. Nature's holocaust.

I hear a rustling at my bedside and perk up to look. There's a fat cat licking its lion-sized paws beside the bed. "Hey, you," I say to the cat, who pays me no attention. I don't remember seeing this orange ball of fluff last night. In fact, there's a big black hole of things I don't remember from last night.

I smile when I see a bottle of water and two white pills in a clear glass container on a tissue next to a note in Leo's handwriting. "Take two and call me in the morning." There is a bucket next to that with another note: "Just in case." That one makes me chuckle.

I swallow the pills and chug back the water. It's exactly what I need. I throw the covers off me and get up. To my utter surprise, I'm completely naked! I instinctively leap back into the bed, gathering the blankets to cover myself while I look around in a panic to see if anyone is in the room with me, or anyone looking through the windows at me. The cat scurries off, probably as frightened as I am. I am alone in the room, and the floor-to-ceiling windows overlook the pool I jumped into last night. Leo's backyard overlooks the valley, so no neighbours are going to peep on the nude girl in his bed.

Now that I've established that I'm alone—a small victory—I have to fill in some blanks from last night. Where are my clothes, and how did I wind up without them, in Leo's bed? I close my eyes and think. I was very drunk. The last thing I remember was Leo trying to kiss me, our noses touching... I know I turned away. I remember his back to me. I remember putting my hand on his waist, wet and cool, his skin quivering from my unexpected touch... whispering, "Happy birthday" next to his ear, so close that I could feel the fine peach fuzz on his lobes touch my lips... I shiver at the memory.

I need to find my clothes and get out of here. I look around the room but don't see anything at first glance. With the sheets wrapped around me like body armour, I get out of the bed and perform a formal search. I'd look under the bed, but there is no under the bed. The box spring is right on the floor: no bed frame. I check the dresser, and find only Leo's neatly folded clothes and a pile of condoms in the top drawer next to his boxer shorts. I feel myself blush and slam the drawer shut right away, deciding my clothes are elsewhere.

Not sure what to do, I wander out to the hallway and check

room by room. Each room is empty or sparsely decorated. I make my way down the stairs. The walls are empty. No pictures or mementoes. I find my way back into the living room with the giant TV and not-so-giant leather couch. Leo is sleeping on the couch with a thin blanket covering just his groin area. His chest is bare. It looks as good as I remember it from last night. I roll my shoulders and shake my head to get rid of the feelings and continue the search for my missing clothes.

Where would they be? I survey the room. My eyes land on the bookshelves, the only place in the whole house that contains a hint of Leo, with some personal effects other than clothes and condoms. My clothes are not on the shelves, but my curiosity gets the better of me, and I approach the pictures I remember passing last night. When I get a closer look, I have to do a double take.

I reach out and pick up one of the pictures: the one of Leo with his arm around the shoulders of the old woman.

CHAPTER 40

I hear a shuffling behind me and panic, fumble the picture frame and am forced to make a split-second decision to drop either my sheets from around my body or the frame from my hand.

"Well, a happy birthday to me indeed!"

The picture frame is still in my hand.

I place it back on the shelf and awkwardly gather the sheet back around my naked body while avoiding eye contact with Leo. He is now wide awake with a huge smile on his face, his arms crossed behind his head, propping him up for a front and centre view of my...

"Where are my clothes?" I ask, not returning his happy mood.

Leo gets serious, probably noticing how shocked I look. But dropping the sheet is only part of it. The old woman in the picture with him is the real source of my shock.

"I'll get them—wait here." He rises, letting his own sheet fall to the ground.

I close my eyes quick to give him privacy from his nakedness but peek when I think he's not looking—half disappointed to find out he's wearing boxers.

"Caught you looking!" Leo yells from another room.

He returns, still in his boxers, with my shorts and tank top folded neatly in one hand and my backpack in the other. I take last night's outfit from him with my free hand.

"Where are my...." I don't see my undergarments.

"You weren't wearing any," he says without looking at my face. "But maybe there is something in the bag. I didn't want to snoop. You remember where the bathroom is."

He moves out of the way, and I head to the bathroom to get dressed. He follows me with backpack in hand and leaves it at the bathroom door for me. I shower and dress, making a point to put on my underwear. What was I thinking?

When I make my way back to the living room, Leo is sitting on the couch and rises when I enter the room. He looks freshly showered himself and is wearing jeans and a white tee. "I don't have a coffee maker or anything, so I'll run out and grab us a Starbucks. Just make yourself at home, OK?"

He's so eager to please. Guilt, guilt, guilt.

"Hey, Leo? Who is that woman in the picture with you?"

He looks at the picture I placed back on the shelf. He hesitates, his expression soft.

"That's my grandma. The woman who raised me."

I sense he doesn't like to say much about himself. He seems pretty private. Of course, I know that they knew each other, seeing as Kay and I ran into her at the funeral, at which Leo was also present.

"Whose funeral was that, a few weeks back?" I ask.

His expression changes quickly and he looks right at me and makes a point of ignoring my question.

"How do you take your coffee?" he asks. His avoidance of my question and the tone in which he asks his tells me I've crossed over a boundary he doesn't like.

"Black, please." I smile genuinely, not wanting to upset him.

When I had first realized I was nude in Leo's bed, I'd wanted to run out of here. After seeing that photograph, I need to learn more about the old woman. She hasn't approached me again, and now that Kay is gone, I expect her to try again, seeing as I haven't left as she had requested. I don't know if she and Jordan are working together, but I get the feeling they don't know there are others working to stop me from finding David. The old woman knew there was a hitman following me, but didn't seem to know it was Mister, yet Jordan did. And neither of them seemed to know David's name. The old woman referred to him only as "the donor," while Jordan flat out told me when he confessed to ransacking our room.

CHAPTER 41

For someone who seems so private, the ease with which Leo leaves me in his home alone while he makes a coffee run surprises me. But after snooping through his entire house, all the rooms, every cupboard, all the shelves, I understand why. Leo has almost nothing of personal value in the entire home. It's as if he were in the witness protection program. And I shamelessly tell him that as we share a cup of coffee on his back patio.

"You snooped the whole house?" he asks, incredulous, and laughs earnestly. He doesn't seem to mind that I did that at all. He sits quietly for a few minutes, holding my gaze. He looks like he's considering his next move.

"The funeral was my dad's. I inherited this house from him. I was raised by my grandmother because my mom was an addict and my dad was a dick. That's the same reason there is nothing in this home. I packed all his shit up and donated it. I haven't quite gotten around to doing anything with the place." He pauses, waiting for my reaction.

I don't give him one. I want him to feel comfortable enough to tell me more.

"I am who I say I am: Leo, CEO. Current project at the Grand Canyon. Would love to take you there one day." He winks at me. "No witness protection program, Scouts' honour."

I don't know who the Scouts are, but I now realize that the old woman is the fraud and Leo is a by-product of that. I don't think he knows who the old woman really is like I do. While the old woman engineered it so we would land near the funeral, or she planned to be at our landing spot to meet us, my running into her grandson at the casino was a pure fluke. It makes me wonder how long that old woman has been here, waiting for me to show up in the silver suit she put me in. I bet she hadn't counted on me catching the eye of her handsome, rich grandson.

"One more question," I say, changing subjects completely, now that I'm satisfied with Leo's connection to the old woman. "Did we..." I feel my face heat up into a blush. "I was naked and... last night, did we... you know?"

Leo throws his head back in a cackle.

"Grace, *when* I make love to you, you're going to remember every move, every touch, every kiss," he teases.

Back to being old Leo. And me, back to making a fool of myself. I also think it's funny that he says "when" not if.

"You wished me a happy birthday and then passed out drunk in the pool. I carried you inside to bed. Your clothes were dripping wet. I intended to strip you down to your undies, but imagine my delight when I found you weren't wearing any!" I roll my eyes at him. "You're welcome for washing your clothes, and thank you for not wearing panties." He smiles and gives me a naughty sideways glance and smirk.

"I have to get going. Thanks for having me last night." I really mean it sincerely, but I've never been good at saying goodbye gracefully. I need to get back to my duty: finding David Williams. I've decided to keep looking for him. Marc's death may be a long way away and may be the result of Dr. Messie being a psychopath, not because I find the donor.

"*Wait,* Grace! Don't go!" He starts after me as I make my way to the door. "Hey! C'mon! I kept my promise! I didn't take advantage of your drunkenness and hot body! Do you know how hard it was to just tuck you in and walk away? And when I say hard, you know exactly what I mean," he teases me again.

He is on a roll with his timely, back-to-back jokes. "Wait, wait! Grace, I'm kidding. Please?"

I stop in my tracks and look back at him, remembering something.

"Hey, can I keep a souvenir from your house?"

Puzzled, he looks around his empty house.

"That phone book." When I was snooping, I found a phone book in his kitchen next to a spot where there might have been a phone once upon a time. "I'm looking for someone," I offer as explanation.

"Sure, but only if you let me drive you to where you need to go. And promise that I'll see you again at the tables, or even better, at my birthday party on the weekend?"

I nod yes to both, but I have no intentions of going back to the casino again or attending his party. I intend to find David, stab him with the syringe, catch the shuttle back home before Jordan dies, and pray I don't kill Marc in the process. When I get back, I'll have to figure out how to stop Dr. Messie, now that I know what he really is. But first, find David.

CHAPTER 42

Three days. Three days. That's the magic number. The number of days that stand between me and the last shuttle. The number of days I've spent walking up to countless David Williams' homes, looking to feel something, whatever something is, and feeling nothing at all. Three days of wearing the same outfit without a real shower, bathing in casino sinks. Three days of sleeping on parks benches, thankful that Vegas is awake all night so I don't look too much out of place. It's also the number of days since Kay left me and since I spent the night at Leo's—thankfully not *with* him, per se.

And it's been three days since I've checked the pager for messages. The last was the one where Marc told me he may have to euthanize Jordan without my consent. In fact, I discarded the pager, threw it out, smashed it to bits before tossing it, in case I felt the need to dig it out of the trash can later. I don't need the buzzing to remind me that there is a family on the other side that I am letting down. What's it going to say that I don't already know? Will it convince me to finally return home? Will it change my mind about finding David? No. It will not. And I've decided that when I find David, I will stab him and follow him and make sure someone kills him. And if no one else does... I've resolved to finish what I've started myself.

To save Jordan. To risk losing Marc by killing David.

But here I am. Three days in, and three days away, and I have nothing to show for it other than a heavy heart and no more money. I feel like giving up because I'm not going to succeed, anyway. I'm worried there may be a message waiting to tell me Jordan is dead. I'm afraid I'm going to return home, and there will be no one waiting for me. I'm going to be hopelessly lonely.

When Kay left me, and I went on a drinking binge and called Leo, I was desperate. But my desperation has turned to despair and now to defeat. I have to get back to the last shuttle in *three damn days,* and I'm no closer to finding David than I was *three damn weeks* ago. And here I am again, back at my blackjack table, next to Leo the anchorman, who has seen me naked, drunk and stupid, exactly where I promised him I would be and myself that I would not be.

"I guess that phone book didn't help?"

I hold back tears as I nod in reply. I can't even look at Leo.

He gears up for another try—he is persistent. "What kind of guy would I be if I just let you sit there and wallow in misery?" But he seems very nervous today, probably because of how I look—or smell. I can't imagine how I must appear to him right now. Especially since when he last saw me, I was wearing this exact outfit, only three days cleaner.

The waitress, Polly, interrupts at just the right time, asking for my drink order. As an inside joke to myself, a way to poke fun at irony, "I'll have a Pepsi," I tell her. I want to know what this preferred drink of the next generation tastes like, this stupid, stupid drink that helped us profile David. I run through that list now in my head: allergic to shellfish, Pepsi, broke a leg... I have asked so many Davids in the last damn days I've been reciting the list in my dreams.

"Is Coke ok?" Polly asks.

I almost cry as I nod yes. I won't even get to try Pepsi. It's like a cruel joke. Nothing is going my way.

"Awwww, pet, don't cry—keep your chin up. You'll get a winner at the right time when you least expect it. Don't spend all your money chasing it, though."

Usually, their coded advice helps me. But I don't think I'll find David, ever.

Leo gives my shoulder a squeeze and tries to lighten my mood. "Don't worry, I prefer Pepsi over Coke too."

His humour won't help me today. "I feel like a complete failure, Leo." And tears spill over. "I didn't get the part," I say. "And Kay, she left me. She went home."

"Aw, Grace. I'm so sorry—I don't know what to say," and he sounds like he really doesn't. He keeps quiet, and so does the whole table.

I don't play the next hand; I let it go by. Leo ignores the next hand, too.

"I know this great little place that serves ice-cold Pepsi and a killer spicy shrimp and steak dish. I really hate shrimp, though, so you can have an extra skewer of them. Actually, I'm allergic to shellfish."

His hand is still on my shoulder, and I look at him like I'm waking from a dream. I don't respond, and maybe Leo takes my peculiar stare as an opportunity to continue.

"I know, I know, why go to a seafood restaurant if I'm allergic to their main dish, right? My dad used to take me there when I was a kid, after my physio appointments."

I am still staring and not responding, and he continues talking—rambling, actually—I think out of nervousness and maybe feeling uncomfortable under my bewildered stare.

"There was a point in time when he tried to be a dad to me, you know... He wasn't all bad when I think about it... I broke my leg pretty bad and did years of physio to be able to walk properly. Anyway, the place is special to me. It reminds me of my dad before he stopped being a dad. The late Mr. Williams. He was an asshole, but ever since he died, I find myself trying to remember the good in him if there ever was any. Will you let me take you there?" Leo is looking concerned and genuinely trying to get me to cheer up, not his usual hitting-on-me style.

"Your last name is Williams?" is all I can say in my stupor.

"No, no, my parents never married, but I am named after him: David. Leo's my nickname, after my zodiac sign, born in August, you know? Happy birthday to me..." He hums the birthday tune nervously under my stare.

"Huh," I say and finally manage a smile, which eases Leo, or David.

"So, how about that dinner," he asks more confidently now that he's shared something personal and private and sensitive.

I think he realizes that's what keeps me interested and not his flirting. But he doesn't realize what he is actually telling me: that he is the one I've been looking for. I make eye contact with him. He has beautiful hazel eyes just like Marc. I'll know when I know...

"I'd love to," I respond as Polly returns with my Coke.

A winner at the right time, when you least expect it.

CHAPTER 43

Leo takes me back to his place first to "freshen up," as he had said politely. He offers to wash my clothes and the contents of my knapsack while I shower. The drive was pretty silent other than me apologizing for missing his party last night. Leo (or David) was quiet the whole drive. I just stared at him, wondering how I hadn't seen it before. Initially, I was also curious if maybe the David I seek was his father, and not him. But when I think about it, I mean really think about it, Leo feels right. When he touched me that first time, hugging me when I thanked him for finding my pager, when our noses grazed, when my lips brushed his earlobe that drunken night he dragged me out of his pool... Leo is my soulmate. Leo is Marc. I can feel it in my own soul.

I put on the undershirt and jogging pants that Leo left me while we wait for my clothes to dry. I take my time, inhaling the smell of his shirt as I pull it over my head. I'm not wearing a bra, and I find myself hoping he'll notice.

"Hey," he says as I approach him, and by the way he looks at me, I can tell he notices how the material falls on me.

I sit right next to him on his couch, almost touching him. I'm looking to feel what I should be feeling, making sure I'm not crazy. After all, I had missed him right in front of me from the moment we arrived. Leo was in my face that whole time. At the funeral, every time I was at the casino. And he is drawn to me, too. He said so in not so many words that night we almost kissed.

"This was in your backpack. I didn't think you wanted it washed."

It's my syringe. He has it in his hand. My pulse quickens. I should take it and stab him with it. I should. That's why I'm here, isn't it?

"Thanks," I say as I take it from him and place it in the pocket of the jogging pants I'm wearing. *Not yet,* I tell myself. I don't actually know if I can do this, go through with any of what I have planned. I don't know yet.

"I'd rather stay in—can we just order something?" I suggest.

Leo is only too relieved that I'm leading the conversation to slice the tension. I feel unspoken apprehension between us and I sense he does too. It's electrifying, actually. I can hardly take my eyes off his... Marc's eyes... Leo's eyes. I can't look away.

He keeps swallowing awkwardly. I'm making him very nervous, I can tell.

"Do you still want seafood?" Leo gets up. "...'Cause that place delivers, the place my dad used to take me to..." His voice trails off as he walks toward the kitchen.

I hear him rummaging through cupboards and drawers before he finally finds what he wanted and returns with a flyer in hand, standing in front of me.

"No one knows that about me," he confesses, but to what I'm not sure. I raise an eyebrow at him, waiting for him to elaborate. "About my dad. I don't talk about him to anyone. Those people at the funeral, other than my grandmother—I didn't know any of them. Which is probably why I couldn't keep my eyes off you."

He hands me the flyer, and I quickly choose something, not really hungry or caring if I eat, even though I've lived off chips and chocolate bars for three long days.

"I have daddy issues too," I tell him. I might as well tell someone. "My dad committed suicide. I found him dangling from the rope myself. He didn't leave a note. And I didn't recognize anyone at his funeral because no one was at his funeral except for a few gambling acquaintances if you can even call them that. It was difficult to deal with what he did, the way he left me and my brother with no explanation. That was only three years ago, and since then, I've pushed everyone away from me."

"Is that why you're so attached to that watch?" He nods at my wrist.

"It fell off his wrist when I tried to reach for him. When it hit the ground, I thought I heard it break. But it didn't break. The sound I heard was actually my dad's neck snapping. You know what gets me? If I had just gotten home a minute earlier, I would've saved him, and a minute later and I wouldn't have watched him die."

I touch my wrist now. It brings me comfort. I almost cry. I almost let Leo all the way in. Tell him everything about Marc, Jordan, why I'm here. I want to tell him to run away from me. That I'm here to harm him. I want to tell him I'm sorry I'm still considering it. Or am I? Maybe I'm just indulging in having Marc's soul beside me. As if talking to Leo is like talking to Marc, but a version of Marc who doesn't know me completely. And since I will leave Leo behind (or kill him), what's the harm in sharing?

Over the next few hours, I let Leo wine and dine me. I let him look at me in a way only Marc ever has. I don't push him away when he comes in for a hug. I don't let him kiss me, though, afraid of the irreversible guilt a kiss will bring.

I tell him I have no place to go. He tells me I'm home and I don't have to leave. I feel at home. I feel like I belong here, to him. It's tempting to forget my life and start fresh. If it weren't for the messages that are probably waiting for me on that pager from a family I am letting down, I might just do that. Stay with Leo. Instead, I decide to enjoy his company for the three days before the last shuttle home. I'll allow myself to feel his kindness before I leave him or kill him. That's it. That's all I will do. I can't get attached. I have people counting on me.

We talk for hours upon hours, well into the night. I find out more about his past. Apparently, his grandmother fled Nazi

Germany during the Second World War, marrying his American grandfather. They couldn't have children, so they adopted David Williams Sr. It's interesting, that he believes that story. I actually wonder how much of it is true. Because if it is, this old woman has been around a long time indeed.

Leo tells me how David Williams Sr. impregnated his mother, a stripper with a habit who later died of said habit, leaving Leo to be raised by his busy, detached father until Grandma stepped in. Leo also tells me her name. It's a name I will never forget.

Adalia Messie.

Not entirely German, if you ask me.

CHAPTER 44

When I'm sure Leo is asleep, I find his phone and dial the pager number from memory. I need to know if Jordan is still alive before I make the decision to hurt Leo—a decision that may result in Marc's death. I won't hurt them for nothing.

I listen to messages from Charlie begging me to come home. From Marc, telling me how much he loves me, so much. He misses me. How he'll be waiting for me when I come off that plane no matter what. I miss him too. I hope he'll be waiting for me.

None of the messages are about Jordan dying. So I leave a message of my own. I whisper into the phone. "I found what Jordan needs. I found your past life. I will be home in three days. Please don't do anything until I get back." I hesitate, thinking about what to say next. "Marc, please forgive me. What I'm doing, it's for Jordan. I hope you understand. Please, be there when I get back. I need you to be there." I hang up. *I love you, Marc, please don't die*, I mutter into the dial tone.

I retrieve the small syringe from Leo's jogging pant pocket. This small tube will save my son. I weep until I fall asleep, with the syringe tight in my grip.

CHAPTER 45

We walk along the path and chat. Leo brought me to the Grand Canyon to walk off the big brunch he cooked for me when I finally gave up on the idea of sleeping sometime around noon. He failed to mention it was such a long drive. And when we arrived, we had a wine and cheese picnic, right up by the edge with beautiful views. He failed to mention the pre-packed picnic, too. He is trying his best to be romantic and sweet. I think my quietness is making him nervous.

A reddish moon peeks out from the clouds, highlighting the curvy path along the Canyon. We're walking where we shouldn't be, breaking the rules. But I've never been here, and he wants to take me right to where the best views can be had. He walks on the cliff side like the gentleman he is. And I'm glad for it. I'm not drunk, having had only a small glass of wine, but I'm dizzy and borderline delirious from lack of sleep. I cried the whole night. I barely slept. And in the car I dozed but tried to stay awake, not wanting to miss the sound of Leo's voice. I want to embed it into my head, commit it to memory. I don't ever want to forget Leo.

Leo chats endlessly about what his company is working on here at the Canyon, sometimes stopping to point at things of interest, animated and proud. I'm not as chatty. My mind is occupied, and I can't even hide it. I nod occasionally to feign interest while I muster up the courage to do what I have to do. All this time, all the sacrifices, all of it was leading up to this. In two days, I must catch that shuttle. In two days, I need to inject Leo with the syringe. I will have to kill Leo. But I'm frozen with fear inside; I'm afraid of what will happen if I go through with it and equally afraid of what will happen if I don't. Either way, I don't want to forget Leo. Whether I go through with it or not. I want to remember Marc's past life, and carry Leo in my heart and soul for all my lives to come.

I've already weighed the pros and cons of being a hero or giving up, but deciding who will die isn't like choosing a link-car colour or decor for your container home. Does Jordan die? Or will Leo, then Marc? If I do nothing, Mother Nature will cruelly take her course and take my son's life. Fate will play out like it's supposed to, without interference from me. But Jordan will die, and I still can't get that image out of my head, of the adult Jordan telling me to let him. If I go through with the plan, I will be a murderer, not only of Leo or David, but maybe of Marc, my soulmate, who is waiting for me. They will both die. Well, Marc might make it... *might,* if Dr. Messie's cocktail is what the old woman Adalia says the doctor hopes it is.

The talking has paused—ceased, actually—and I sense it's my turn to say something. I think Leo has asked me a question, but I have no idea what it was.

"Huh?" I ask and look over at him to find that he has stopped walking and his expression is serious; not the usual fun guy. Serious, curious, concerned.

"You didn't hear a word I said."

I don't reply, which is an affirmation of his observation.

"Grace." I love how my name sounds when he speaks it. I memorize it. "Whatever is on your mind, whatever you are thinking, whatever decision you're conflicted with, you can tell me. I want to help you. You can trust me."

And I really want to.

I look at him. I mean really look at him. This sweet, kind man. What am I supposed to say? I let out a sarcastic laugh. "You can't help me, Leo. No one can help me."

"Is there someone else in the picture?" he asks gently, his face showing a pang of jealousy. "If so, he's not right for you. I saw that bruise on your leg."

Confused, I look down at my leg and realize what he's talking about. The bruise from when I banged my way out of the glass room, on the way here, is still fading. My thigh took quite the beating. And Leo is concerned that someone hurt me.

It always feels good to tell him things. And I'm not sure if it's his concern for me, or the hurt on his face when he thinks of me with someone else or even my lack of sleep. Perhaps even the feeling of wanting to unburden my sins on someone who won't know me anymore makes me tell him things. If I tell him, he'll leave me alone. I'm so stupid.

"Leo, I tricked you into falling for me so I could kill you and take your soul. Oh, and by the way, I think I fell for you, too. And... I'm sort of struggling with the decision of killing you or letting my son die."

"What the hell are you talking about?" He is staring at me as if I am utterly insane, which I feel as though I am, and the air around us is suddenly tense when a moment ago it was easy, almost romantic. His shoulders are stiff and square. He's looking at me, into me, like he is seeing me for the first time and doesn't know who I am.

"Hello-o? Do you want to tell me what the hell is going on here? What are you ranting about?"

I don't like distraught Leo. I like romantic, flirty Leo; cute do-anything-for-ya Leo. Disbelief is thick in his voice, accusing me, and I'm shocked at myself that I blurted that out and I wonder if should keep going and just say everything. If he thinks I'm crazy, he may leave me alone.

Here goes... I repeat myself, but this time deliberately, and not as harshly, I come clean. I confess. I tell him everything.

"I'm not a showgirl trying to make it in Vegas. I know this sounds crazy, but I've actually come here from another time. You're my son's father—or at least you will be, in another eighty years or so when your soul is reincarnated. We're soulmates. We find each other in every life."

I'm expecting him to burst out laughing, call me crazy, back away from me slowly. Maybe he'll stay clear from the casino for a bit and lock his doors, buy blinds and keep them closed to avoid the crazy girl, not answer his phone.

But he does nothing. His expression hasn't budged one bit. Neither of us speaks for what feels like hours but is more likely a minute or two.

I shift my weight from one foot to the other, feeling heavy on my feet with anticipation of what comes next. An uncomfortable amount of time passes by, and I feel my heart pulsating in my ear. The silence is killing me.

"Say something," I whisper. "Please." Even less than a whisper.

I feel my face heat up, and tears begin to well in my eyes, and I bite my lip hard to try to hold them back, prevent my emotions from getting in the way of the decision I have to make. I obviously haven't made a decision to flee home or hurt Leo, and for the first time, I admit it to myself. I don't know if I can go through with this. I don't know if I possess this fatal flaw that Kay thinks I do.

I half-sob, "I'm so sorry, Leo," and at that, he finally breaks his silence.

"What you're saying is crazy, insane, not possible."

"I know," I reply.

"And you're not insane or crazy."

"Right."

"So why are you saying these things? Is that your easy way out? You finally agree to get to know me, we're getting along, I trust you with things about me I've told no one, and I thought you did the same. I, I ..." His voice is steady but not calm. "I fall in love with you," the word "love" stings my chest, "and you're breaking up with me by pretending to be nuts?"

His voice is no longer steady; it cracks as he accuses me of breaking up with him and I feel like I've been punched in the stomach. I didn't realize we were even together to break up, but I don't voice that. And I'm equally shocked at his confession of loving me and confused.

"What is wrong with you?" It's funny that he chooses the same words as Kay. "Why are you doing this? Why are you pushing me away? Is it your dad?" It's funny that he uses the same words as Marc. "What are you afraid of, loving me?"

He pauses and waits for me to respond, but I don't.

"Is that it?" My silence must be a response in itself for him, and he softens his tone. "You do love me, don't you?"

Tears spill out over my lower lids, and I don't try to stop them anymore. I don't hold anything back, or try to hide who I am anymore.

"Yes, Leo. That's what I'm afraid of." And I'm being completely truthful. No more lies. "I love you now. I will love you in the future. I have loved you in all my past lives and will love you in all my future lives. We're destined to be together and to lose each other over and over and over because I'm so stupid and scared and selfish..."

"No." He steps into me and takes my trembling hand, reaches for my face and pulls me to him and I'm afraid.

I reach my hand up to his chest to stop him from coming too close, but he's pulling me in, and I'm afraid I won't do it, that I don't have it in me to hurt him. Or am I afraid that I will and that I am perfectly capable of hurting him? I can't—I can't kill him, I'm in love with him, Marc, Leo.

He pulls me right into him, my feet shuffle toward him at the imbalance. Again I resist, grabbing fistfuls of his shirt and pushing at his chest, and when he doesn't give up and let me go, when he whispers my name and that he loves me, I realize he's won me over and I melt. We're so close his breath is on my lips—the scent of jostaberries subdues me—and he kisses me. His lips are soft and intoxicating and worst of all, they tell me everything I need to know. Any lingering doubts about whether or not he is Marc vanish with each touch of our tongues. The kiss is so passionate I can't stand a second more. And with this kiss from my soulmate, my decision is made.

My hand stills over his beating heart.

"You love me," he hushes at me, and I cry harder and return his kiss harder. He pulls my hips in closer. Our foreheads are touching, our eyes locked. "You don't have to be afraid—if your crazy logic is real, we'll see each other in all our future lives. You and I, we're soulmates."

"I know." I sob as I stab the syringe into his soft neck and hear it open and dispense its pink liquid into the donor that is Leo.

"That's exactly my point." I sob harder as I bring my knee up hard between his legs and pull my other hand free and shove him in the chest as hard as I can.

I see the surprise in his eyes, which I try not to look at, and before I lose my nerve, I go hard at him and shove him toward the edge that he is already so close to.

He doesn't react at first, and I take full advantage of his shock and kick and punch at him. I lose my balance and fall on my rear. On my back, I use my feet to push him. Strangled animal sounds are coming out of me. "I'm sorry, I'm sorry," I'm cry-yelling.

He comes out of his confused state to defend himself, but he's too close to the edge when he begins to rise, and I give him one final shove with both my feet, which makes him stumble and he falls.

Right over the edge.

I collapse in the dirt, screaming so hard my throat is burning, my eye sockets might explode, the vein in my head feels like it's on the verge of bursting. I'm shaking, screeching like an animal being tortured. I don't look over the edge, I can't bring myself to, but to my horror, I hear him calling for me. I hear my name. It's like hearing my dad saying my name before he died, only worse because I didn't kill my dad.

I cannot save Leo. I can't—I made my decision. I chose Jordan. I chose: "Jordan! Jordan! Jordan!" I'm yelling his name to convince myself that taking Mother Nature's job into my own hands was righteous. A mother's job is to protect her children.

I don't know why exactly, but I drag myself over to the edge. Perhaps because I love Marc and won't be there when he dies—if he dies; there is still a chance—but I can be here when his past life, Leo, dies at my hands. If Marc goes through code 33, maybe he'd be at peace knowing why I did it. I don't have to let Leo die alone. I love him too.

Leo is clinging to the edge but slipping. Seeing him gives me a sudden change of mind, and I reach for him even though I'm too far to do anything. "I'm sorry," I cry again. "I didn't want to do this, I had no choice, I'm sorry."

But when I look at him, when I look into his hazel eyes, which I can hardly see, he seems calm, peaceful. I don't know if it's just the light of the moon or if it's my perception. What's even stranger is that he is not pleading. He's not even reaching for my outstretched hand. And his calm quiets me, silences my tears. Every version of Leo or Marc calms me now, today, in the future, forever.

"Rachel, I want you to know that I've loved you all along," he says, and before I can respond, before I can ask him who Rachel is, before what he says sinks in, he releases his hold on the ledge.

Never breaking eye contact with me, not even to blink, he falls back, with his arms outstretched. He doesn't yell, scream or squirm. He just falls into the black hole beneath him and the night darkness eats him up. He's gone.

And I'm confused.

CHAPTER 46

I gather myself as best I can. My legs are the consistency of jelly. My emotions are numb. I reach our picnic spot, the hood of Leo's car, and polish off the last of the wine. Jostaberry. I commit the taste of Leo to memory, savouring the last drop, running my fingers over my lips, which ache for his. I take the car keys and his phone from the hood, and I get in on the driver's side. I breathe in the leather. I commit the smell to memory. The drink tray holds the cork from the wine bottle. "I'm sorry," I say to his memory.

Time to go home.

I need to make my way to the place in the desert where that shuttle will leave. Someone will be there. At the same time every morning at sunrise until the last shuttle. And I'm two days early.

I drive like a maniac, breaking speed limits while checking my rear-view for State Troopers. Part of me wants to get caught, punished like the criminal I am. Is being a Hamartia a crime? I think so.

During the drive, I use Leo's car phone to make a call. I dial the pager and check for messages. Nothing. No response at all.

I leave Marc a message.

"Marc. I'm on my way home. And I'm sorry. I'm sorry for everything. I love you. I love you. And if you're not there when

I get back, I will never be able to live with myself. I need you to be there. Please... just be there, OK?"

Sadly, I make it to the place in the desert on time, without interruptions or interference. No sirens behind me. No one to arrest me for murder.

The sun isn't up yet, but I see the small shuttle that will take me to the plane. I'm not allowed to bring anything back with me. "It may contaminate the future," is what they said in the orientation. Bullshit. I tuck the cork from the wine bottle into my pocket before abandoning everything else in Leo's car.

I don't look back.

CHAPTER 47

I can't breathe. The anxiety forces the air out of my lungs in short breaths that I can't seem to catch. I've been gone nearly three long weeks. I miss Marc immensely; I can't contain it. I have no bags, nothing to declare. It's not like I'm carrying a box labelled "Jordan's soul repair kit." But I still have to wait my turn behind normal people coming back from normal trips. This is an airport, and I still shake my head at how they mix me with regular guests, just like on our way to Vegas.

The journey back to my decade was much like the journey to Vegas, except instead of crawling through the roof of an airplane to get to a glass room, there was a small jet waiting in the desert. The pilot, wearing a white suit, handed me a glass with fog rising from the murky liquid it contained. I took it without saying a word and chugged. I didn't ask him who he was and he didn't offer to tell me. He said nothing. Absolutely nothing. He just pointed me to the back, where I saw the familiar glass room. We were airborne in minutes. It was a turbulent take-off. When the glass shattered away from my feet, and the wind sucked me out of the plane, I was terrified. Only instead of fear of hitting the ground and dying, I feared getting back and finding Jordan dead, or Marc missing, or both. And then, Kay would out me to the world, and I'd be euthanized for my crimes.

I arrived at the airport like a regular passenger, greeted by Dr. Messie's people, congratulating me on my safe return. Like a hero, not a villain. Now, just on the other side, I hear the flashing of holograms being taken, the chattering of excited fans and critics eager to meet me. They are probably hoping the clone was a success. So am I. I hope Marc is on the other side.

"Passport?"

"Huh?" I move to keep up with the line shuffling forward.

"Next."

Now I can see the doors open and close. Each time they open, the jabbering dies down, people shush each other. Holograms flash, capturing the anticipation of my arrival. When Charlie said the media was crazy over the story, I never pictured this. They're treating me like a celebrity.

They don't know what I've done.

I slide my hand over the counter to scan my fingerprint, revealing my passport-a-gram to the customs agent. I nod "yes" and "no" where appropriate, adjust my watch, feel for the wine-bottle cork I'm smuggling back. I straighten up, take a deep breath and prepare to walk through those doors.

I'm nervous, anxious, a mixed bag of emotions, and a wave of nausea passes through me. I hold my breath and walk up to the doors; sensing my presence, they open before me. The crowd hushes down again but this time, I walk through the threshold, and it's not a false alarm.

Right away reporters start shouting questions, microphones dangling in my face. I hear more flashes. My image projects in the air, live holograms. I see people as far as the room is deep, but I don't see him.

I don't see Marc.

Where is he? Did he come? Did he make it? Have I destroyed him?

For a few moments, I am still, I'm not moving from the doors, and they are partially closing and reopening when I don't move away from the sensors. I scan the faces in the crowd, slowly at first, pausing at each face. I don't want to miss seeing him.

I'm trying to remain calm, but he'd be calling out for me, wouldn't he? He'd be right here, right now, right at the front, no? That was what he said in his message. I'm quickening my scanning as the panic rises inside me at the realization that he might not be here. I sacrificed him, didn't I? This was a risk I took to save our son.

I'm paralyzed with fear, worry, and regret. But I did what I had to. Marc will understand. *Come on!* Where *is* he?

Oh no, that's it, I've done it, I've really done it. He's gone. My palms sweat, my stomach aches, I'd cry if I wasn't about to faint or throw up or scream or rip my hair out.

I'm trying to call out his name "Mar, Mar... *Marc!*" I've found my voice. His name was stuck in my throat in the form of a bitter lump, and now I'm calling out his name. *"Marc! Maaarc!"* I start yelling it. I'm nervously pulling at my earlobe, grabbing at the back of my neck, and now I'm screeching *"Marc!* Marc Marc!" I'm no longer scanning faces. The microphones are still in my face, crowding me, but I don't hear any sound.

Am I losing my mind or is the crowd quieting for me? I don't know. I suddenly gain feeling in my legs and try to move forward but these people, these people just won't get out of my way—why are they here, in my face, in my way. I can't breathe!

Any intentions of calmly walking out and finding Marc, my soulmate, waiting to whisk me away are gone, and I'm frantic. I'm crying and yelling—not even yelling his name, just yelling at the injustice, the unfairness. Selfish Dr. Messie's family who sacrificed someone's future for immediate gratification and interfered with past lives in the first place. I'm crouching down, wanting to just shrink away and disappear.

He's not here, I can't believe this, he's not here.

He is gone.

I killed Marc.

I'll see him in my next life like I did in my past lives. We're destined to be together and destined to be ripped apart by the same reasons we're together.

I need to move. I need to get up. There are too many people around me, but they are quiet now. I am quieting down as well, and I steady myself on the railing. I have to get up. I have to finish what I've started. I need to go to our son.

With my eyes closed, I will myself to breathe slow and stop the insanity for a moment. The crowd now completely drowned out, I hear only the holograms capturing my image, and I feel like I'm in a trance or something. The world seems to be shifting around me. I feel the crowd moving, the air suddenly easier to take in. The crowd is moving away from me, and I open my eyes as I hear yelling. It's not me; I'm not yelling anymore.

"I'm here! I'm here!"

The crowd is indeed moving, actually splitting and parting like the Red Sea, and then I see him. Holy shit, I *see* him!

"I'm here! Right here!" And he's shoving the few people out of the path, and I come to as if awakening at last from a daydream, like my ears have popped and I am now fully present. My heart is racing.

"Marc!" I yell. I have got to get through this crowd. "Marc!" Get the hell out of my way... He's fifty feet away, twenty...

Dodging and shoving people, not breaking eye contact with me now that he has it.

"I'm here, right here!" he yells.

"Marc!"

Ten feet...

...five...

I grab the railing and awkwardly try to monkey-bar over it as best I can. I feel people help me keep my balance and I half-leap, half-fall over the railing. He's right under the stairs now, and I just about throw myself over the barrier and land clumsily in his embrace.

"Marc..."

"Yes, I'm here." And he feels good.

I'm dead weight in his arms, and I let my knees weaken as I begin to weep. He holds me up, and I'm wailing and mumbling his name between sobs and tears of relief and joy. He's got me so tight, and I love it. I bury myself in his arms and neck, and I inhale his scent, and I release myself and cry out all the pressure, the pain, the suffering: it's pouring out, and he's here. The anxiety of not knowing, of choosing who will live and die, just bursts out of me in the form of weeping.

I don't let go, but he pries me from my death grip to look me in the eye. He grabs my face in his hands and makes me look at him, puts his forehead to mine firmly. I stare deep into those hazel eyes. Leo, Marc. When we lock eyes, I swear that he stares into my very soul and whispers, precisely articulating each word, "You are my queen…"

CHAPTER 48

I gasp when I see Jordan. He is so thin and pale. Mid-afternoon sunlight streaming in from the window doesn't seem to bother him. Even from where we stand, I can see his eyes are wide open. He isn't squinting as one normally would in response to the bright sun. A white sheet over his small body shows the outline of his slender frame. His bare arms are tucked at his side on the outside of the blanket. They made Marc and I dress in gowns and scrub before we entered, but it seems like I won't be able to touch my son or kiss his cheek, as he is protected from contamination by a transparent plastic tent. His chest rises and drops slowly under the sheet with each laboured breath he takes. They seem to be minutes apart, and when he finally does take a breath, it's not a wheeze, or as if he is fighting for air. It's a little breath, shallow and quick, and it escapes through his little lips as soon as it's drawn in.

Marc places his hand on my back, nudging me forward, but I'm frozen in place. I want to go to Jordan but am afraid. This is not the same room as before, with Walt and the other boys. This is a pre-surgery room. There are dozens of beds lined up like an orphanage, but no patient occupies them. Jordan is the only one to have his soul repaired ever. But the facilities have been ready and waiting. It's so presumptuous of Dr. Messie to have gone through the trouble to build a whole wing in his clinic for those waiting for surgery, based on a medical trial that wasn't even approved. Although that angers me, I am also grateful for the privacy the big, empty space allows me to see my son, even if I can't touch him.

Marc nudges again and finally whispers, "Go on."

It's the first thing he has said to me since our embrace at the airport. Right after our short reunion, we were whisked off to the clinic. We had a five-link-car police escort followed by media link-vans. All the linkways were closed, and only we were permitted to mount them. Marc must've been as overwhelmed as I was, all this attention, all of this for one child. I just stared out the window, squeezing Marc's hand while I watched this new, ambitious world outside my window. Crowds of people stood on every corner, waved at us, cheered. Young children held up handmade posters: "Save Jordan—save the world!" These people were eagerly awaiting my arrival, and now they wait to see if Jordan lives. If he does, they can save their own sons, daughters and loved ones. And here I am, unable to move in his direction, to go to my son, the first who will be saved.

With a deep sigh, I unglue my feet from the floor and make my way to Jordan's bedside. My legs feel as heavy as two cement blocks, but my head is as light as a feather. I reach his bedside and extend my hand to touch the plastic tent and let him know I'm back, as promised.

"Ma'am, I'm afraid you mustn't do that."

I hear an unfamiliar voice and jerk my hand back, look around the room for the intruder. I thought Marc and I were alone. There is a nurse standing in the far corner, near a glass wall. I feel exposed, knowing what that glass wall insinuates. There are probably people on the other side, watching us. I look to Marc, but he has no expression.

"I just want to touch him," I say meekly, on the verge of tears.

"I'm sorry, ma'am. But that's impossible." She sounds so robotic.

"Please," I say, and to my surprise, she walks right over to Jordan's bedside and starts unplugging things, unlocking the bed wheels.

"The doctor is ready. We must bring him now," she says firmly.

"No, no, wait! Please!" I beg. I haven't had a chance to say hello, or tell him he's going to be OK, or anything at all. He doesn't even know I kept my promise and came back for him.

The nurse pauses. Her face softens. She touches my shoulder. "It is a miracle he has hung on as long as he has, waiting for you. If we don't get the cloned soul implanted right away to repair his, he will die."

I look over at Marc, who still remains expressionless. He is probably used to seeing Jordan in this state, but I am not. So nurse or no nurse, glass wall or not, I am going to talk to Jordan.

"Jordan, honey, Mommy's back. Do you hear me?"

Jordan doesn't flinch. His eyes are vacant, not even blinking.

"You're going to be OK. We found a cure. You hang on just a few more minutes..."

The nurse is wheeling him away, and I jog beside his bed, out the room, toward the doors at the end of the long, empty corridor, where a team of people dressed in white wait for his arrival. Dr. Messie is standing at the front of them.

"Jordan, I love you! Don't you die on me, OK? You fight!"

I know he is going to make it because I met him in Las Vegas, yet I still fear that this is the last time I will see him. What if adult Jordan or Adalia found other ways to stop me that I don't yet know about? I grab at the plastic tent but miss as Marc grabs me around my waist, pulling me back, allowing the nurse to pass freely.

"Jordan, I came back for you! Just for you—I know you're going to make it!"

They say that before you die, your whole life flashes before your eyes. But what they don't tell you is that before a child dies, that child's life flashes before his mother's helpless eyes.

A million things run through my head. The feeling of him in my belly, kicking, and the excitement that used to bring me of waiting to meet him. Me humming to him as a baby when he cried in my arms, which now ache to hold him one more time. Jordan as a toddler, rolling around on the ground with Lucy, giggling while she licked his face. The sound of my boy's laughter echoes in my head. Pictures of him and I lying on the roof of our container, watching the stars, when he was starting school. I hear his voice asking me questions about what's out there. I smell his hair when he came home from playing outdoors just a few months ago. It was typical boy-smelling hair as he rushed past me to the tray of brownies on the counter. Brownies are his favourite.

I close my eyes and cry out as the door at the end of the hallway closes. Marc holds me from behind. My knees buckle, and he has to hold me up. In my head, I see adult Jordan asking me to let him die. I feel his lips graze my cheek as he kisses me goodbye. I touch my cheek now to preserve that feeling. I hear him tell me he loves me and see his back turned to me as he walks away. I pray that is not the last time I see my adult son. I should've talked to him, about normal regular stuff. I should've asked him about his life, did he have a girlfriend? Where did he live? What did he like to do?

"He will make it," Marc says confidently as he steadies me and guides me in the other direction toward the waiting room. He seems so sure; he is not at all distraught, like me. I am the one who should know Jordan will make it—I met the adult version of our son. Why is Marc so sure and at ease?

We head back to the waiting room, which is empty of people, but full of white leather and chrome chairs, glass walls. No one is waiting because no one else is having this surgery. We are making history. I sit down in one of the chairs, my head between my hands, my elbows resting on my knees. Marc doesn't join me. He stares through the glass wall at the room next to us, the room where Jordan was just moments ago.

"I came as soon as I could."

I look up to see Charlie walking into the room. What a sight for sore eyes. My brother greets me with open arms. We hug, and I cry into his chest.

From the corner of my eye, I see Marc watching us, emotionless. Poor Marc—he must've gone through hell in my absence.

CHAPTER 49

"I've missed you so much," I tell Marc as I lie on his warm chest, his heartbeat soothing me. Although weeks have passed since we've been reunited, between Jordan's rehabilitation at the clinic, where he still lives, and the interviews with the press, we haven't had any alone time. We haven't even shared a meal together yet—not one dinner.

"I can't believe it's over," I lie. "I still can't believe that Jordan is going to be OK." More lying, as my guilty mind replays adult Jordan telling me he is dead anyway.

That conversation with Jordan troubles me. Not just that I disobeyed him telling me to let him die, but him speaking about me in the past tense and insinuating Marc will also die. I don't have a plan to ensure his safety in the future, other than not letting Jordan work for Dr. Messie as he said he would. That will keep Jordan safe. But keeping Jordan safe won't stop what's coming anyway. The holocaust Jordan spoke of. We're all doomed.

It's already started. People are lining up by the thousands to profile their past lives. All the while, I'm standing back and watching Dr. Messie gain more and more popularity and support, knowing full well what the outcome will be, and I'm doing nothing to stop it. Dr. Messie has a whole clan of followers and guards surrounding him, making it hard to approach him, much less confront him. He is never alone.

What can I do about it? I can't tell anyone. I'll risk all of our lives if I try to uncover his scandal. He is too powerful. I haven't had the courage to tell Marc anything at all about what I did to get here today. I haven't told him about Jordan interfering, so how can I tell him why he interfered without telling him he did? I especially haven't told him that I almost killed him.

I miss Kay. I need to talk to her, but she won't talk to me. She hasn't returned my calls. I've shown up at the casino where she works, but she won't see me. She's probably not sure about me. I guess she's figured out that I found David and killed him, seeing as Jordan is alive and well. She's probably relieved that Marc survived, but not enough to let me off the hook for taking the risk. She also hasn't outed me, which I'm relieved about. I suppose "what happens in Vegas, stays in Vegas" is ringing true so far.

"We should celebrate," Marc interrupts my thoughts. "Go out for a special night, just you and me."

"Where?" I ask.

"You pick."

I smile at the thought that a few weeks ago, him being indecisive was what I hated about him, but today I love how he puts me first. His simple act of asking me to choose is about making me happy, not about him being indecisive.

"How about our favourite restaurant, where you proposed to me?" I suggest.

"Of course, yes."

"Do you remember that night?" I ask, reminiscing. "I was so sick, and poor you, determined to propose anyway. I tried so hard to hold it in, but I couldn't. And just as you finished popping the question, I ducked under the table to puke. I didn't even make it to the bathroom. You just held my hair and asked if that was a yes or a no."

Marc laughs robustly like he is hearing the story for the first time. "Well, it obviously wasn't a no," he replies.

"Damn, Marc, you were always so good to me. I really love you." I prop myself up on my elbow so I can look at him. "I can't believe I am lucky enough to be your wife. Thank you for holding my hair."

He kisses me in reply, his lips soft and warm. "I love you too, my queen," he replies.

He's been addressing me by that new term of endearment since my return. I like how it sounds. I love how he looks me in my eyes as if seeing right into my soul each time he calls me his queen.

I rest on his chest again. Neither of us speaks anymore. Although I feel guilty for almost killing this man, my soulmate, I am more than relieved that the prophecy the old woman laid out for him was not to be. That Marc survived is a miracle. The guilt I feel is still very real, though. It doesn't matter that no harm came to him. I still have time to figure out how to stop Dr. Messie, but that I had it in me to risk Marc's life sickens me. Not like the night he proposed, but like a fatal character flaw that I possess. "Hamartia."

I tickle my fingers on Marc's chest, his skin producing nervous bumps under my touch. I feel his heartbeat quicken under my cheek, and he doesn't move. I let him lie still as I plant small kisses on his chest and work my way down. The pace of his breath picks up. I fumble with his pant buttons; he doesn't help.

I like the control.

I work my way down, preparing to take him in my mouth. Three quick beats later and his resistance to touch me fails all at once, like he's an addict and I'm his drug. He pulls me back up, desperately, by my hair. Holding the side of my face and back of my neck, he turns his body into mine and kisses me hard before he flips me onto my back.

He's in control now.

My body has been craving this, craving and missing him. I pour my guilt into every kiss. We kiss harder, quicker.

Taking my clothes off is like an emergency—we can't get them off fast enough, and so we don't bother. He manages to open the top buttons of my blouse, shoves my bra under my breasts, and his thumb touches the tip of my nipple, making it hard. Urgently his mouth moves down my neck, tonguing my breast. My back arches in response.

He moves down. I'm overcome by emotions, guilt, lust, sex. He is rough and passionate as he hikes my skirt up and his hand finds the wet between my legs. He strokes me. Our lips meet again, eyes open. It's like he's looking right into my soul, with his eyes gazing into mine.

He doesn't bother removing his pants, just lowers them so I can grip his cheeks with my heels as he enters me roughly. We rock, not slowly, but furiously, urgently, never breaking eye contact. I cry out as he grunts and moans. Our souls meet on another level as we surge together, ripples running through my body in time with his rhythm. I feel his manhood pulsating inside me. He collapses on me, his breathing laboured, his body limp, his face in the pillow, exhaustedly panting next to my ear.

My emotions get the better of me, and I'm overcome by tears of joy, relief, tears of guilt and longing. I'm surprised to hear his breath catch, and he sobs too. His body is heavy on mine as he trembles. I squeeze him with my arms and legs as hard as I can to show him I understand, and maybe to silently apologize for almost divorcing him, for being a miserable wife, for almost murdering him. He recovers, pulls himself back to look at me, nose to nose, his eyes wet.

"I am so, so sorry," we both say it, simultaneously.

I'm apologizing for being a bad wife. What is he so sorry about?

We dress in silence for our dinner date. I was grateful for the uninterrupted shower so I could cry and think. Marc seemed to welcome my silence. Something isn't sitting right with me. A worry creeps up, but I shove it away. I can't address my insecurities right now. I have bigger problems; mankind has bigger problems. I can't address that aching feeling that Marc might be having regrets. He doesn't seem like himself. I can't address that he seems like a different Marc right now.

His apology is bothering me.

CHAPTER 50

We're alone enough to speak freely, but it's awkward being solely with Marc. This will be our first meal together, and it will be a good start. It's also symbolic that we're going to our restaurant, where he proposed.

He is unusually quiet as we walk along Yonge Street toward the old, historic tower with the rotating restaurant at the top, where we will celebrate our reunion. I wonder when it stopped looking like the replica at the Canadiana hotel in Vegas, shiny and new.

I think we're both making an effort not to talk about the drama. Not to talk about Jordan being the first success story of soul cloning, and the unintended consequence of that, putting our family in the media's centre of attention. Marc has avoided all the media, quite well, actually. No one wants to talk to him, they want to talk to me, and Marc usually stands content in the background.

The news can't get enough of Dr. Messie. He gives interview after interview in press-release forums, with his team of experts in matching white outfits behind him. He seems really comfortable in front of the limelight. He is usually the only speaker. A younger version of that old woman stands at his side, his assistant with no name, Adalia. It makes me sick, knowing the kind of man he really is. When I see the old woman in her youth, I wonder if she already knows too—has Adalia figured him out yet?

The media are on high alert, anticipating Jordan's recovery so that they can talk to him, the nine-year-old boy miracle. If only they knew the miracle was that Marc isn't dead. Every newscast offers updates on the first person to undergo a successfully cloned soul repair. All the holograms around town, previously plastered with Dr. Messie's face, now bear the face of our son, smiling and alert. His eyes are red-rimmed from being asleep for so long, his cheeks gaunt from the weight loss, his skin pale from lack of sun. But his eyes are full of life, a sign that his soul is intact. The slogan in silver, bold cursive writing reads "Give Us Your Body, We Will Find You a Soul." It's below the logo and name "Recycled Souls."

"It's a beautiful evening, isn't it? Not too cold," Marc says.

The small talk is a clear sign that he is also feeling the awkwardness. When you take Jordan out of the equation, maybe we don't have anything to talk about. It's strange, but I had more conversation with Leo than I do with Marc.

Normally, I would welcome the quiet, holding hands, strolling over to have a great meal. But Marc feels weird to me when we're not talking about important things.

"Ya, not a cloud in the sky. We're going to have really great views from up there." I nod upward, as we approach the tower. His grip tightens on my hand.

The tower was built more than a hundred years ago, sometime in the late nineteen-hundreds. Standing more than fifteen hundred feet high, it survived all the rebellions of the mid-twenty-first century, and even the Third World War just after that. I know these facts because Marc told them to me, the night he proposed. He had stated that it represented us; that nothing could bring us down, no war, no rebellion, or anything else, for hundreds of years to come. He had rubbed my swollen, pregnant belly as he told me we were the best thing that ever happened to him.

The tower was deemed a UNESCO World Heritage site and still boasts a full-service revolving restaurant at the very top. To get to it, you have to take an old, restored glass elevator up one hundred and forty-seven flights. The elevator faces outward. I recall the views of the setting sun over the lake being breathtaking.

Marc seems nervous as we step onto the elevator, which is full of people heading up for dinner. He grips my hand tighter. A voice on the hologram tells us facts about the tower, giving details on the history, the survival of the tower, rebellions, and wars. I look over at him and smile, reminiscing about his proposal speech, but he is focused straight ahead, watching the old numbers on the elevator light up as we ascend. 19, 20, 21, 22... The higher it goes, the more people talk about the views and the beautiful sunset, how the people down below look like little ants. I hear a child ask a parent to point out his own city in the distance.

66, 67, 68...

Marc hasn't stopped staring at the numbers lighting up, and I can't stop staring at him, bewildered. He's not afraid of heights. He's the thrill-seeker, the guy who jumped out of a plane on his eighteenth birthday. It's part of what I hated about him, taking dumb risks but then being so nervous about serious stuff. And yet here he is, nervous on an elevator. I can actually see his pulse beating in his neck above his collar.

Is that... sweat? Just under his hairline.

I look away from him and try to enjoy the sunset with the other patrons of the restaurant, push away my thoughts. What am I actually thinking, anyway? I don't know.

Maybe he is getting sick, a fever. A rock appears in my stomach. Maybe the soul loss is gradual. Maybe he is going to die. Maybe... I push the thoughts out of my head. That can't be it.

...145, 146, 147...

The elevator pings on arrival and the doors open. Marc releases the breath he must have been holding. He looks over at me and smiles, letting me get off first, but not the other patrons as he hurries out behind me.

At dinner, Marc sits next to me in the booth rather than across from me. "I just want to be near you," he tells me. It seems to me like he is avoiding the window.

"Are you OK?" I ask.

"You know, I'm not, actually. I don't feel well, sorry," he answers with relief.

Relief about what, I don't know.

"I must be coming down with something. I just feel a little dizzy, but I'm sure it'll pass."

The dizziness explains why he was uncomfortable in the elevator. Maybe the motion was making it worse. That's what I tell myself, anyway, as I run through the list of Metagenesis symptoms in my head. No, that can't be it. I push the thoughts aside again.

"We can do this another night, you know. If you're sick, you're sick." Maybe I should tell him about what I've done, come clean. What if he is experiencing the beginning of soul loss? Maybe we should go see Dr. Messie.

"No, no, no. We're going to have a great evening. Please, don't worry about me, it'll pass. Last time it was you who got sick—now it's my turn," he jokes.

"Actually, it wasn't last time. We come here every year for our anniversary, Marc."

I didn't think memory loss was a symptom. Or maybe it is— just not of Metagenesis, and something is terribly wrong.

"You know what I mean," he replies and kisses me on the forehead as the waitress comes by to take our order.

"Do you need more time? Another few minutes?" she asks.

"No, we don't need to look at the menu—we always order the same thing. Tradition," I say and smile deliberately at Marc, waiting for him to place our order, which he doesn't. He just smiles back at me patiently.

"We'll start with the chef's signature salad," I tell the waitress. "Not too much dressing, and switch the goat cheese for blue cheese. And for our main..." I use my index finger to find what I'm looking for on the menu that we haven't read. "We'll have the house steak, cooked medium, with the traditional sides, extra onions."

"And to drink?" she asks, and Marc orders the most expensive bottle of champagne.

"To celebrate," he says.

I excuse myself and head to the bathroom. When I return, I sit across from him rather than beside him. We wait in silence until our meal arrives, and when it does, Marc greets it eagerly. The bleeding steak is the first thing he samples, eyes rolling back in his head with pleasure. I don't react.

"What's the matter? Aren't you going to try yours?" he asks me.

I watch as he takes another bite of his meat.

"For someone who's not feeling well, you're certainly hungry," I reply.

"I think maybe I was just starving, you know? With everything that's going on, sometimes you forget to eat. It's like the dizzy thing might just be low blood sugar or something. I think I just needed some food." He scarfs down another greedy bite. "This is really good stuff."

"You say that every time we eat here," I lie with a regretful smile.

Marc is a vegetarian.

CHAPTER 51

"I propose a toast," I say, holding up my champagne glass. Marc dabs at his mouth with a perfectly starched white napkin and places it back on his lap, then lifts his glass to meet mine, still mid-chew. He smiles crookedly at me. I feel my own lips quiver with nervousness.

"To you and your queen, whoever she is, and whoever you are."

His glass remains frozen in his hand, not reaching mine. His smile wavers, but doesn't disappear.

"Who is she?" I ask somberly.

"Pardon?" He swallows the rest of his food, confusion on his face, glass still in hand.

"Who is she?" I repeat to humour him. I know he heard me.

"Grace, what are you asking me? Who is who? Are you accusing me of something?"

"Yes," I reply.

"What are you accusing me of, exactly?" He rests his glass down but hasn't looked away from my glare.

"I don't know, actually, so why don't you just tell me? In fact, why don't we both come clean, tell the truth, and stop living a lie."

"Grace, what's going on?" he asks.

"Who is Rachel? And who are you?"

When I say "Rachel," any sign of trying to deny whatever he is denying is gone from his eyes. He gets up to put his jacket back on, no longer bothered by the height of the view. His smile is completely gone now, replaced by a steely expression. We stare at each other. Neither one of us flinches or dares to look away. He's not answering my question, but I can tell I hit a nerve. Rachel is someone important. There is a link here: Leo's soul, Marc's soul, it's all the same. They're just reincarnated versions of each other, right? I think about how Leo's eyes look like Marc's eyes, and the last thing Leo said to me before letting go to his death, never breaking eye contact with me.

"You screwed up. Marc was a vegetarian," I confess.

He lifts his arm to beckon the waitress over and asks for the cheque, all without taking his eyes off from mine, like Leo, falling to his death all over again.

From the waitress's point of view, we must look like we're facing off in a staredown. She doesn't ask if there was a problem with our meal or why we are leaving without eating it. It's almost untouched, and she doesn't even offer to pack it up so we can take it home.

The ride down the elevator is uncomfortable. It was full on the way up, but no one is leaving the restaurant at prime dinner time. We're alone. Marc stares at the lights again, as we descend.

"You're afraid of heights?" I ask in a cruel tease, having no idea what the situation is, yet trying to maintain control of it.

"I was pushed to my death in a past life," he replies coldly, without shifting his eyes from the lights until we reach the lower floors. When we get to the tenth, he makes a point of staring hard at me, showing me he has the upper hand in what happens next. "Ever been to the Grand Canyon, Grace?"

I swallow hard.

CHAPTER 52

We reach the bottom floor. Marc motions with his hand for me to step off first, but I don't feel comfortable. In fact, I'm suddenly afraid of him, whoever he is. I don't understand what is going on. His gaze is expressionless, cold. He doesn't move when I don't get off the elevator, but tilts his head toward the door, raises his eyebrows, narrows his stare for me to go first. I step off hesitantly, the hair rising on my arms and back of my neck as I pass him on my way off. I can feel his eyes never leaving me, burning a hole in the back of my skull as I exit. I have no idea what to expect next. When he follows me off the elevator, he is too close to me; I feel his breath move my hair, without touching me.

"Go left, Grace. Don't raise any flags, walk normal, put a smile on your face." He speaks through my hair right next to my ear before placing a firm hand on the small of my back, directing me in case I don't know left from right. Then he moves his hand around my waist and holds my belt taught, making it squeeze my empty, nervous stomach.

"Where are we going? Where are you taking me?" He doesn't respond. "Please say something." The cruel tease I had in my voice is now gone, replaced by a shaky, scared voice, my mouth dry, my tongue thick. I hate that I sound so weak.

"Marc, are you going to talk to me?"

Without saying a word, he leads me down a corridor and through an employee-only area, to the back of the building, and out through the back door. We're in the garbage disposal alley now, and when we get there, he finally lets go of my belt. I don't waste two seconds. I spin around right away to face him. I don't trust him and am not sure what to expect, but he is just standing there, looking just as untrusting as I do, just as nervous and as scared. For a brief second, I see the fear in his eyes. But he recovers his stance quickly and his expression firms up the moment we lock eyes. But it was there, fear, it was, I saw it. It reminds me of how I felt during the last conversation with Leo, right before I—

"Talk," he commands.

"What?" I reply.

"You said we should *both* come clean. That implies you are keeping something from me too. So, *talk*."

"Who are you?" I ask. "And Rachel? And, and... Are you even Marc? Or Leo?"

"That's not how this is going to work," he cuts me off, his voice full of intolerance toward my questions. "You're going to tell me everything first. Don't leave anything out. You tell me what you've done. You're keeping something from me, and I want to know what it is."

I laugh without humour at the irony. Me, keeping something from him, but what the hell is he keeping from me? He eats meat, he's afraid of heights, he knows something about the Grand Canyon and Rachel... I turn from him, start to walk away. I'm not ready to talk, and I'm afraid to listen. I want to get the hell out of here, find Dr. Messie, find his assistant Adalia, find someone who will make sense of whatever the hell is going on here, with Marc, or Leo, or whoever the hell this man is.

Stupid move that was, turning my back to him.

"Get the fuck back here," he barks as he grabs my arm to pull me back around.

When I try to shake loose of his grip and refuse to turn around to face him, determined to get out of this alley, he twists my arm behind me. With his other arm, he squeezes his forearm under my chin, pushing against my windpipe in a choke. My feet lift off the ground, and he slams me up against the brick wall. I'm stuck, between his body and the brick wall, pieces of cold brick dust coming loose under my cheek, into my mouth, up my nose.

His body is hot and pressed right up against me so I can't move. With my free arm, I try to pry his forearm away, so he stops choking me; it's getting hard to breathe. My left arm is still twisted at my back, I'm gasping for air; what the hell is going on? I'm starting to see stars. The harder I squirm to free myself, the worse his hold on me becomes.

"When I release you," he whispers, "when I release you, you're going to talk, Grace. Do you understand? No more dickin' around. No stalling tactics. Just talk."

I try to nod yes, but the movement only squeezes more air out of my burning lungs.

He's implied that he's setting me free, right? So why isn't he? The panic is making it even worse. He doesn't let me go, he doesn't. He squeezes rougher against me, he's choking me harder, the alley feels darker. There is a ringing in my ears; I'm afraid that I'm going to pass out, and I'm trying to nod cooperation, but he just squeezes tighter, even pushing his body violently into mine. He is squeezing the little air out of my lungs, which I can hardly get through my airways because his forearm is blocking it, crushing me between him and the cold brick scraping my face...

I'm trying to focus, keep my eyes open, which feel like they are bulging, the blood vessels screaming for air.

All at once, just when I think I'm done, on the verge of passing out, he releases me, and I drop in a coughing heap to the ground. I'm gasping, writhing on the ground, grabbing at my throat, massaging it to open more and take in more air.

More.

Air.

I try to turn over to draw breath in from above, but he flips me over and ties my hands up behind my back. It's my belt; I recognize the clink-clink of the clasp. He must've removed it. He ties my arms tight. I wince in pain—my shoulder feels like it might come loose from the socket when he lifts me by my tied arms and flips me onto my back. I'm still struggling to catch my breath when he sits hard on my chest, straddles me, and retrieves a knife from up his sleeve, placing it against my neck. The knife smells of ripe blood and peppercorn, making me want to cough or sneeze. It's his steak knife from the restaurant. I feel its grooves digging in, pressed up hard. I look up at him. He appears calm; he's not even breathing through his mouth, like taking me down was stress-free.

"Ready to talk, Grace?"

I remind myself that I had seen fear there only a few moments ago; that he isn't this cool, calm guy; no way, Marc would never hurt me.

"You first," I reply, stupidly, to which he responds by pressing the knife harder into my throat. He doesn't even blink. Maybe I misread that bit of fear; this is not Marc—*this is not Marc,* I repeat in my head, over and over.

"OK, OK. Just, can you get off me? It's hard to talk when I can hardly breathe."

He shifts his weight only slightly, making it a bit easier to breathe, but not by much. Of course, he doesn't get off me, and he increases the pressure of the knife even more. I know he's cut me before I feel the warm goo of my blood because he glances at my neck for a second before locking his eyes back on mine. Was that unease I sensed?

"I think you already know," I begin, "that I killed a man named Leo to save Jordan's life. At the Grand Canyon." I begin to cry as I say it. There is so much guilt built up in me. "I knew that killing him to clone his soul would risk killing Marc. I thought I'd never see you again." I'm sobbing hard. "But I did it anyway. I did it to save Jordan—I risked killing you for him." He loosens the knife a bit on my neck. He doesn't ask me to continue, but I do anyway; the floodgates are open. "I regretted it right away. It's like I don't even know myself anymore. How am I capable of murder? Dr. Messie lied to me, to us! He didn't tell us that I would have to kill you to save Jordan—I didn't find out until I was already there. I shouldn't have done it. Especially after I found out that Dr. Messie created this disease in the first place; that without him, no one would even know what the hell Metagenesis is, anyway. People are not meant to interfere in past lives, it's dangerous."

Marc removes the knife from my neck completely and gets up off me in a hurry. He is pacing back and forth. I'm on the ground and don't move, my body happy to have some breathing room. My arms are numb underneath me; the belt and the weight of his body were cutting off my circulation. I'm crying hard, the guilt and regret pouring from me. Marc puts his hands through his hair, distraught, doing that deep sighing thing he does when he's stressed. Knife still in hand, he stops pacing.

"My name isn't Marc," he begins, his back to me. He is shaking.

I cry harder, hearing him say that. I don't understand, but somehow I do understand. Somehow this is my fault—I feel it. I've messed with Marc's past life. Dr. Messie's concoction is partly responsible, but I carried on with the deadly plan, despite warnings.

"Are you Leo?" I ask in a small voice, sobbing uncontrollably.

He turns to look down at me. The fear I thought I saw before is definitely there now. He looks scared.

"I was, once, but that's not my name, either. I was Marc once, too; it just isn't my name now." None of this is making sense to me. "I don't want to tell you my name." He pauses, gauging my reaction, but I don't react other than my uncontrollable weeping.

I wait for him to continue, crying at his feet where he now stands. "I don't know how much you know about Metagenesis. But where I'm from, we don't actually go and visit past lives. We know about them; get them mapped out like one would map out a family tree. So I am Leo, I am Marc. Those were my lives, my souls. We're the same person, the same soul, reincarnated over and over again. I know what happened to them, bits about how they lived, who they loved." He looks at me. "How they died." He laughs just then. "But apparently not how they ate." He shakes his head. "I did know about the heights, though. I just didn't think you would be taking me to the highest point in the world for dinner." He crouches down beside me. "I have nightmares about that fall like I was actually there. I dream of Rachel's face looking over me, desperate and regretful, like she doesn't have a choice. And even though I don't know why she wants me to die, I tell her I love her and I let go so she doesn't have to live with the pain of killing me, like I could've climbed back up but I chose not to." He is looking off in some distant future, thinking about his Rachel, his sacrifice.

"That wasn't a dream," I whisper. "That's how Leo died. And it wasn't Rachel, it was me."

"I know," he replies. His eyes meet mine. "Because the next thing I knew, I was at the airport, and you were calling Marc's name. I went through thirty-three deaths looking for him, for the moment he died. You've heard of code 33, right?" Just like one of Marc's messages on the pager, he assumes I do know and offers no explanation. "Grace, your name will be Rachel, when you're reincarnated, in another hundred years or so, where I'm from. You're my wife's past life."

"So it's true, our souls keep meeting in every lifetime?" I'm asking, but it's more of a statement. I haven't moved from the ground. I feel like I belong at his mercy, underneath him, my character out in the open, my wrongdoings exposed to be judged and punished. I don't completely understand what the hell is going on, but I know I'm at fault.

"Grace, if I let you live, Rachel will die." He lets that last sentence linger between us. He is just staring at me as I lie there, helpless, crying in my own misery and pain and guilt. His eyes show misery, pain, and guilt, too.

"Why do we keep meeting this way? It's cruel punishment. Inhumane," I whimper to him, the significance of what he is saying suddenly hitting me. He's here to kill me, to clone my soul and save Rachel.

"About what happened between us earlier," he says, his eyes filling with tears. His cheeks redden with shame, his eyes shift to the side. "I'm really sorry. I shouldn't have, you know, I shouldn't'tve..."

"Are you talking about making love to me, Marc?" I make a point of saying "Marc," pronouncing it carefully, like that name is as fragile as freshly made glass. "Don't be sorry, because I'm not. If what you're saying is true, if I am going to be Rachel, and you were once Marc, and Leo, then we are each other's soulmates. And I love you."

He looks at me, his eyes wet with tears that are now running freely down his face. His eyes are vibrant when they cry.

It would be easy to hate this man if I didn't know how he felt right now. Struggling with the decision to kill me or let someone he loves die. I remember the feeling, from when I decided to kill Leo to save Jordan.

I don't want to resist my death. I want to end it, end my life for him. I owe him that. End my life and let him return to Rachel. I am not afraid anymore, and I'm ready to die now that Jordan will live. I deserve whatever happens next, but I still flinch when he reaches for me suddenly.

There are butterflies in my stomach, and an involuntary cry escapes me; I'm shaking with the unknown. But he just turns me over, unties my wrists. I sit up. He takes my hands in his, massages them; the circulation is coming back to them. He is staring at my hands. He is rubbing tears away from his cheeks with his sleeve.

"You look just like her, you know. Your eyes, your scent, the way you talk...and feel..."

"Are you going to take my soul?" I ask meekly.

"No, no." Confusion on his face. "You don't understand. I wasn't sent here for your soul to save Rachel. Metagenesis, soul loss, it doesn't exist anymore. Just like travelling through past lives, people just don't do that. I'm stuck here—there is no return for me."

"You're right, I don't understand. You said if I live, Rachel dies. That can only mean…"

"He has her. Claudio. He took her from me. He told me I had to go back, kill you, and he would let her go. But by the sounds of it, all the stuff you just said... killing Leo ended up killing Marc, which is how I ended up back here, the only open portal; then that would mean if I kill you, Rachel is dead anyway."

"Did you say 'Claudio'? How far in the future are we talking here? What the hell is a portal?" I'm still crying, but his hands holding mine feels so genuine, my fear is dissipating.

"I have a lot of explaining to do. Let's get out of here. I won't hurt you, Grace." He grabs my face between his hands like he did when I first arrived back and he greeted me, calling me his queen. "I love you, Grace. You are Rachel in every way. I will do everything to save you now and in the future. We have to stop Claudio." He gets up and extends his hand to me. "Let's go home," he says.

We walk home together, hand in hand in silence. It's funny—not funny ha-ha, but funny weird—how this evening started off and where it ended up.

CHAPTER 53

I can't keep up with everything Marc is telling me. He seemed to keep up with my confession just fine. I told him everything, right from the beginning of Jordan's diagnosis to the moment we saw each other. But Marc's story, it seems so farfetched. I need to itemize it, put it in order, like a timeline of events in a history school project, except his story is the future based on history we are making.

"Why don't we back up a bit? What's your name?" I ask. Starting from the beginning is always a good place. I push the now-cold scrambled eggs around on my plate, hardly touched. Marc's steak and eggs are just as cold, I'm sure. It's weird to see him sitting in front of a bleeding piece of meat. I keep looking at him, trying to see something different, but not. In the morning light, his eyes appear amber, just like I always recall them.

"Just call me Marc. I can't go back, anyway. Marc is my name right now in this place in time. It's like I'm picking up where he left off. Think of it that way."

"OK, well, then... Marc..." He looks like Marc, smells like Marc, makes love like Marc. This should be easy, but it still feels off.

I look out the window and watch the naked tree outside our home dance in the wind. Marc and I used to sit underneath that tree on warmer days when we were first married before Jordan was born. He would talk to my belly and sing, off-key, to our baby. It was sweet and romantic. He would rub my swollen feet and let Lucy, who was a puppy then, tickle them with her whiskers, which used to drive me mad and make him laugh. This Marc doesn't have those memories. But I simply have to accept that. He gives me no choice.

"Let me get this straight, let me see if I really understand." I look back at him, with my hand up to pause him from going back to his long-winded explanation. Right from the moment we woke, he hasn't stopped talking. Last night, when we reached home, we were both so exhausted, we didn't talk. We left all the questions unanswered. You would think that with everything that went on between us—him evolving from wanting to kill me to wanting to protect me; me coming to the realization that I killed my husband, or not really, since his soul came back to me anyhow, which I still don't understand—you would think all of the above would've kept us awake all night talking, trying to make sense of each other's situations and lives. But no. We came home and went straight to bed, where we wept and made love again. But this time, the lovemaking wasn't urgent and rough. It was patient and slow as if we were getting to know each other, which I suppose we are. I lay still while he traced his fingers along the contours of my body, letting him familiarize himself with each curve. I want to let him know all of me and will never withhold anything from him again. Then we held each other until we fell asleep. Not a word was spoken between us.

"So, in about a hundred years from now, where you're from, there is a cure for old age. Dr. Messie and his team of experts will discover the secret to longevity in *this* near future, which is why he is still alive in *your* future."

Marc nods. "Yes, exactly. He is almost two hundred years old."

I put my hand up again. "OK. Weird. But, OK. I got this. So, Rachel goes missing one day," he nods, sadly, "and you receive a message saying that if you want her to live, you'll cooperate."

Another sad nod.

"You're told that in Rachel's past life, she was me, a criminal who brought the human race to the brink of extinction by stopping Recycled Souls from continuing. Am I repeating this right?"

He gives me another sad but approving smile.

"Dr. Messie is developing longevity. But you need to kill me so that Recycled Souls can be brought back—or rather so that it is never destroyed in the first place. Recycled Souls is the key to further the development of keeping the human race alive, indefinitely, immortally, not just longevity. Because I, Grace Dartmouth, am responsible for the end of the original Recycled Souls. I saved Jordan's life, but became obsessed with not letting anyone else travel back to clone souls. I revolted against them without explanation."

"That's right. You died in the explosion in the Recycled Souls laboratories, taking all the data and all the ways to travel back to past lives with you. Like a human bomb. Jordan was burned but survived. I think he tried to stop you. He was only eleven when you died. Only two years from now. Anyhow, Rachel has a fear of fire, you know."

He looks at me with pity. I touch my cheek instinctively at the spot where adult Jordan's burn scar was. That's why I wasn't part of his life, and why he became sad when I asked him about his face. How could he tell me I was dead?

"But something must have survived. The data and ways to travel back. Jordan came to see me in Las Vegas. How'd he get there? Someone had to help him," I ask, puzzled.

"I guess we'll never really know. It's not like you can ask him," Marc replies.

We both ponder that for a few moments.

"Anyway, apparently, even though you're the one who ended things with Marc, you couldn't deal with him abandoning you guys completely," he continues. "They say he left town the day you came home. But I now know that he probably vanished when you removed Leo's soul. When you implanted Leo with that syringe, you killed them both. It makes sense. You saved Jordan, but because of his warnings when he interfered in Vegas, your next step would've been to stop Dr. Messie. I guess you figured killing the research would prevent other people from going back. That's probably why you started that fire."

The fire Jordan couldn't save me from, I remember.

"Well, I must've done something right. You say there are no longer past life travels. Recycled Souls no longer exists?"

"Yes, but Grace, that wasn't enough. Dr. Messie is the problem. And unfortunately, the new formula that you tried out on Leo leaves the body open to another soul, not just what you guys call lost soul."

"That's where I get confused..." I sigh deeply. He has explained this part already, but I just don't get it. "Back up. Again. And tell me that part. Again. Like I'm a four-year-old. Explain it like I'm four." This is exhausting.

Marc scoots up on his kitchen chair. "OK. So. When you gave Leo that dose of soul release, it's like his soul dislodged from his body. It left him before he even died, and his body became, I don't know..." Marc gazes around as if he can pluck the answer from the air if he looks hard enough for it, "...maybe like a host, you could say. Ya, like a host for all future versions of his souls. And Leo's next life, your Marc, he vanished. And had I not been sent back to occupy Marc's body, he would've remained vanished, like a lost soul. You were not the first to travel back and try this, but you were the first to try that exact strain of soul release. So the difference is, instead of vanishing altogether like all the other lost souls did, people can travel back to actually relive a past life. So I'm essentially having a do-over of one of my past lives— Marc."

"Still confusing, really, really confusing. Why don't you just move on to the next part?"

Marc smiles patiently, taking a moment to look at me before continuing. "Since you were the only one to try out Dr. Messie's newest experiment, only one person was ever subject to that strain of soul release, Leo, Marc, me. I'm the only one whose past life was left open for me to inhabit."

"But why wasn't that destroyed with the lab? You said I'm going to bomb the place, right? How did the resources to send you back survive if the rest of it didn't?"

"Because the means of travel is me. I had to leave my body to come here. That's why I can't go back. I won't have a body to go back to. My body has lost its soul. I didn't arrive through a life travel airport like you. I had to do deep meditation practices, alone. It took months and months of deep trances. They call it soul searching. I never saw another person or left the room I was in. Then, all of a sudden, through my trances, I was facing my worst nightmares, code 33. I was looking for the right moment until I found it, staring at you in the face, falling to my death in the Grand Canyon—a recurring nightmare I've had all my life since I was a kid. The next thing I knew, you were calling for me in a crowd of people, and I was waking from a dream to the reality of running to you. I didn't realize the dream of falling was real. I didn't realize I was actually at the Grand Canyon until you asked me about Rachel."

This is a lot to take in. Hearing his experience, what he went through, all he risked for Rachel. The way his voice softens at the mention of her, and how he lost her, fills me with envy and pain. It reminds me of when Marc, the real Marc, used to feel that way about losing me. And now my Marc will never know that I wanted him back and he was right all along.

"Why the hell does Dr. Messie want Recycled Souls back? He knows it's the cause of Metagenesis and that people lose their souls then vanish or die. He knows he's the cause of this all," I ask, frustrated.

"Rumour has it he is dying. I can only guess that maybe he wants to go back to his past life so he can live another two hundred years or whatever. Maybe keep repeating the pattern so he can live forever? I don't know. All I know is that we need to stop him."

"How?" I ask.

Marc shrugs in response, resting back in his chair, looking down at his lap. I'm trying to picture him meditating for months on end, alone, searching for his souls through his mind while suffering code 33. Giving up his body, his life in the future, for Rachel. For me. I push my twinge of guilt aside, vowing to make it up to him. I vow to end this once and for all.

"I have an idea," I tell him. He looks up at me curiously. I smile at him. "OK, sort of an idea. But it needs work. I'll fill you in on the way. And don't forget what I told you. You are

Jordan's father, as far as he knows. When we eat in the cafeteria, order the veggie wrap, OK?"

"Got it!" He laughs. "Veggie wrap. Mmmm..." He rubs his tummy, faking hunger before finally deciding to eat his steak, realizing it's the last real food he's going to have for a while. Lucy, having sat through our whole meal quietly now perks up next to Marc, hoping he'll throw her a piece. Marc squeezes Lucy's ears and pats the top of her head.

"No shot, Lucy," he says with a full mouth.

It's amusing how she doesn't seem to notice the difference in him. I thought dogs were intuitive. I guess not our dumb dog.

CHAPTER 54

When we arrive at the clinic, something isn't right. The atmosphere is thick with apprehension, nurses speaking quietly, voices hushed, heads lowered. The visitors are also speaking in low voices. My heart skips a beat when I realize the hush dissipates into silence as Marc and I walk past. They look to the side as I try to meet their eyes. What's going on? I wonder, as Marc squeezes my hand. He must feel the tension too.

When we arrive at Jordan's room, it's empty. I pause abruptly at the doorway and take a step back. Marc stumbles into me.

"Nurse?" I say to no one. There's no nurse here in the room. I turn around, rush over to the nurses' station, my hand steadying me on the wall as I go. I don't feel so good. Where is my Jordan? Why is everyone looking at Marc and me with pity? We were here just twenty-four hours ago, yesterday morning, and we were looked at with pride, the first of the future generation of saved souls. People were smiling at the site of us like celebrities.

"Nurse?" I reach the station, Marc at my side, supporting me.

The nurse turns around. Sorrow fills her face when she sees it's me. "I'm so sorry," she says. "I'm so sorry, he's gone—we lost his soul to Metagenesis."

"Jordan?" I mutter as my knees weaken, feeling her hands grab for me and Marc's hands under my armpits before I almost black out at her condolences.

"No, no. It's Walt," she says as she steadies me.

"Oh no," I say with relief, followed immediately by guilt for feeling relieved that Walt is dead and not my own son. "I think I need a minute," I tell them. My knees are so weak I don't think they can hold me up.

I let Marc lead me to the room the nurse points toward. He sits me down in an oversized chair, squeezes in awkwardly beside me. It's a white room, the same room that all those lost souls were in before, but it's empty.

"Jordan... I thought it was Jordan."

He puts a finger up to my lips to hush me. "I know, I know." He holds me in his arms and hugs me until I release him.

"Walt is gone," I mutter quietly, unable to cry. All I feel is a numb shock. My mouth feels like I've eaten a pound of crackers, yet it's salivating, craving liquid.

"Let me get you some water," Marc volunteers as if reading my mind.

He pats my shoulder and leaves, detouring to speak to the nurses first. I can hear them talking in the distance. But just like when Jordan told me he was dying, I feel like I'm not in my mind or body, so I have no idea what's being said, but I see one of them hand Marc a drink in one hand and a small backpack in the other.

Walt is gone, another casualty to Metagenesis. I am saddened for my son, who has lost his friend and saddened for the boy whose body gave up waiting for his soul to return. I am angry at Dr. Messie, who is to blame for all of this. But I snap back to reality when Marc hands me a glass of water, which I don't take. I look up at him urgently.

"When?" I ask.

Marc looks back at me, squinting, the lines in his forehead deepening. "When, what?" he asks, shrugging his shoulders curiously.

"You were just talking to the nurses. Did you ask when he

died?" I ask. "I don't want to miss his funeral."

"Not too long ago. Did you know Walt had no family left? Poor kid." Marc's face shows sadness for the boy. I don't think the liking he had for him was faked. Walt is, or rather *was*, an insatiable character, funny, outgoing.

"I know, which is why I'm asking. When exactly did he pass, Marc? This is important. I'm sure Jordan won't be allowed to leave, but one of us should go to the funeral."

"I don't know, a few hours ago?"

Startling Marc, I leap to my feet. "Don't look surprised or people will wonder what's wrong with you. They bury Metagenesis victims within a few hours, an old tradition from when they thought it was contagious. If we're going to the funeral, we need to go now," I tell him.

"Shouldn't one of us stay with Jordan? He's really distraught. His best friend just passed away." The way he thinks of Jordan is comforting. Knowing that he is taking on the role of Marc warms me from the inside. I nod at the bag in his hand and give him the questioning eye.

"It's Walt's," Marc says and puts the drink down to open the bag and inspect its contents. "He died alone. No one will come to claim his things. I figured we're his only family, so I just asked the nurse if we could keep it." I recall Jordan asking me if I ever wondered about why no one came to visit Walt. He had a family. They probably just went looking for a donor soul and never made it back, courtesy of Dr. Messie.

"Can I see?" I ask.

Marc turns his palm up in a be-my-guest motion. I reach in, feeling weird about going through his things. I am also angry that this little bag represents this boy's whole life. This is all that is left of him and his whole family. I find what I'm looking for: the decorated framed photogram of Walt with the lady I presume was his mother. Walt had her eyes.

"I'll go—you stay with Jordan. And I'm taking this with me," I say, photo in hand.

"Why don't I call your brother to meet you there, so you're not alone?" Marc suggests.

I nod in agreement. "Ya, that'd be great, thank you," I reply as I second-guess our plan. I'm worried about how Charlie will react to the get-rid-of-Dr-Messie-scheme Marc and I discussed on our walk over here. It probably shows on my face, because Marc brings me in close for a warm hug.

"You'll be fine. Charlie will understand." When we part, Marc gives me a reassuring smile. "I believe in you, Grace, and he will too."

Believe in me? How does he even trust me? I know that I won't hurt him again and that I want to make things right, but I don't know why he knows it too.

Making things right means getting rid of Dr. Messie—committing murder, again. And this time, I won't lie to Marc, Charlie or Kay. They will know everything. I can't do this alone.

I kiss Marc goodbye. "Tell Jordan I'll see him soon. I don't have time to get sanitized to see him and make it to the funeral on time."

I rush off to the cemetery for Metagenesis victims, saddened by the loss of a great kid, nervous at confessing to my brother and losing his respect. Fearful of my plan failing.

Here goes nothing...

CHAPTER 55

We're sitting back to back, leaning on each other, as we've always done since we were kids. Except then, we would talk about everything: music, fashion, cute guys, and girls. But today, just like when Dad died, we're both silent. Beaten down by the gravity of what's happened in the last months.

We're away from the sadness by Walt's casket. Only a few people linger, hovering over the hole in the earth that waits to swallow him up and claim his body and the photogram I placed on his chest. It's not raining or miserable at all. Not like how you'd picture a child's funeral to be. The bright sunshine seems to take away from the despair that is the end of this boy's life. He is gone. Barely a child and not quite a man, born in an unfair world. Born during a time when having an old soul is the same as being given a death sentence.

I think I have survivor's guilt, which must be what this rock at the pit of my stomach is about. The ache where my heart is, the hole left behind. It's guilt for surviving, and guilt for the other thing—for what I did to Leo. The tears haven't started until just now.

Somehow I made it through the entire funeral, the speeches and the nice "so sorry"s without emotion. But now, I sit here at the edge of the cemetery, a safe distance from the remaining mourners. I've said my goodbyes. I'm leaning on my big brother. I allow my pent-up emotions to roll quietly down my cheeks, to the corner of my lips, and salt my taste buds. Yup, guilt tastes salty and bitter, and I've earned it.

"Charlie, I have a confession," I whisper with my eyes closed, the sun painting my inner lids a bright orange.

My brother doesn't respond. Maybe he knows it will be easier if he doesn't speak. He's right. I can't even look at him. I'm glad we're back to back. I'm glad Charlie can't see me and judge.

A minute passes by, maybe two. I don't say anything, and he doesn't ask me to. If I didn't say anything more, I know Charlie still wouldn't persist and I'd be off the hook. We'd never talk about this again, nor would he ever refer back to this moment in time. That's how I know I can trust him with my confession.

But it's more than that: I have to trust my brother. I have to share this burden with someone else. I can't hold on to this guilt, and I need my brother's help to undo my wrong. I relax my shoulders—I didn't even realize they were so tense—and I let out my confession.

I don't feel like myself as I say it, like the words being spoken aren't even coming from me but from another source altogether. It gives me goosebumps as I say, "I'm a murderer. I murdered him, I looked him right in the eyes when he died, I killed him... everything is my fault."

Charlie's posture stiffens—there's no going back now.

CHAPTER 56

My brother slides a spoon across the table toward me to make his point. He twists it as he does, so it catches the sunlight and sparkles. The reflection dances on the wall and other patrons of the restaurant follow the bouncing beams around the room.

"You see, now that I've moved the spoon from here to there, we're talking about it. And that means we're not talking about whatever else might've been on our minds. Now just consider how everyone else's future may also change as a result of this spoon," he says.

It's been a few days since my confession. I wanted to give him time to absorb all I told him, which was everything. Today I want his advice and help. His opinion matters greatly to me. I wish I had sought it earlier.

"So to answer your question," he continues. His fingers are now twisting the spoon, obnoxiously blinding some of the customers, who throw dirty looks in our direction. "Those people at that table over there," he nods to his left without taking his eyes off me, "they are so annoyed with me right now. And if I keep this up," twist twist "that man's likely going to say something. Or maybe they'll start talking about me to each other and lose the spot in their own conversation. But if I had bugged them one minute later, they may have finished their conversation, or one minute earlier, they wouldn't even have started it." He rests the spoon down and sits back. "So even though I have nothing to do with their lives or their history, I've affected their future with something as insignificant as this cutlery."

I think about what he says. Jordan interfered. He wouldn't have interfered if he didn't think the future could be changed. He knew that coming back would have an impact, and that was why he did it. Whatever I do from now on will change not only the future, but it will change the past, as he will no longer have to go back to Las Vegas to warn me. And if I'm never warned, then I will never make these decisions, and this conversation with my brother will never happen, and these people sitting in this restaurant will continue with their conversations without the distraction of Charlie's spoon.

"So how do we know what came first? The action? Or the consequence?" I ask.

He hasn't answered my question at all.

"You don't." He shrugs. "But sometimes timing is everything." He pauses, and I sense where he is going with this. We haven't talked about Dad in a long time. "Just one minute can make all the difference," he says.

We look at each other thoughtfully, remembering Dad, and the one minute Charlie knows I wished I could go back to.

"So, what's the plan?" Charlie asks. And although he doesn't have the answer to my questions and can't ease my mind about my plan, I feel like he's telling me we have to stop Dr. Messie at just the right time and place.

"I'm not quite sure," I reply. I have ideas but haven't settled on just one.

I use his spoon to stir in more sugar. The lemonade tastes sour today. I miss the creamy milkshakes of Vegas.

I'm staring at him as he slowly stirs his own drink, to which he had also added more sugar as soon as the waitress set it down. I guess his taste buds are also dull and numb. He seems deep in thought, and I know he probably has a bunch more questions but is waiting for the best time to ask them. I'm sure he's hoping I have an idea, which I do, but I need to gauge how he's taking my confession. I really need him on my side so I can live with myself if it goes wrong. He seems to be feeling me out, to see if I'm ready for action or ready to give up. I'm also feeling him out, to see if he will take action with me or give up on me.

My idea is to kill Dr. Messie. But I have two ways of going about it.

Although Charlie and I are two years apart, sometimes it's like we're twins. As kids, we always worked well together in the casinos and running the household when Dad was on a gambling binge. But confessing to plotting a murder is more than some little white lie, hustling people for money or lying about Dad's whereabouts to the authorities in order to keep our small family together.

This is different. The stakes are high. This is not even about my son's life anymore, and not about Marc's, either. Marc is gone—sort of—and Jordan is safe, at least for now. But we need to stop Dr. Messie. Ever since he announced to the whole world that a cure has been found, thousands upon thousands of people have signed up to try it. Of course, they can't all go back at once, but Dr. Messie's new company, Recycled Souls, is already building a larger state-of-the-art shuttle, made completely of glass, to transport people back in bulk. I remember the assistant mentioning something about moments in other dimensions and being able to watch them when we looked around curiously at the glass walls the day we agreed to the trial. I wish I could go back to that day and scream at myself not to go to Vegas in the first place. I can't undo that mistake, but I can try to halt the trickle effect it is causing. If we don't do something before the first shuttle is scheduled, those people will interfere with past lives, and that will be the beginning of the human extinction Jordan warned about.

But what can we do about it? Go to the media? I can't prove anything. Jordan is alive and recovering, the first ever to survive Metagenesis and the recipient of a new soul. Marc seems alive and well. I made it back safely. Who will believe me? I can't talk to Dr. Messie. His only interest is money and saving his own skin.

So I sit with my brother, and we sip sour drinks. I deserve a bunch of "this is all your fault" and "why didn't you just..." or "what the hell were you thinking..." But instead, Charlie waits for me to tell him my plan. Even after spilling my guts to him, confessing to murdering my soulmate, causing a chain reaction that will cause human extinction, his response is still that there must be a plan to fix all of this. He doesn't bother with the blame game. He patiently converses with me, answering my questions as best he can without the judgment I deserve.

I smile at him, stirring a drink that is already stirred, and by the amount of sugar added is now far too sweet to consume, while he probably schemes a plan of his own. My smile grows wider as he senses that I'm smiling, stops stirring and smiles as well, revealing his dimple. He places the spoon down softly, playfully twists it to catch the light again. He folds then unfolds the white napkin, raises his eyes to mine, and an unspoken understanding is made that we're both ready for action. Appreciation builds for my brother now that I've told him I am the most horrible person ever and he still supports me. I love his attitude. I love that he knows I'm in a fighting mood and with a smile and eye contact alone I know he's going to fight right along with me, his screwed-up little Hamartia sister with a fatal flaw. He doesn't even ask why I waited so long to tell him. He doesn't even seem mad.

"So do you want to hear what I'm thinking about doing?" I ask, satisfied that he's on my side.

"I thought you'd never ask."

I love his reply.

CHAPTER 57

For the third time, I sit across from the man dressed in white behind his desk like it's a throne, and he's a pharaoh. The first was in his regular office, with the plaques and awards on his walls, when he told Marc and me Jordan was dying. The second was where we sit now, in his home office made of glass, when he told us I could save Jordan. And now, today, I'm here to tell him I know why.

"What brings you here, Grace?" he asks coldly.

It's the first meeting I've had with Dr. Messie alone. All other meetings and appointments were about getting Jordan better and his recovery process. But I sense he knows that I know something because I haven't once thanked him for his cure and for saving my son. I've refused to shake his hand or even fake a smile in his direction. When questioned by the media, "How will you repay Dr. Messie for choosing you to be the first?", I answered, without taking my eyes off the good doctor or offering even the slightest grin, "I will dedicate my life to ensuring no one ever suffers from Metagenesis again." I had meant it, only not in the way the media portrayed my statement.

"It's nice to finally meet with you, alone," I say with a straight face and no smile, insinuating that there is nothing nice about meeting with Dr. Messie at all. I am also miffed that they wouldn't let Charlie come in with me. I had to leave him waiting outside, on the curb.

"Or are we... alone?" I inquire as I glance around at the glass walls, showing the corridors and other rooms but not the people who may be in them. I hope his entourage are on the other side.

"Oh, Grace. I think you know that we are," he replies coolly.

It explains the heavy security I went through to see him. His team patted me down, checking for anything that could be a weapon while telling me it was an extra precaution now that Dr. Messie was a celebrity. His family line consisted of notable scientists, explorers of past lives. But Dr. Messie, he just cured the disease of all diseases. I push aside the feeling that coming to see him is a mistake, especially now that we are alone for sure. I should've known he wouldn't want others listening in on our conversation. I have a plan, but he may have an agenda of his own, or he wouldn't have agreed to meet me. I can't let him see that he intimidates me.

"I know what you've done," I state as confidently as one can when sitting in front of a mass murderer, alone.

If he's surprised, he doesn't show it. "And what's that, Grace? What is it that you know?" His tone is condescending. He is humouring me.

"You should know that if anything happens to me, I've taken measures to ensure you're exposed. So it's in your best interest to keep your hitmen away from me and that I remain very much alive."

"If something was going to happen to you, Grace, it would have already."

The way he sits across from me, beefy hands folded comfortably across his large midsection... This isn't at all what I had in mind. It's scary how calm he is, and I don't like the way he is overusing my name.

"You have to stop," I tell him, trying to get on with the plan despite the growing dread passing itself off as a lump in my throat. If we're alone, this plan goes nowhere. "If you don't stop, or if something happens to me, whichever..." I try to sound nonchalant about the "whichever" part, shrug my shoulders for effect. "I will expose you for all that you've done and all that you and your family have been responsible for. I will make sure the whole world knows you are a fraud. You created Metagenesis, and saving souls means murdering innocent people."

There. I've said it, without shaking or stuttering once. And I wait for it. I wait for his reaction. I saw a twinge of something when I accused him of creating Metagenesis. His eyebrows twitched slightly.

"You know, Grace," *stop saying my name*, "I don't think I gave you enough credit. You *do* seem to know more than I had expected. I mean, when my main driver disappeared suddenly, not making it back with you on the shuttle, I assumed he had betrayed me. Perhaps he felt guilt over all the others he had killed in the name of saving souls and decided to confess to you. But he didn't know that little bit, about the family... how'd you put it... creating Metagenesis?" He pauses for a reaction, which I don't give him.

"The murdering, yes. My driver knew that because he was to carry out the murder of David, as he had so many others before. So I find it interesting that you know that fact about how Metagenesis began."

He waits for me to reply. I don't. I am afraid I may have slipped, said more than I should have. Charlie told me to keep calm. But we didn't expect that I would be having a full-on conversation with Dr. Messie. I don't let my face betray me, nor my voice. I sit perfectly still and stay as expressionless as I can, keeping my mouth shut for fear of my voice shaking or losing my composure.

Dr. Messie meets my silence with his own silence. Neither of us says anything. For me, I'm afraid to speak; for him, it's his method of intimidation. I don't even think he's blinked. And it's working. He's scaring me.

He moves suddenly to the edge of his seat, and I involuntarily jerk back. He smiles at me, knowing he has the upper hand. I curse myself for being so easy to scare and remind myself to remain calm.

"Grace, Grace, Grace." He shakes his head, feigning disapproval. "You know what I've done. But let's not be silly here. Because I know what *you*'ve done. My main driver didn't kill David, did he?" he asks, searching my face for a reaction I try to hold in.

Leo, I want to correct him. His name was Leo. I feel my throat closing, my face heating up. *Shut up and stay calm!*

"Yes, yes, that makes sense now. I don't know how you know about my family..." his eyes look up and around, searching for the right word, "...traditions. But I don't want to leave you with any misgivings." His eyes come back to me; his expression will haunt me forever, I'm sure.

"In fact, Grace, I believe you and I are quite a bit alike. Out to save the world. Except, I didn't kill anyone I loved. My soulmate. The person with whom I created a child. You did that, all by yourself. Maybe my driver did betray me, and that's why he didn't make it back here. Maybe he told you everything to clear his conscience and decided not to kill anymore. It's not the first time a driver's remorse has outweighed his duty. So you took things into your own hands." He's half-right. "You played God." His smug smile is infuriating. "When faced with the choice to save humanity or save one child, you chose to save one child. You sacrificed many for the one. Let's face it, Grace. You're not going to tell anyone about anything you think I've done because that would mean having to admit what you did. How can you prove that I'm killing people without admitting that you did the same? It's actually like we're the ones who worked together, you and I—we're partners in this undertaking."

"I am nothing like you!" I finally let it out angrily, despite instructions from Charlie to keep calm at all times.

Screw it. Time for Plan B.

"*You* are a criminal! A man without a conscience!" I yell. He leans back in his seat, satisfied at my outburst. "You're not even a man, you are a *monster*! And I am *nothing* like you!" Tears threaten to spill over, but I force them back enough to say what I need to say, to get it off my chest, to express the pain I've been carrying and probably will carry forever. "I travelled back in time to the unknown at the chance to save my son. No guarantees were made to me, no promises. I was cut off from my brother, my husband, my dying son, thrown into an unfamiliar environment with nothing but constant reminders about Jordan's dwindling health to keep me going—only to find out that I would have to commit murder at a chance to save my child!"

I rise out of my seat, lean across his desk and invade his personal space.

"I jumped out of a plane, I risked not ever making it back to see my son alive again, *or* my husband, for that matter! I may have killed, but it wasn't for you. It was *because* of you that I had to do it!" My voice is shaking, but not with fear, with anger toward this complacent man. I want to grab his smug, ugly face and claw his stupid eyes out of his fat head!

I take a few deep breaths, trying to calm my nerves, proud of myself for getting in his face, but annoyed that he doesn't seem to care and worried about disobeying Charlie. I sit back down and make a show of bringing my anger down a few notches, breathing in through my nose and out slowly through my mouth.

"I tried to save my son despite all the odds against me. And I succeeded." I pause, narrow my eyes. "Do I strike you as the kind of woman who would simply sit across from you without a plan and let you intimidate me into keeping quiet?" My voice is steady, my nerves as calm as the still waters in the caves he doesn't know his hitman died in, at the hands of my son. I can still salvage this plan.

"At the press conference before the launch of your first shuttle next week, you will announce that there are complications with the travel ports to past lives. You will stall for months until Metagenesis starts to die down—pardon the pun." I wink at him. Now he looks pissed at me. "Then you'll announce that a local drug has been created and start giving out placebos. People will eventually stop dying because no one will travel back in time, and the rest should be history." I smile at my own inside joke to myself about history since it seems history is what you make it.

"Grace, get the hell out of my office."

He kicks me out so straight-facedly that I let out a surprised laugh, my jaw ajar in shock. That was easier than I thought.

He presses a button on his desk, sounding a bell, and at that, a door opens behind him, and a young woman in white appears to escort me out. Finally. This is the part I've been waiting for. I rise to leave but make a point of being rude enough so that the woman feels the need to come in and physically help me to the door. I cooperate with her, but only a bit, walking ahead of her, but slowly enough to shout at Dr. Messie.

"Well, Dr. Messie, if you change your mind an hour before the press conference, look for me at the... oh, who am I kidding? You know exactly where to find me! We're not so anonymous, are we?"

And I look straight at the woman holding my arm and shoving me out the door as I say it; she tucks her hair behind her ear, as always.

"Trust me..." I say to Dr. Messie, or rather to her, and then I mouth her name so only she can see me and hold her eyes as I do it. "Adalia Messie."

I wink at her just before the rest of the security crew grab me and roughly drag me out of Dr. Messie's home, through the gate, and out onto the curb, where Charlie is pacing back and forth.

But not before I saw the woman's expression change. Adalia knows I was talking to her.

Plan to get Adalia's attention to meet with us: checkmark!

"How'd it go?" Charlie asks. His face was anxious until he saw my satisfied expression.

"Perfectly," I reply.

"You saw Adalia, then?"

I nod yes.

CHAPTER 58

"That's crazy!" Kay looks at me, at Charlie, back to me. "Crazy," she repeats, shaking her head, wide-eyed. "Have you both lost your minds? Grace, Jordan is still healing. Shouldn't you be focused on that? You just got back from gallivanting through past lives finding him a cloned soul. You killed your husband..." She spits the word "husband" at me, and I flinch as though I've been slapped in the face. "Do you really think pulling off this scheme will redeem your bullshit?"

I don't interrupt her or reply. Her questions are rhetorical, really. She isn't expecting answers. She's angry with me. She's ignored all my attempts to contact her since my return, and I'm sure she wouldn't even have let me past her front door had I not had Charlie by my side. We weren't even offered seats in her living room upon crossing her threshold. In fact, if it weren't the first snowfall, I'm sure we wouldn't be granted permission to stand in her small foyer and watch her pace back and forth in anger. I decide she needs to vent and have no choice but to let her.

She is glancing, bewildered, from me to Charlie and back to me with each step she takes. Each time she comes back to me, her eyes narrow more.

"Shouldn't you be by his side, even right now, like you're his

Siamese twin?" Marc is with him, I think, but don't say. "Why are you even here? Your kid just escaped death, and you concoct this big, elaborate plan to break into the Recycled Souls laboratories and sneak onboard a past life flight with me, Charlie and Marc—or fake-Marc, whoever the hell he is..." she flails her arms while throwing out our names, "...with all of us in tow, and you think no one will notice? What the hell are we going to do when we get there? Whose soul are you going to kill this time? Did you even think about what might happen if we get caught? We'll be euthanized!"

She stops pacing now and bombards my personal space, leaning in a few inches from my face, causing me to back up until I'm against the wall with no place to go.

"You should've left when you were told to!" Her face is as red as I remember it on the day she left me in Vegas. "You should've listened to *Jordan!*"

Her eyes shoot daggers at me when she says "Jordan" as if I don't know who she's talking about.

"You're not a hero, for shit's sake! Neither of you! And nor am I!"

Hearing Kay swear is foreign and shocking because she has always considered vulgarity to be synonymous with negative energy. She's throwing her hands up now, shaking her head more vigorously, her eyes wild.

"Peter will finally get to rest in peace, we'll make sure," I offer meekly.

"Don't you bring Peter into this! Don't you ever say his name again!" she screams. "You two are shit-brained idiots! This is outright the most ludicrous thing, the most, the most irresponsible... this is like..." She turns her back to us, probably looking for the right words. When she's flustered, the idioms don't come as quickly, I've noticed since I've been the cause of her frustrations lately.

"Kay," Charlie interrupts, getting impatient with her dramatics and saving me from my scolding. "We're trying to prevent a holocaust. If we don't stop Dr. Messie, millions will die. He parades around like a god. We may not have a choice but to stop him in the past and make sure he loses his soul forever. And like I explained, his assistant will be our way in and hopefully Plan A will work: just kill him, here and now, so no one has to go back anywhere. We just need Adalia to get one of us close enough. So how about it? Are you in, or not?"

Kay snaps her head around and looks right at me—not at Charlie, who asked the question—and she answers with as much disgust as if she has just been asked, in public, if she had herpes.

"Of *course* I am!" She practically spits it out at my face. "We'll also have to blow up the building to make sure no one starts the research where that asshole left off. Did you even think about that in your plans, smarty pants Grace?" She shakes her head in disbelief.

"Blow up the building," I repeat under my breath, remembering Marc talking about what will happen to me, and Rachel's fear of fire. I'll have to make a point of not being the human bomb. If Jordan had never interfered, it's pretty clear to me that I would've died in a fire sometime when he's eleven.

CHAPTER 59

Sitting in the furthest corner of this underground casino brings back memories—some fond, others not. Actually, most not fond, as even the fond ones I have are soured by my guilt. I met Marc at the casino. The real Marc is dead because of me. I met Leo in the casino; he is also dead because of me. You would think the presence of Charlie and Kay would at least remind me of good old times, but the silent treatment Kay is giving me reminds me that I questioned her loyalty, reinforcing that I deserve to be ignored.

Marc puts his arm around my shoulders. Kay looks annoyed as he does it, at me, not at him.

Every old screen in the casino is broadcasting the countdown to the upcoming press conference. Reporters interview hopeful families of sufferers from Metagenesis. Dr. Messie is expected to announce the flight manifest of those who will travel back on the first shuttle. Twenty lucky participants will be named today.

The patrons of the casino continue gambling, but the mood is hopeful as they all watch the screens, anticipating the announcement. This will be one of the days they expect to talk about for years to come with their grandchildren. They'll all remember where they were the day the first shuttle was announced.

The waitress brings us a tray of drinks. Kay's face changes momentarily for the waitress and then immediately back to ugly when she leaves. I giggle at how she does that.

"What's so funny, Grace?" Kay asks and shakes her head with distaste.

I don't respond. We're all on edge, hoping that Adalia will show up. We've been here for a half-hour already. The press conference should be starting soon, and still, there is no sign of her.

"Are you sure she caught the hint?" Marc asks. "Were you clear about the meeting time and place?"

"I told you, I didn't see her alone. It was hard to get my message across—I was lucky she finally showed to escort me out of Dr. Messie's office. I was staring right at her when I said 'trust me' and 'you know where to find me' and 'one hour before the press conference.' There wasn't much more I could say without officially inviting her to a meeting to conspire to murder the man we were standing right in front of."

"I'm sure you did your best, Grace—she'll show," Charlie reassures me.

"Is there anything Grace does that would upset you, Charlie? You do know what she's done, right?" Kay says.

"You know what? I am sick of your sourpuss attitude. What's done is done—get on with it." Charlie stares hard at Kay.

Kay opens her mouth to respond, inching up in her seat and ready for an argument with my brother, but then Marc interrupts by putting his hand up to halt her. Apparently, he's the only one she isn't upset with as he is the victim in all of this. It doesn't matter that his intention was to kill me.

"Not now," Marc says calmly. "We have company." And he nods in the direction of the doorway.

Adalia is wearing an all-black, fitted jumpsuit—quite the contrast from her usual all-white suits. She has on a baseball cap and is clutching a small purple bag under her arm. She looks very much out of place among the gamblers in the room, as she scans the underground casino for us. When she finds us, she visibly takes a deep breath before walking over to us, cautiously, still scanning the room as she makes her way.

Marc and Charlie rise from their seats to greet her, but she doesn't sit down right away. She looks at us one by one, making eye contact with each of us, trying to tuck her hair behind her ears, but it's tied back, and there is nothing to tuck.

"I shouldn't be here," she says.

"Adalia, please, sit down." Marc offers her a drink, which she declines, but she does take a seat.

"What do you want?" Adalia asks.

We all exchange looks with each other, deciding who will explain. I'm so tired of explaining things, but this is my mess, so I need to clean it up.

"We need to stop Dr. Messie. We know what he is doing: creating more soul loss. We know he is a murderer."

I let that information sit while I search her face for a reaction. She doesn't seem surprised.

"What makes you think I will help you?" Adalia asks.

"Because you tried to stop me in Vegas. You warned me."

At this statement, Adalia does seem a bit surprised, and I question my approach. Maybe she's not ready to betray Dr. Messie.

"I tried to stop you?" she asks, tilting her head with confusion.

"Yes. You didn't tell me your name, but I knew it was you. I recognized you, the way you... your voice." I don't want to call attention to her nervous habit of tucking back her hair, or the way she told me to trust her, or the way she said she's anonymous. Those were the things that gave her away, not her voice.

"If I didn't tell you my name, how do you know it?"

I feel Charlie, Kay, and Marc all staring at me, waiting to hear what I will say. Will I tell her I met her grandson, Leo? How do I explain that I killed him and still get her to cooperate and help us?

"You told me, you also approached me. That's why I left to return home so suddenly," Kay jumps in.

I make eye contact with her, and I almost want to cry. She makes a small movement with her head, a knowing nod that goes unnoticed by everyone except for me, and I'm grateful to my best friend for saving me again. This small act of lying for me, so I don't have to tell Adalia the truth is her way of trying to forgive me.

For a few minutes, we sit quietly. I nervously stir my drink with my straw, and Charlie finishes slurping his. The waitress comes back with a new tray and fresh drinks, and we all watch in silence as she clears the table and places a snack platter in the middle. No one reaches for the snacks. The countdown on the screen is done. Dr. Messie is taking the podium.

"I sent you back in silver outfits so you would stand out. I wanted to make sure I would recognize you, in case I forgot what you looked like by the time I had the courage to go back and fix my family's wrongdoings. It's also why you had such little money, you know, the piggy bank?" Adalia looks at us, maybe deciding how much to tell us and if she can really trust us.

Dr. Messie has started his speech about how we've all suffered long enough. I couldn't agree more with Dr. Messie on that note.

"Claudio is my brother," Adalia offers, watching him on the screen, announcing to the world the names of those who will travel back.

I keep a poker face, so I don't startle her into stopping. I want to hear more. But she doesn't offer more. And for a few uncomfortable minutes, we stir drinks nervously and nibble on the snacks none of us are really hungry for while she watches Dr. Messie talk about the mission that is history in the making, saving lives.

"Adalia," I say. "We want to kill your brother."

Adalia looks away from the press conference to meet my eyes. Her hands tremble, causing the ice cubes to clink in the glass she holds. She places the drink down on the table, wiping her hands on her thighs. We hit pause on snacking and drink sipping. Dr. Messie looks unstoppable on the screen. The patrons of the casino cheer and clap at their hero, who will save mankind from extinction. We hear someone declare "it's a miracle," and some people hug each other as if they've just won a war.

"What do you need me to do?" she asks.

"We want to inject him with a syringe and kill him, so he loses his soul. Can you find a way for any of us to get close to him? Or will you give him the serum? But we don't want the strain of soul release you gave me. We want the one that doesn't work, so he will never be reincarnated again," I respond, and then hold my breath.

Everything rests on Adalia being ready to betray her family's legacy. Having a brother of my own, I try to imagine being asked to deceive him and knowingly let him die of Metagenesis. I think of Kay and her brother and all she was risking just to spare his suffering.

I continue with our wish list. "And we would like you to find a way to stop the experiments on Peter. Kay would like to be there when his life support is removed."

I offer Kay a supportive glance, which she doesn't return. She's just staring hard at Adalia. I can tell Kay is holding back tears.

"OK. I'll help you—with Peter, that is. I can find an excuse for him to be taken off life support. But Claudio..." She trails off, hesitates, looks at each of us.

I fear she's going to say no. I can't read her expression, and my heart is pumping through my chest with panic.

I throw Plan B out on the table to fill the dead air surrounding us.

"What if we travel to his last life and kill him there?"

Charlie looks over at me, surprise on his face. His jaw clenches.

"That is if you can't get us close to him in this life?" I'm prepared to argue, beg and plead, but Plan B has gotten a reaction out of her.

She draws a long, deliberate breath, and at last, Adalia meets my eyes, removes her cap and lets her hair fall around her face; she quickly tucks it behind her ears.

"The only way to truly stop him is to kill him in a past life. I know who he used to be. It's imperative that we go back to Claudio's very last life." She stops, puts her cap back on. "I've thought about what you're suggesting before, but I didn't have the guts to try it alone." The determination on her face betrays her trembling hands, which fidget with her purse strap. "I'm coming with you. If you fail, and I get caught, I'll be dead. I want to go with you, but I'm not coming back." Her eyes drop down to her lap. Her voice is barely above a whisper; I have to lean in to hear her. "There's only one way to stop the genocides…"

CHAPTER 60

As I sit next to my new Marc onboard the flight to the past, my heart aches for the real Marc. The Marc who held my hair when I vomited after his proposal; the Marc who was present at Jordan's birth, who made me laugh all the time and loved me even when I became uptight after Dad died. The Marc whose world I crushed when I almost divorced him, who left me beautiful messages on that pager. The Marc I killed.

I play back the events that got us here, to this very spot onboard a flight as unregistered guests travelling back to the 1930s. The guilt I feel over what I've done has not subsided, and likely never will. I constantly obsess over other ways I could've dealt with the circumstances I was thrown into. Nothing will fix the void I created when I removed Marc's soul. Nonetheless, I hold on to the desperate hope that I will somehow earn his forgiveness—if not through my Marc, who is gone, then through doing the right things from here on in.

I hope that going back to put an end to all of this through Dr. Messie's past life will help me move past my guilt. My real Marc is gone. He is not here to grant me forgiveness. But in travelling back and removing Dr. Messie from ever being reincarnated again, I hope to earn forgiveness from this Marc, who now squeezes my hand, seated next to me. Perhaps sensing my mood, my guilt exuding from every pore of my body like a bad storm, Marc offers me a kind smile.

This Marc almost killed me to save Rachel, and then he didn't. He was strong enough to let me live. Ironically, I thought being strong was making the decision to kill Leo. But Marc choosing to let me live, that was heroic. I think back to the moment when I thought he would kill me, be done with me, strangling me. He could've let me die right then. He almost did.

I remember looking into the eyes of a man who looked just like Marc, someone I loved and who loved me and who only a few hours earlier had made love to me. At the time, it seemed fitting that he would kill me—I deserved to be killed by my soulmate. Looking into his eyes, I had felt confusion, just like Leo. But I wanted him to kill me. I wanted to die at his hands. I wanted him to do it so badly.

Realizing that Marc wasn't Marc because I killed Leo was a crime I deserved to pay for with my life. I deserved the death sentence.

Guilty Grace speaks up within me all the time. I try to beat her into submission, quiet her so that I can live with a peaceful conscience that new Marc insists I deserve.

As if reading my mind, Marc tells me, "Everything is going to work out, you'll see."

Marc always reminds me that Dr. Messie is the real evil, who put us all into an impossible situation and turned us all into desperate people keeping loved ones alive. He insists that I acted with blind love for my child. He tells me this all the time. He leaves out the part about the fact that he chose to fight Dr. Messie instead of selfishly saving Rachel. He is a good man, and I will cherish him forever.

I repeat good thoughts over and over in my head as I squeeze Marc's hand in return. He is stuck here, but he doesn't have to be stuck with me, and yet he has chosen to be. I can't be as horrible as I feel I am. There is hope for me yet.

Redemption is just around the corner—in the year 1933, to be exact, in a place called Munich. It makes perfect sense that Adalia went back to that year and never returned. That's how she got to be so old when I met her. And the genocides she mentioned, well...

Dr. Messie's past life was as a politician by the name of Hitler. We're going to stop the Metagenesis holocaust—maybe even two.

EPILOGUE – JORDAN

Jordan turns the old envelope over and over in his hands. The lettering on the front is written in a hand he doesn't recognize, but the names in the neat font are frightfully well known.

Charlie and Grace.

Jordan swallows hard. His late uncle and mother, both of whom died: his mother in a tragic fire in the labs that he tried to stop; his uncle of Metagenesis only months after. The burn mark he sees every day in the mirror is a constant reminder that he couldn't save his mother. What would this envelope be doing among Dr. Claudio's things? Jordan has few memories of his parents. His father, Marc, was rumoured to have abandoned his family, but his mother always insisted that he died of sudden Metagenesis, just before the cure was found that saved Jordan. When his mother, then his uncle, died shortly thereafter, Jordan was left to be raised in foster homes. He has no belongings from his childhood.

Dr. Claudio always maintained contact with Jordan, taking an interest in his first successful cloned soul transplant. He knew how desperate Jordan was for information and stories about his parents. What's in this envelope that Dr. Claudio never shared with Jordan?

Jordan tucks the letter under his belt, deciding that it's not meant for him to find. He leaves Recycled Souls laboratories, where he was recently employed to help families deal with Metagenesis. After the fire, it took ten years for the formula to cure. It needs to be aged like a fine wine. They are finally getting back to travelling to past lives to clone souls again. And it couldn't have come at a better time. The population has dwindled down significantly, by the hundreds of millions— entire countries abandoned. Humans are going extinct. There were tens of thousands of recipients of new souls before the big fire, but Jordan was the first of those lucky ones. Because of that, his life's mission has always been to give back. At last, the first shuttles are scheduled to start up again, now that the medicine to inject is properly aged.

And now this...

In the solitude of his link-car, he opens the envelope, revealing a letter that will change the path of his life forever. A letter that reveals the truth. A letter from his grandfather.

Dearest Charlie and Gracie,

If you've found this letter, then the measures I had in place to keep me alive have failed, and I am dead. If I'm dead, Dr. Messie is the one responsible. I never had the courage to stop him, but I must tell the truth when I'm gone so that perhaps someone else will. I am sorry I never had the courage to tell you before now that I am not a good person.

Before I met your mother, I was a hitman for Dr. Messie. I'm sure you've heard of him—he is the one whose family discovered reincarnation and life travel. What you probably don't know is that they've been travelling to past lives for decades now. And interfering with past lives is the cause of Metagenesis. Dr. Messie knows this, and he doesn't care.

My job was to travel back to other lives and commit murder. But when I arrived in New York all those years ago as a young man, I fell in love with your mother, a local from that century, and decided to change my ways and not return. I changed my name and went AWOL. I proposed to your mother at the Statue of Liberty—or, more accurately, a replica of it in Vegas, where we moved to. It's a good place to run to if you want to be hidden. She picked up a job at a diner. We married. We had you kids. Life was good.

But Dr. Messie sent someone back to find and retrieve me and teach me a lesson on loyalty and duty. Driver's remorse was my crime. He had the new hitman execute your mother right in front of me. He called her a casualty of society. I had a choice to come back to Toronto present-day with my children or to die with your mother in Las Vegas. That is the story of where you came from, and when, and the truth about your mother and my past.

Jordan stops reading to check his surroundings and make sure he is still alone. He knows his grandfather committed suicide many years ago without explanation. But this letter is stating otherwise and somehow implicating Dr. Claudio. The rest of the letter reveals how Dr. Claudio is the reason for the plague of Metagenesis and details how the cure will only bring more loss.

Jordan decides to carry on what his grandfather never had the courage to do. He'll have to destroy the barrels of medicine. But he'll have to do more: stop the extinction where it began. The cure began with Jordan.

He'll have to find Grace, his mother. And he knows the diner. His mother used to speak of it all the time, with the thousands of flavours of milkshakes. He wonders if Grace ever ran into her parents there.

The letter closes with:

Losing your mother was the worst day of my life and a tragedy from which I will never fully recover.

I write this letter in hopes that it will start a movement in the right direction. I did not have the courage to undo my wrongs in my life, but perhaps in my death, they will finally be rectified. Society is wrong.

Please forgive me, Camilla, Charlie, and Grace.

And it is signed:

Eddie

ACKNOWLEDGMENTS

Finding out HAMARTIA was going to be published is right up there with the day my children were born, my wedding day, and seeing Prince in concert. All of which wouldn't have been possible without you, Greg. Thank you for encouraging me to chase my dream and for continuing to sleep next to me in spite of the hammer I keep under our bed. I love you.

Thank you to my editor Vicky Bell who delicately tried to cure me of writing in shouty caps and run-on sentences that make no sense but would if I'd just learn how to use a comma, in the right place.

Maria, the book cover is just like you, one-of-a-kind: thank you.

Christine, when I said, "I'm writing a book," and you said, "It's about time," that was the moment I realized my dream wasn't stupid. Thank you for believing in me enough to make up for all the times I didn't. xoxo

Thank you to my beta readers, Gregory, Emina, Dé, Jill. Without you guys, Charlie would've been a woman, Kay might've been perfect, and the story's rhythm and pacing would've resembled sneakers tumbling in a dryer. But mostly, I wouldn't have continued were it not for your (backhanded?) compliments about how surprised you were that I could write so well.

Last but not least, thank you to my sons, Gregory and Liam, to whom I dedicate this book. When I lack the confidence to do something for me, I start by doing it for you. You are my weakness and my strength. Eu te amo.

ABOUT THE AUTHOR

© Christine Albee

Raquel Rich loves to travel, suntan, walk her dog, and is obsessed with all things Beauty & the Beast. She despises cold weather, balloons, and writing about herself in the third person but noticed all the real authors do that. Born and raised in Canada to Brazilian parents, she lives in the Toronto area with her family. She's married to the guy she's been with since she was fifteen (her baby daddy) and her superpowers include being a mom to their two awesome grown-ass boys and one fur baby. Hamartia is her debut novel.

Connect with the author
www.raquelrich.com
Facebook @AuthorRaquelRich
Twitter @Raquelriosrich
Instagram @rich-raquel

COMING SOON

An ethical dilemma becomes a fight to undo an apocalypse
in Hamartia's sequel, Deus Ex Machina

Printed in Poland
by Amazon Fulfillment
Poland Sp. z o.o., Wrocław